MW00474461

ON THE ROCKS

NO LONGER PROPERTY OF
DENVER PUBLIC LIBRARY

Praise for Georgia Beers

The Secret Poet

"[O]ne of the author's best works and one of the best romances I've read recently…I was so invested in [Morgan and Zoe] I read the book in one sitting."—*Melina Bickard, Librarian, Waterloo Library (UK)*

Hopeless Romantic

"Thank you, Georgia Beers, for this unabashed paean to the pleasure of escaping into romantic comedies…If you want to have a big smile plastered on your face as you read a romance novel, do not hesitate to pick up this one!"—*The Rainbow Bookworm*

Flavor of the Month

"Beers whips up a sweet lesbian romance…brimming with mouth-watering descriptions of foodie indulgences…Both women are well-intentioned and endearing, and it's easy to root for their inevitable reconciliation. But once the couple rediscover their natural ease with one another, Beers throws a challenging emotional hurdle in their path, forcing them to fight through tragedy to earn their happy ending." —*Publishers Weekly*

"The heartbreak, beauty, and wondrous joy of love are on full display in *Flavor of the Month*. This second chance romance is exceptional. Georgia Beers has outdone herself with this one."—*The Lesbian Book Blog*

One Walk in Winter

"A sweet story to pair with the holidays. There are plenty of 'moment's in this book that make the heart soar. Just what I like in a romance. Situations where sparks fly, hearts fill, and tears fall. This book shined with cute fairy trails and swoon-worthy Christmas gifts…REALLY nice and cozy if read in between Thanksgiving and Christmas. Covered in blankets. By a fire."—*Bookvark*

Fear of Falling

"Enough tension and drama for us to wonder if this can work out—and enough heat to keep the pages turning. I will definitely recommend this to others—Georgia Beers continues to go from strength to strength." —*Evan Blood, Bookseller (Angus & Robertson, Australia)*

"In *Fear of Falling* Georgia Beers doesn't take the obvious, easy way... romantic, feel-good and beautifully told."—*Kitty Kat's Book Review Blog*

"I was completely invested from the very first chapter, loving the premise and the way the story was written with such vulnerability from both characters' points of view. It was truly beautiful, engaging, and just a lovely story to read."—*LesBIreviewed*

The Do-Over

"You can count on Beers to give you a quality well-paced book each and every time."—*The Romantic Reader Blog*

"*The Do-Over* is a shining example of the brilliance of Georgia Beers as a contemporary romance author."—*Rainbow Reflections*

"[T]he two leads are genuine and likable, their chemistry is palpable... The romance builds up slowly and naturally, and the angst level is just right. The supporting characters are equally well developed. Don't miss this one!"—*Melina Bickard, Librarian, Waterloo Library (UK)*

The Shape of You

"I know I always say this about Georgia Beers's books, but there is no one that writes first kisses like her. They are hot, steamy and all too much!"—*Les Rêveur*

The Shape of You "catches you right in the feels and does not let go. It is a must for every person out there who has struggled with self-esteem, questioned their judgment, and settled for a less than perfect but safe lover. If you've ever been convinced you have to trade passion for emotional safety, this book is for you."—*Writing While Distracted*

Calendar Girl

"*Calendar Girl* by Georgia Beers is a well-written sweet workplace romance. It has all the elements of a good contemporary romance… It even has an ice queen for a major character."—*Rainbow Reflections*

"A sweet, sweet romcom of a story…*Calendar Girl* is a nice read, which you may find yourself returning to when you want a hot-chocolate-and-warm-comfort-hug in your life."—*Best Lesbian Erotica*

Blend

"You know a book is good, first, when you don't want to put it down. Second, you know it's damn good when you're reading it and thinking, I'm totally going to read this one again. Great read and absolutely a 5-star romance."—*The Romantic Reader Blog*

"This is a lovely romantic story with relatable characters that have depth and chemistry. A charming easy story that kept me reading until the end. Very enjoyable."—*Kat Adams, Bookseller, QBD (Australia)*

"*Blend* has that classic Georgia Beers feel to it, while giving us another unique setting to enjoy. The pacing is excellent and the chemistry between Piper and Lindsay is palpable."—*The Lesbian Review*

Right Here, Right Now

"The angst was written well, but not overpoweringly so, just enough for you to have the heart-sinking moment of 'will they make it,' and then you realize they have to because they are made for each other."
—*Les Reveur*

"[A] successful and entertaining queer romance novel. The main characters are appealing, and the situations they deal with are realistic and well-managed. I would recommend this book to anyone who enjoys a good queer romance novel, and particularly one grounded in real world situations."—*Books at the End of the Alphabet*

"[A]n engaging odd-couple romance. Beers creates a romance of gentle humor that allows no-nonsense Lacey to relax and easygoing Alicia to find a trusting heart."—*RT Book Reviews*

Lambda Literary Award Winner *Fresh Tracks*

"Georgia Beers pens romances with sparks."—*Just About Write*

"[T]he focus switches each chapter to a different character, allowing for a measured pace and deep, sincere exploration of each protagonist's thoughts. Beers gives a welcome expansion to the romance genre with her clear, sympathetic writing."—*Curve magazine*

Lambda Literary Award Finalist *Finding Home*

"Georgia Beers has proven in her popular novels such as *Too Close to Touch* and *Fresh Tracks* that she has a special way of building romance with suspense that puts the reader on the edge of their seat. *Finding Home*, though more character driven than suspense, will equally keep the reader engaged at each page turn with its sweet romance."—*Lambda Literary Review*

Mine

"From the eye-catching cover, appropriately named title, to the last word, Georgia Beers's *Mine* is captivating, thought-provoking, and satisfying. Like a deep red, smooth-tasting, and expensive merlot, *Mine* goes down easy even though Beers explores tough topics."—*Story Circle Book Reviews*

"Beers does a fine job of capturing the essence of grief in an authentic way. *Mine* is touching, life-affirming, and sweet."—*Lesbian News Book Review*

Too Close to Touch

"This is such a well-written book. The pacing is perfect, the romance is great, the character work strong, and damn, but is the sex writing ever fantastic."—*The Lesbian Review*

"In her third novel, Georgia Beers delivers an immensely satisfying story. Beers knows how to generate sexual tension so taut it could be cut with a knife...Beers weaves a tale of yearning, love, lust, and conflict resolution. She has constructed a believable plot, with strong characters in a charming setting."—*Just About Write*

By the Author

Visit us at www.boldstrokesbooks.com

ON THE ROCKS

by

Georgia Beers

2021

ON THE ROCKS
© 2021 By Georgia Beers. All Rights Reserved.

ISBN 13: 978-1-63555-989-7

This Trade Paperback Original Is Published By
Bold Strokes Books, Inc.
P.O. Box 249
Valley Falls, NY 12185

First Edition: December 2021

THIS IS A WORK OF FICTION. NAMES, CHARACTERS, PLACES, AND
INCIDENTS ARE THE PRODUCT OF THE AUTHOR'S IMAGINATION OR
ARE USED FICTITIOUSLY. ANY RESEMBLANCE TO ACTUAL PERSONS,
LIVING OR DEAD, BUSINESS ESTABLISHMENTS, EVENTS, OR LOCALES
IS ENTIRELY COINCIDENTAL.

THIS BOOK, OR PARTS THEREOF, MAY NOT BE REPRODUCED IN ANY
FORM WITHOUT PERMISSION.

CREDITS
EDITOR: RUTH STERNGLANTZ
PRODUCTION DESIGN: STACIA SEAMAN
COVER DESIGN BY ANN MCMAN

Acknowledgments

I hope you're ready for more of the Martini cousins, 'cause I was. Honestly, this series wrote very quickly, and I think it was because I liked these women so much. I loved the Bar Back and I loved their affectionate snark and I really loved watching them fall in love. It's Vanessa's turn this time around.

All my gratitude, as always, to the folks at Bold Strokes Books. I'm so glad to work for a company full of people who are professional and know what they're doing. My part is easy: I write the books. The rest of it is the hard part, and Radclyffe, Sandy, and all the BSB staff take care of it seamlessly.

To my editor, Ruth Sternglantz, thank you for being not only professional, but fun, always up for answering my dorky questions, during or not during business hours and for always being happy to educate me. I appreciate you.

To my friends and family: thank you so much for the support. I've been doing this for a while now, and it's a weirdly solitary job, but I am lucky to be surrounded by people who love me even when I'm freaking out about my work in progress or stopping mid-conversation to jot down a cool name or job in my Notes app. They get me, and I can't ask for more than that out of life.

And finally, to my readers: the past year and a half has been the weirdest, craziest, scariest thing I've ever lived through, and being alone didn't help. I'm an introvert and I enjoy being by myself, but lately, I have learned what it is to be lonely. What helped tremendously was your support. The social media posts, the emails, the likes, all of it helped me feel a little less isolated, and for that, I thank you from the bottom of my heart.

Chapter One

"Alcohol. Now. Please."

Vanessa Martini dropped on the couch in the back room of her cousin's bar like her skeleton had suddenly disappeared from her body. She gestured to Julia, then pointed at herself. "Actually, you can just pour it right into my mouth. Glass be damned."

"Wow," Julia said, clearly amused as she chuckled from behind the practice bar and Vanessa heard ice dropping into a shaker. "Rough day, huh?" Jules was one of her very favorite people on the planet. She'd help. Vanessa just knew she would.

"You have no idea," Vanessa said, raising her voice over the sound of the ice being shaken. "Who invented second graders anyway? Any idea? I'd like to give them a stern talking to, whoever they are."

Julia approached her and handed over a rocks glass with a creamy white concoction in it. "Here you go. Something smooth and yummy that will take that edge off."

"Thank you," she said as she accepted the glass. "I'm all edges right now. Nothing but edges. I'm completely edgy." She sipped, let the drink coat her tongue, rolled it around in her mouth a bit, trying to pick out flavors. Julia wasn't kidding. It was creamy and smooth, a little frothy, with a hint of…coffee, maybe? A dash of cinnamon? "Oh, that's fabulous," she said and sighed as if her world had just been righted. Which was often how it felt when she was with her cousins in the back room of Julia's bar that they'd affectionately dubbed The Bar Back. For obvious reasons.

"You like?" Julia asked.

"I love. What is it?"

"That, my dear cousin, is a Cinnamon Roll, and it will be one of the rotating specials once the holidays hit. It's RumChata and Kahlúa. We'll rim the glass with cinnamon and use a cinnamon stick for a stirrer."

"Well, it's definitely doing the trick." Vanessa wasn't lying. She took another sip and felt the warmth of the alcohol seeping into her, slowing everything down just enough for her to feel like she could breathe again. "If you had a fireplace back here, I'd probably never leave." She glanced up at her cousin and gave her what she hoped was a grateful smile. "Thank you."

"Anytime. You know that. Wanna talk about it?" Julia was tall and beautiful, with rich brown eyes that reflected her feelings and loads of deep, dark waves that were the envy of anybody with unspectacular hair. She and their other cousin, Amelia, were Vanessa's people. They'd gotten her through high school, college, her parents' divorce…Every major event in her life had her flanked by Julia and Amelia. They were her strength, and she wouldn't have it any other way.

"Yes, please." She made herself sit up like a normal person instead of a bored teenager. Talking would be good. None of this stoic, keep-it-all-bottled-inside crap. No way. Vanessa knew the way to help solve a problem was to get it out of her head and into the presence of other people with opinions. Speaking of other people, she glanced around, searching. "Wait. Where's Savannah?" Julia's new girlfriend was notoriously calm and rational, and she made for a terrific opposite to Julia's tendency to go with whatever emotion hit first.

"Hey, *I'm* here," Julia said with a feigned pout. She knew the score.

"I know you are, and I appreciate you so much, but you know that she—"

The back door opening cut her off midsentence. "I'm here. I'm late, but I'm here." Savannah McNally walked in on cue and pulled the door shut behind her. "Getting cold out there."

"Oh my God, did I conjure you?" Vanessa asked, wide-eyed and laughing.

"It happens," Savannah said with her signature grin. "I go where I'm summoned, and something told me I was supposed to come here."

"Was it your phone that told you that you were supposed to come here? 'Cause, you know, dinner with your girlfriend?" Julia wiped down the practice bar as she spoke.

"Hmm." Savannah rubbed her chin and made a show of thinking.

"I mean, maybe?" She drew out the *maybe* as she leaned over the practice bar and kissed Julia. "Hi, baby. Pizza's on the way."

"Hey there, gorgeous," Julia said back.

Vanessa groaned. "God, you two make me sick. Have pity on those of us who are single and have nobody to goo-goo over."

"We do excel at the goo-goo," Julia said, her face still very close to Savannah's.

"We do," Savannah agreed.

"Ugh," Vanessa contributed and fell back onto the couch again, making the other two burst into laughter. The two of them hadn't been together long at all, but Vanessa knew in her heart this was it for her cousin. Not to be too corny by quoting eye-roll-inducing lines from rom-coms, but Savannah completed Julia—she really did. It was clear to anybody who had eyes.

Julia filled Savannah in. "Vanessa came here all ruined about her day, asking me to pour alcohol into her face, but when I tried to get her to talk about it, her response was to ask where you were. It didn't hurt my feelings at all. No, it did not."

"Aww." Savannah squeezed Julia's chin, then turned around and took a seat on one of the three barstools that lined the practice bar. She spun herself so she faced Vanessa. "Talk to Auntie Savannah."

It was amazing how seamlessly Savannah had become part of the group. Their threesome had become a foursome, and none of them even blinked. Savannah just…belonged.

"Okay, so it's been about two and a half months of second grade for me." Vanessa began unburdening. "And I love it. I do."

"Better than the fourth grade?" Savannah asked.

"Ninety percent of the time, yes."

"And the other ten percent?" Julia handed Savannah a glass of white wine, and she sipped after she posed the question, her eyes never leaving Vanessa's.

"The other ten percent is named Oliver Chapman."

"Uh-oh. Problem child."

Vanessa sighed. "He is, and I don't think it's his fault. But when you look up *acting out* in the dictionary, I'm sure there's a picture of him. He is seven years old going on fifty. He doesn't want to share. He doesn't want to listen. To me or anybody else. He's a very angry little boy."

"That's so sad." Savannah's voice was soft because she took care of everybody. That was Savannah. She looked for the good in every person and usually found it. "I wonder why."

"Has something changed at home for him?" Julia asked, and Savannah nodded her agreement.

Vanessa shook her head. "I don't know. I talked to Miguel, the first-grade teacher who had him last year, and he said the kid was a delight. Not a red flag in sight." She held up her now-empty glass for a refill as Savannah's phone pinged.

"Hold that thought," she said, one finger raised. "Pizza's here."

Savannah headed out the side door to meet the pizza delivery, while Julia mixed another drink, and Vanessa thanked God it was Friday. As a rule, she rarely drank on a work night aside from a sip here or there, but the week with Oliver had been rough, and sitting at home alone stewing about it wasn't going to do her any good. No, she needed her peeps to keep her sane.

Ten minutes later, they each had a paper plate with amazing Vinnie G's pepperoni pizza on it, Julia had mixed fresh drinks, and Savannah had moved to sit next to her on the couch. Clea, Julia's bar manager, popped her head in, and Julia excused herself to head out into the bar to see what was up, putting on the whole I'm the Business Owner persona that Vanessa loved and Julia was finally settling into.

"So no changes at home," Savannah said when it was just the two of them and seemed to be thinking about it as she chewed.

"I mean, I don't *think* so, but I'll find out. He's only been acting like this for the past couple of weeks, so something's definitely up with him." Vanessa thought about Oliver Chapman. A little tank of a kid, small but solid, with a mop of dark hair and startlingly green eyes, which she rarely got to see because he rarely gave her his full attention. "I sent an email to his mother after the kids went home today." She clenched her teeth, made a face.

"Your favorite," Savannah said with a laugh, already familiar with her. "Parent-teacher communication."

Vanessa dropped her head back and rolled it back and forth, making a strangled sound that made Savannah snort-laugh. "Listen, I love my job 'cause I love kids."

"The parents, not so much," Savannah supplied.

"Not so much." Vanessa laughed. "You get me, girlfriend of my cousin. You so get me."

"I do, cousin of my girlfriend. I do."

They toasted with pizza, touching their slices together before taking tandem bites.

The side door opened with a burst, startling them both, and Amelia Martini entered. She wore jeans, a black tank top, a black-and-white flannel shirt, and no coat.

Vanessa's teacher instincts kicked in immediately, and she scolded, "Meels, it's, like, thirty-five degrees out. That's all you're wearing? Let me guess—the hot flashes are back?"

"Back? Did they ever leave?" Amelia asked as she shut the door behind her and helped herself to a slice of pizza. "Call me crazy, but I'd rather not spontaneously combust and end up a pile of ash in the middle of the parking lot. Have you seen how people drive out there? I'd get run over in a heartbeat."

"Which wouldn't really matter if you were a pile of ash," Savannah pointed out with a half shrug.

"Look, you"—Amelia pointed at Savannah—"just because you're Julia's girlfriend, that doesn't mean you can be all logical and practical and stuff with me."

Savannah grinned as Amelia approached the couch and kissed them both on the cheek. Julia reappeared, kissed Amelia hello, and reclaimed her pizza.

They were all together, and this was when Vanessa felt the most relaxed. The most herself. These were her people, and they grounded her. They knew her. They loved her. They were her family.

Julia squeezed onto the small couch, so she could sit next to Savannah. Amelia grabbed the desk chair from the corner and rolled it over to the coffee table, and the four of them ate in silence for a moment or two before Amelia said, "Okay, what'd I miss? Anything? Catch me up."

Yeah, this was her family.

Vanessa retold her story.

❖

I think it would be a good idea for us to sit down together and talk about what might be going on with Oliver. Please let me know at your earliest convenience if any of the dates below work for you.

Grace Chapman sat at the desk in the corner of her too-small-to-actually-be-called-a-dining-room nook and reread the paragraph again.

And again. The email was from Ms. Martini, Oliver's second-grade teacher. Her first name was Vanessa, which Grace didn't think she'd known until that moment.

"Pretty," she whispered to the room as her eyes roamed over the name again. She'd met the teacher once, during orientation the week before school started, and she had a vague recollection of Ms. Martini. Blond hair, blue eyes, very, very chipper. She remembered wondering if it was hard to keep that level of cheer and thinking that if she was around it all the time, she might have to kill somebody.

But back to the matter at hand: Oliver was acting out in school. She sat back in the plastic chair that wasn't really meant for the desk and folded her arms as she gazed into the living room at her son. Oliver was enjoying some of his two daily hours of screen time playing his LEGO game on his iPad. These days, she was torn between worrying about him playing computer games too much and letting him be because it was the only time she could get some peace. It was the holiday season, so The Petal Pusher—the florist where she worked—was slammed with orders and deliveries. Grace could already feel the blisters from being on her feet all day. Her fingers were sore from arranging flowers with thorns. She'd definitely have to wear a lower heel tomorrow. Maybe some gloves, too.

"Hey, buddy, what do you want for dinner?" She said it loudly, hating that she'd become that, a loud person. But it was the only way to get her son to hear her.

He shrugged, not looking up from his game, and mumbled the kid equivalent of *I don't know* that contained no actual words, only sounds with inflections.

With a quiet sigh, she pushed herself to her feet and took the four steps into the apartment's tiny galley kitchen. She'd stupidly thought once Mike had moved out, the cramped apartment, which was actually half a tiny house, would feel a little bigger, but somehow, the opposite had happened. The walls had begun to close in. She was sure of it. Every morning when she woke up, she felt like the entire duplex had shrunk by six inches, and one day, it would just absorb her completely.

Stupid. Silly. She knew it. But these were the places her brain took her. She opened the fridge and scanned the meager contents, annoyed at herself yet again because she was supposed to stop at the grocery store on her way home, but she'd run late at work, and there'd been no time before she had to pick up Oliver from his after-school program. Sitting down with Mike and revamping their schedule wasn't something Grace had any desire at all to do, but she had to. She couldn't keep up this pace.

It was going to be french toast, she decided. She had all the ingredients.

"How about breakfast for dinner?" she called. Gave it a beat. "Oliver?"

"What?" came the little voice, dusted with irritation as it seemed to be a lot lately.

"French toast?"

"Okay." At least it was an agreeable response and not a temper tantrum. Yeah, those were new. As she pulled eggs and milk from the fridge, she recalled two days ago when he'd thrown a tantrum in the shoe store. He was seven years old. Seven, for God's sake, not three. And yet he'd thrown the box of sneakers he didn't want and shouted that he hated her. And while she knew he didn't mean it, that he was just being a kid, she'd felt the prick of tears behind her eyes, which mixed with the embarrassment of other customers looking at her.

They'd left the store immediately. New-shoeless.

Even as a toddler, Oliver had never acted like that. He'd never really gone through the terrible twos, at least not to the extent everybody had prepared Grace for, warned her about. He was a good boy. He'd always been a good boy. Sweet. Kind. Funny as hell. He made her laugh all the time. Well. He used to. Now he was sullen. His temper was short. He seemed to have lost patience with her.

Out of the corner of her eye, the computer caught her attention. She'd left open the email from Ms. Martini. They needed to see Oliver's teacher. Why was she nervous about it? She shouldn't be. Oliver was seven. She'd had many parent-teacher conferences about him, and she'd have a ton more before he graduated from high school. It was no big deal. But until now, they'd almost exclusively taken place online. The in-person conference wasn't as common as it once had been. People were busy. Time was precious. FaceTime and Zoom were things now. She sighed, knowing what her actual worry was—if Ms. Martini wanted to talk in person, it was likely things were too much of a concern to address them online. All right. She would deal with that when the time came. She'd go in, they'd talk, she'd come home. Easy-peasy.

"Son of a bitch!" came Oliver's little voice, then a clunk.

Grace stopped beating eggs and hurried around the corner to see the iPad on the floor and Oliver's arms folded across his chest.

"Buddy, what happened?"

"Stupid game doesn't work," he muttered, and if she wasn't his mother and didn't speak Oliver, she'd have had to ask him to repeat himself.

Five-four-three-two-one…Grace had learned the countdown technique long ago exactly for moments like this. In her head, she debated over which problem to address first, the swearing or the mistreatment of belongings. "What did we talk about the other day?" she asked, impressing even herself with the calm tone of her voice as she reached for the iPad. Not broken, thank God. In no way could she afford a new one right now. She held it up and used a sterner tone. "Oliver. What did we say?"

His dark eyebrows were a sharp V above his nose, but he said quietly, "It's 'spensive."

"It's expensive. Right. And what are you supposed to do when you get stuck on a game?"

Oliver let go of a sigh, and Grace almost smiled. Already practicing for teenagerdom. "Ask you."

"That's right. Ask me."

Mike would've put the iPad away, and that would've been that. He always had an easier time being strict. Instead, though, Grace took a seat on the arm of the chair where Oliver sat and handed the iPad back to him. Hiding her smile at his obvious surprise was harder than she expected.

"Show me where you got stuck. We'll figure it out together, okay?"

Damn if he didn't seem relieved, and he looked up at her with his big green eyes, so like hers, and smiled at her. More tears behind her eyes because, my God, how long had it been since he'd smiled at her?

"And can we watch the language, please?" Yeah, she should've gotten on him in a big way about that—and she'd have to talk to Mike about censoring himself a bit better around their son—but she was honestly so happy to see his face light up that she didn't want to spoil it.

"Yeah. Sorry." He grimaced, then made a show of scootching and patted the small space of cushion next to him. "Wanna sit?"

She did. More than anything. She squeezed herself onto the chair, and they ended up shifting so he was in her lap. He didn't even complain that he was too big or squirm to make his discomfort known. Who knew how long this would last? Grace certainly didn't because seven was almost eight, and eight was closing in on nine and ten, and everybody knew nine- and ten-year-old boys didn't want to sit on their moms' laps or hug their moms, right? So she soaked it in, hugged him close, and helped him get unstuck in his building game.

The french toast would have to wait.

CHAPTER TWO

*W*hy am I so damn irritated?
    And then the snort. Sarcastic. Something Grace's teenage self would've used on her parents or siblings. *You're not worth words* was what it said.

Lots of reasons to be irritated. First of all, it was November. This was when busy time at The Petal Pusher began, and it wouldn't let up until after the first of the year. And even then, there would only be a small break before orders for Valentine's Day and Valentine's Day weddings started rolling in. Her boss, Ava Green, was not happy that Grace had asked for an extended lunch, even if it had to do with her son. She'd be passive-aggressively annoyed with Grace for the rest of the day, Grace was sure of it. And that would be fun. Second, Mike had a meeting he—quote—couldn't get out of, and yes, Grace made the air quotes in her head because, really? He couldn't get out of a meeting when there was an issue with his child? Apparently, the answer to that was yes, so he'd opted to let Grace deal with things on her own. Which wasn't really new and not totally unexpected, but still. Irritating. Third, it was freaking cold out, and she'd worn a jacket that was much too light. The wind picked up Grace's hair and whipped it around her head as she walked from the parking lot to the school, following the signs to the office entrance. Hands pushed way down into her pockets, head bowed, she held her coat as tightly around her as she could until she was able to find the door with the buzzer and camera. She announced herself, the door buzzed so she could pull it open, and the wind blew her into the building like a dead leaf.

She stood there for a moment to catch her breath, get her bearings. She was at the end of a long hallway, the standard gray vinyl flooring reflecting the bad lighting from above.

Schools all smelled the same to her, especially elementary ones. Crayons and construction paper and electronics and rubber. Funny how you could be out of school for over a decade, well into adulthood, and still recognize the smell, still feel like you should be running to class before you got caught lingering in the empty hall after the bell.

Check In Here. The big sign on the door to her left directed her inside, and she entered the administration office. Three women sat in the open area behind a long, high counter. The one closest to her, who couldn't be much older than her own twenty-nine years, smiled up at her. Her nameplate said she was Ms. Parker.

"Can I help you?"

"Hi, yes, I'm Grace Chapman. I'm supposed to be meeting with my son's teacher."

"Which teacher is that?"

Duh, Grace. She closed her eyes, gave her head a little shake. "Sorry, yeah. Um, Ms. Martini?"

"Oh, Vanessa. Sure. She's in room seventeen." Ms. Parker jotted something into her computer, then handed Grace a laminated Visitor card to clip to her jacket, then pointed to a binder on the counter. "Sign in right here and then drop the pass back off when you leave." She stood up and pointed. "Down this hall to the end, make a left, her room will be on the right."

Grace thanked her and pushed out of the office and into the belly of the school. At this time of day, it was bustling. She imagined some kids were at lunch, but she also passed plenty of full classrooms, small heads bent over desks, laptops open on the desks of older kids.

Ms. Parker's directions were perfect, and in less than three minutes, Grace stood at the open door of room seventeen. The room was empty, except for the very pretty woman at the teacher's desk in front, typing with impressive speed on the laptop in front of her. Her blond hair was pulled back and fastened low against her neck, and she wore a flowing printed skirt and a simple blue top. Before Grace could rap her knuckles on the doorjamb, Vanessa Martini looked up from her work and met her gaze with light blue eyes.

"Mrs. Chapman?" Ms. Martini asked as she stood from her desk and crossed the room, hand outstretched. Her smile was cool, and it surprised Grace how easy that was to detect. Reserved for the parents of problem children, Grace thought as a seed of dread bloomed somewhere near the pit of her stomach. "Come in. Have a seat." Ms. Martini gestured to a chair that had been placed next to the desk. It was slightly smaller than a regular chair—likely pulled from one of the students' desks—and as Grace sat in it, she wondered if that was intentional.

"So," Ms. Martini said. Then she inhaled, exhaled, and folded her hands on her desk. "We need to talk about Oliver." When she said his name, her face softened just a touch.

"I know your email said he's been acting out." Grace swallowed and held Ms. Martini's gaze, even as those beautiful eyes, like azure crystals, stayed cool.

"He has, and it's not like him from what I gather. He disrupts class. He talks without being called on. He seems…angry." Ms. Martini waited, seemed to be gauging Grace's reaction to that. "In the second grade, the kids have pretty much got sharing down pat, but Oliver has decided he doesn't like that. Everything is his."

Grace swallowed again, feeling scolded herself, even though she was fine with sharing. Good at it, in fact. She liked to share, really. She nodded. As Ms. Martini seemed to wait, she took a deep breath. "Oliver's an only child, so he doesn't have to do much sharing at home." *Oh my God, did I actually just use that as an excuse?* Before Ms. Martini could judge her further, she added quietly, "His father and I have split."

"I see." Was she seeing things or did Ms. Martini's face get a little harder instead of registering the sympathy most people would?

"I mean…" Grace looked down at her hands, not wanting to get into the details of her personal life, but needing to explain. "It's been a while. That we've been separated. Months. But my hus—Oliver's father, he just moved out. A couple of weeks ago."

"I see," Ms. Martini said again. And again, not a hint of sympathy on her face. Or maybe that was just Grace projecting. She did that. Her best friend Courtney was always telling her so.

"He seems fine at home." She flashed back to him throwing the iPad to the floor. Swearing. Okay, so that was a teensy lie.

"And you said no siblings."

Grace shook her head. No, they hadn't gotten that far. Thank God.

"Is he seeing anybody?"

"I'm sorry?" Grace squinted at her. Seeing anybody?

"A therapist."

A blink. Another. Grace just looked at her. A therapist? Seriously? "My son is seven, Ms. Martini."

"I'm aware of that, Mrs. Chapman. Your son is also having trouble around other kids and authority figures, and it seems pretty clear why." As if realizing just how harsh she sounded, Ms. Martini seemed to make an effort to temper herself and her tone. "Look," she said after a second or two. "Oliver is a good boy, and I don't mean to judge you or your handling of your own divorce."

It sounds like that's exactly what you're doing. Grace managed to keep the words in her head.

"I'm just saying that…have you talked to him about it? In detail?"

It was a valid question, and they *had* talked to him when they'd first decided to split, but then school had started and then Halloween was coming and then it was on them and only *then* did Mike finally find a place and move out. For fuck's sake, had she gotten so distracted by her own emotions that she forgot to check in on her kid's?

She left the meeting feeling like crap. Mike had made her feel like a crappy wife, and now Ms. Martini made it clear she was also a crappy mother. Crap, all the way around. Grace didn't like being made to feel stupid. Or incompetent. But Oliver's teacher had made her feel both of those things. And really, how far off was she?

She pulled the door closed on her car and dropped her head to the steering wheel. Did she have time to sit there and cry for a few minutes? Because that's what she felt like doing.

Her phone pinged an incoming text, and her question was answered with a resounding no, she did not have time.

Where ru?!

Her boss, freaking out on her as usual, and Grace instantly regretted teaching her to use the text function on her phone. In Ava's defense, it was crazed at the flower shop. In Grace's defense, her divorce was seriously messing up her kid.

That should earn her a good cry, shouldn't it?

The afternoon went by like molasses rolling downhill in January, and the fourth time Vanessa caught herself looking at her watch, she managed to stifle the groan before her students caught it. Her mood had slid into that gray area, not great but not awful. Just…meh.

Though he'd likely had no idea she'd met with his mother, Oliver Chapman had a reasonably trouble-free afternoon and even smiled at her once. He had his mother's eyes, she'd learned that day when she'd looked up from her work and seen Grace Chapman standing in her doorway, all windblown dark hair and wide seafoam-green eyes. She was pretty. Like, *really* pretty. Her dark hair only made those eyes more of a feature. She wasn't tall, and she'd worn a jacket, but it was clear she had some curves underneath it. Yeah, Grace Chapman was very attractive.

"Also clueless and kinda defensive," she muttered as she packed up her laptop at the end of the day.

"Are you talking to yourself again?" Danika James wore her usual expression—the one that said, *Honey, if you'd only listen to me when I tell you!*—as she leaned against the doorjamb of Vanessa's room.

"At least that way, I know somebody's listening," Vanessa replied with a chuckle. She took in Danika's lightweight, multicolored dress, along with the enormous tote bag, purse, and computer bag that all hung from her shoulders, all indicators that she was on her way out. "It's crazy windy out. And also November. Where is your coat?"

"How many times do I have to tell you that this body of mine runs hella hot?"

Vanessa shook her head with a grin and joined her in the hall where they fell into step. "A few more, clearly. How you don't freeze to death, I'll never know."

"When you have as much as I do to love, you keep yourself warm."

"Until you get home to Will," Vanessa added with a grin.

"Until I get home to Will"—Danika paused for likely dramatic effect—"and then I keep him warm, too."

True to Vanessa's warning, the wind hit them hard the second they opened the door, taking the words she spoke and whisking them away before Danika could hear them. It was nearing five o'clock, so the building—an elementary school that stood on its own while the junior high and high school students attended classes seven blocks away—was fairly cleared out by then.

"You okay?" Danika managed to make herself heard when there was a break in the wind as they hurried to the teachers' lot, which seemed to get farther away the colder the weather got. "You're quiet, and that's not like you."

Vanessa scratched at her forehead and lifted her shoulders to her ears in an attempt to battle the wind. "Yeah. Just a weird day is all." Not really. That was a lie. But Danika was a prober, and if she let on that anything at all was bothering her, she'd never get to her car or home to her warm house.

"I hear that."

Danika's minivan was first, and they said their good-byes. Vanessa slid into her Prius and immediately heard her cousin Amelia's voice in her head saying teasingly, *It's not a car, it's an attitude*, before starting it up. Made her smile every time. Twenty-five minutes later, she was unlocking the door to her small one-story house.

Stress just seemed to slide off her the second she entered her home. It was the best part of her day. Her shoulders dropped, her breathing evened out, and her heart rate slowed into a more relaxed rhythm. Once out of her coat and having shed all her bags, she went straight to the switch on the wall that turned on the gas fireplace and stood for a moment or two just staring at the flames and holding out her hands as if it was a campfire and she was warming them. In her room, she changed into cozies, gray sweatpants and a navy blue hoodie, and pulled her hair into a messy bun on top of her head, then stared at her own reflection.

Grace Chapman had had an effect on her.

Okay, no. Not exactly true. Well, okay, maybe true, but that wasn't the effect she meant. She shook her head in some weird attempt to loosen up her thoughts, get them in the right order. No, the *conversation* with Grace Chapman had had an effect. Yes. Better.

Her mind drifted as she wandered into the kitchen and absently sorted through the mail she'd left in a pile on the counter all week. Divorce was a subject that, when brought up in any kind of discussion, would move itself to the forefront of her brain and stay there for hours, days, sometimes weeks. Even years after her parents had split, she didn't talk about it a lot—an unusual thing because Vanessa was a talker—but it had messed with her in many unforeseeable ways. It made her grow up way too fast and miss out on much of the formative part of her childhood. It made her wary of long-term commitment and fiercely protective of her mother. So many little things about her—her habits, her behaviors—could be traced back to the effect her parents' divorce had had on her. It would do the same thing to poor Oliver Chapman, unless his mother could see it, grasp it, and do something to stop it.

"She certainly didn't seem to grasp it today," she said, recalling the way Grace Chapman's face had shuttered. Vanessa had been direct. Factual. All right, maybe a tiny bit harsh. But if she didn't tell the woman, who would? She only had Oliver's best interests at heart. That was her job, after all.

None of the rationalization seemed to make her feel better, and she couldn't get those green eyes out of her head. She finished with the mail, did some dishes she'd left in the sink that morning, then stood in the kitchen with her hands on her hips and sighed loudly.

It was time.

It was like the thought whacked her in the head with a two-by-four, and she grinned widely as the three words settled into her brain. She'd been waiting for them, waiting until she knew she was ready. Weird that it would be today, after the way her meeting had stirred up old, uncomfortable feelings. Or maybe that was exactly why. She picked up her phone.

I'm ready, she typed and sent the text, then set down the phone and reread the letter she'd received from the state tax department telling her that property taxes had gone up. Welcome to homeownership in New York.

In less than a minute, her phone pinged a return text. Her cousin Amelia.

You are not. Don't tease me.

Vanessa gave a little snort-laugh. It was exactly the response she'd expected. *I'm serious. I'm ready.*

So you've said. 647 times. And an eye roll emoji. *Not falling for it. Mean to tease me.* And a mad emoji.

Vanessa grinned. She'd been rolling around the idea of getting a dog for months now, and she'd promised Amelia she could help. But every time she'd mentioned it and Amelia got excited, she'd chickened out and changed her mind. She'd never felt a hundred percent ready.

She typed, *I mean it. I'm serious. Tired of talking to myself.*

Serious, serious? Amelia asked.

She gave herself a moment to think about it. To be absolutely sure. It was easy to come up with a dozen reasons why she wasn't ready, but they were weak, and really, was anybody ever one hundred percent ready for any big life change? She was ready enough, and she had been for a while now. *Yes! Very! Let's go look.* Sent.

She could almost hear Amelia's squeal of delight, picture her happiness in the words that came via text. *Hallelujah! I have been waiting for this day! When?* Then came a GIF of Rachel and Phoebe from *Friends* jumping up and down in celebration.

Vanessa laughed. *Online first.*

Deal!

Amelia would start looking tonight, possibly right now. Vanessa knew her well. And dogs were her thing. All animals, really, but dogs especially. Plus, Amelia needed—no, longed for—things to take up her time since her wife had left over a year ago.

And that took her right back to thinking about divorce. She sighed again, and this time, poured herself a glass of pinot grigio from the fridge, against her—okay, not terribly well-enforced—rule, as it was only a Tuesday, and she honestly did try to save her alcohol for the weekends. The truth was, she was rarely successful, as teaching was stressful, and that was before you even factored in the kids or their parents.

Having missed lunch, since she'd met with Oliver's mom during her lunch break, she realized she was starving and quickly threw together a salad. Because she'd planned to get groceries that night, but decided she didn't feel like it, her salad consisted of cucumbers, red peppers, and half an avocado that had seen better days. She was even out of cheese, which was a travesty of epic proportions in her world.

She'd been eating by the fire for no longer than three minutes when her phone rang, and she knew without looking that it was Amelia and a list of possible dogs for her to adopt.

The whittling down began.

CHAPTER THREE

Junebug Farms was a no-kill animal shelter just outside the city limits of Northwood, and though Grace had her doubts about what she was doing, they began to ease the moment she and Oliver walked through the glass double doors.

She'd expected him to take off running through the large lobby area—he'd been there before on a field trip with his class, so he knew the place better than she did. But he stayed next to her, his small, warm hand snug in hers, probably overwhelmed by the sounds. Grace was.

Barking. A lot of it. Other kids, running around, squealing. The lobby was large, two-story, and took all the sound up to the ceiling, seemed to amplify it, then hurled it back at her. Volume aside, though, there was something about the place that calmed her. The smell was definitely an animal one, but not assaulting. Almost pleasant, really, dog food and rubber toys and fur. The folks working behind the horseshoe-shaped front desk all wore smiles and looked happy to be there. It was busy—it was a Saturday, after all—but not stressfully so.

"This way, Mom." Oliver tugged her by the hand toward a door marked by a sign that had nothing but a line drawing of a cat on it. "The cats are in here."

Oliver had always wanted a dog—and that was Grace's pet preference as well—but they couldn't have one in their duplex. A cat was okay, though. It would add an extra twenty-five dollars to the rent each month, but Grace thought if Oliver had something to look after, something he was responsible for, it might help him focus. Soften. Take the shadow out of his eyes.

"Mom. Come *on*."

She picked up the pace, letting her ridiculously excited son tug her along, feeling her own grin because it was wonderful to see him so happy about something. They passed through the cat door, and the sound was cut by at least half. She took a quiet breath and followed Oliver into a space where windowed blocks lined the walls on both sides. There was a room to the right, also windowed, and it contained several plastic chairs. The door to it read *Visiting Room*, and she could see three people inside, all with cats.

"Where is he?" Oliver muttered. "Where is he?" He'd finally let go of her hand and was scanning the cards on each window, looking for the one that said *Rudy*.

Going in blind wasn't something Grace ever did, so she'd researched for hours on Wednesday night after she'd put her son to bed. That was the day she'd decided that maybe a pet would be good for Oliver. He had zero interest in fish, and she had zero interest in anything that resembled a rodent—*not* in her house—which eliminated anything of the hamster, gerbil, or guinea pig variety. When she explained that a dog was out of the question, but a cat was allowed, his eyes—so much like hers it was almost eerie—had widened in obvious excitement. He'd sat up straight in his chair and suddenly looked like such a little man as he seemed to contemplate carefully, then gave one nod and said, "I like that idea, Mom."

Apparently, they'd had a discussion in Ms. Martini's class earlier in the year about pets, and that had led to talking about adoption and shelters like Junebug Farms. All of which meant that Oliver hadn't gone in blind either. In fact, he'd shocked her by saying that, rather than getting a kitten, he'd like to "give a home to a grown-up but sad cat…make him happy again."

Grace had blinked at him, astonished at how adult he'd sounded in that moment. *Seven going on fifty* went through her head, not for the first time, and she'd smiled at him and felt her own pride in him. "I like that idea, Oliver," she'd said.

"Here he is!" her son cried now, skidding to a stop in front of a window, his small finger on the card.

Rudy.

He was not a small cat. Good-sized. Fourteen pounds, his card said. Under characteristics, it listed the same qualities that she'd seen on the website. Loving. Affectionate. Chill.

Wise, Grace thought as she looked at the cat. He lay there calmly, seemingly unperturbed by the small boy bouncing on the balls of his feet in the window. He was shiny black, with white on his chest, his throat, and right up his chin and the center of his face. Each foot was white, as if he wore furry white slippers. He blinked his big green eyes once at her. Those eyes had seen a lot, she thought, feeling the strange sensation that he was speaking to her. And then he turned his gaze to Oliver and stood, then bumped the glass once with his forehead.

Grace stared in shock, because there wasn't a doubt in her mind. She was absolutely sure the cat had just picked her son. They both turned their green eyes to her, and she felt a tingle run through her body.

"Well, we'd better see if he likes you, huh?"

"He does!" Oliver kept bouncing even as he turned back to the window, which was just above eye level for him, and began murmuring to Rudy.

Grace caught the eye of a woman in a Junebug Farms T-shirt, and in a few minutes, they were in the visiting room. The others had gone, and they had the room to themselves. Grace sat on an orange plastic chair and watched her son walk laps around the room, dragging one finger along the wall as he did so. Trying to get him to sit would be completely useless—he was flying on adrenaline—so she let him walk until the door opened and the woman brought in Rudy.

"Take as much time as you want," she said with a big, friendly smile and closed the door behind her.

The next several minutes were like nothing Grace had ever experienced. She'd never really seen actual bonding take place. At least, she hadn't been aware of it. But as she sat there and watched in awe, Oliver and Rudy formed an instant friendship with no help from her. Oliver was down on the floor, on his hands and knees, his head bent at a strange angle only kids could master, and he looked at Rudy upside down. For his part, Rudy sat, blinked, then pushed his head into Oliver's, which made him giggle.

"Mom! Did you see that? He bumped me." The delight in her son's voice was like light, filling the room with its brightness and cheer.

"I did see." She knew from her hours of reading that the head bump was a cat sign of affection.

"I think he likes me," Oliver said as he shifted his stance so he sat cross-legged. Rudy wasted no time crawling into his lap and curling up, his front paws hanging over Oliver's thigh like he'd sat just like that a million times before.

"Sure seems to."

It was fate. Destiny. Preordained. And before long, they were at the front desk, filling out the paperwork—she had done most of it online—to finalize Rudy's adoption. She was signing the last form when she heard Oliver's excited voice.

"Hi, Ms. Martini! I got a cat!"

"You did?" came the voice, and when Grace turned, there was Oliver's teacher, squatting down so she was eye-level with him.

"His name is Rudy. Me and Mom found him online. He's five, and his owner died, so he had to come here to live until he found a new home." Oliver looked up at Grace as if for clarification, and she nodded because damn if her son hadn't actually been listening when she'd explained Rudy's situation. "We're gonna be best friends and make each other feel better."

Um, what?

Grace felt her face flush at that detail she hadn't heard before, and she swallowed hard as her heart squeezed a little bit in her chest. And yes, she caught the glance Ms. Martini tossed up at her, but she looked away before giving herself any time to analyze it. Because who needed that judgment, right? Grace certainly didn't need to hear *I told you so*, which was written all over the teacher's very pretty face.

"Mrs. Chapman. It's nice to see you again." Vanessa was standing now, looking directly at her. Her mouth was smiling. Her eyes were not.

"You, too," she said, and her gaze shifted to the woman standing with her. A little older, light hair, hazel eyes, a hint of dimples similar to Ms. Martini's.

"Oh, this is Amelia Martini, my cousin." Ms. Martini spoke to her cousin rather than to Grace. "Amelia, this is Oliver, one of my students"—she ruffled his hair—"and his mom."

"It's nice to meet you," Amelia said with a smile that seemed much more genuine than her cousin's, and she shook Grace's hand.

That awkward moment that came when new people weren't sure what to talk about pushed its way into the small group and made itself at home, and Grace had the sudden urge to sprint out the door and not look back. She fought it valiantly until she realized she really did need to go out to the car. Tapping Oliver on the shoulder, she told him she was going to scoot out to get the cat carrier they'd borrowed from Mr. Garabaldi, who lived in the other half of the house and owned it.

"Okay," Oliver said. "I'll be right here waiting for Rudy." Again, he sounded like such a grown-up, and Grace felt her eyes mist. She stroked his head and headed out.

Yeah, she had to get out of there. Away from those blue eyes that seemed to see right into her and that weren't impressed with the view. At all.

❖

"Well, she was stupidly pretty." Amelia kept her voice low and only said it once Grace had headed for the door.

Vanessa was glad Amelia had been subtle with the comment, mindful of the boy bouncing on the balls of his feet and waiting for his cat, if she'd understood things correctly. Her gaze followed Grace Chapman's exit without her permission, paying close attention to those swaying hips. "She is," she whispered back. On a delay, she realized Amelia was not only looking at her, but smiling in that way she had. Like she knew something she shouldn't. "Stop it."

"Stop what? I'm just stating the facts as I see 'em."

"Mm-hmm," was Vanessa's reply. But there was no time to elaborate because Amelia spoke again, but not to her.

"There you are!" A tall woman with short, light hair and gorgeously smooth skin was suddenly hugging Amelia. Vanessa glanced down at Oliver, still standing next to her, and shrugged. He shrugged back and laughed his little boy laugh, and it warmed her heart.

"Vanessa, this is my friend Lisa," Amelia said, making introductions. "She's in charge of adoptions here."

"Nice to meet you," Lisa said. Vanessa shook her hand, liking her kind face. "I hear you're in the market for a new best friend."

"I am." Vanessa grinned as she suddenly realized her own excitement. All the trepidation from the morning suddenly melted away, and now? She wanted a dog. Plain and simple. She wanted a dog.

"Pretty sure we can help you with that," Lisa said, laughing as the constant barking suddenly increased in volume for whatever reason, then lowered again. "Follow me."

Vanessa glanced down at Oliver. "Will you be okay here?"

He nodded with the exuberance only a kid could put into a nod. "My mom's coming." He pointed toward the window where, sure enough, Grace Chapman was on her way back in, cat carrier in hand. Good time to leave. She ruffled Oliver's hair and told him she'd see him on Monday and to have fun with his new cat. Then she followed Lisa and Amelia toward the door with the drawing of a dog on it.

If she thought it was loud in the lobby, it didn't begin to compare to Junebug's dog wing, and the sound tripled once the door closed behind them.

"Sorry," Lisa said as she walked down a long stretch of floor with cages on either side. "They get excited when a new person comes in."

There were already a handful of others wandering the floor. Up and down. Peeking, squatting, petting dogs through the grates of the doors. Vanessa did her best to focus on Lisa's moving form and not on each dog in each cage. She knew if she let herself dwell, she'd want to take every single one home with her, and she obviously wouldn't be able to, and her heart wouldn't handle it well. So she walked, eyes forward, until Lisa stopped.

"Here she is." Lisa pulled the clipboard off the cage door.

Her name was Delilah, and she had the most soulful brown eyes Vanessa had ever seen. Even in her online photo, something about them spoke to her, and she knew this was the dog. Delilah lay in a ball, curled up in the corner on a blanket that looked like it had been hand-crocheted. Mostly black with a little brown on her feet, chest, and eyebrows, she watched the three of them, and when Vanessa said hello to her, she lifted the tip of her tail in an almost-wag, but she didn't get up from her spot. She wasn't a big dog, but there was definitely more of her than there should've been.

"Well, there's a lot of her to love, isn't there," Amelia noted, clearly making the same observation, but there was a gentleness in her tone.

"She's eight years old, up-to-date on all her shots. Her owner had to go into assisted living and wasn't allowed to take Delilah." Lisa frowned as Vanessa's eyes met hers. "Trust me when I tell you, it was not an easy decision. The man was heartbroken."

Delilah was sad. Despite those eyes, there was a clear weight hanging on her, and Vanessa felt her own heart squeeze in her chest. How could she not be sad? Her daddy was gone. A lump formed in Vanessa's throat, and she did her best to clear it away, forced herself to swallow. Twice. "Can I go in there?" she asked Lisa, when it was clear Delilah wasn't going to get up and come to her.

Without a word, Lisa used her keys and opened the door to the cage. Vanessa went in slowly.

"Hi there, sweetheart," she cooed. Those brown eyes followed her carefully, likely gauging any danger, but Vanessa just sat down next to her. "You're so pretty." She held her hand in front of Delilah's nose, let her get a good sniff, watched her nose twitch as she did. "Can I pet you? Is that okay?" She stroked the dog's black head. "You're such a pretty girl. Oh, look at these ears," she whispered as she rubbed Delilah's velvety ears. "Hi. I'm Vanessa."

"She's a mix," Lisa said, still scanning paperwork. "Looks like some beagle, some dachshund, and maybe a little Lab."

"You're a dog stew, huh?" Vanessa said and felt her own smile widen when Delilah finally lifted her head and seemed to study her.

"You're welcome to take her for a walk if you like," Lisa said. "Get to know each other a little bit. Up to you."

Vanessa met Amelia's eyes. "You think?"

"Let's do it," Amelia said.

Ten minutes later, they were outside the building, Delilah on a leash between them. Vanessa had laughed when Lisa brought out the leash because Delilah had perked up noticeably, and Lisa told her that the dog hadn't had a lot of exercise the past year or so once her owner had become less active.

"She's really pretty great on the leash," Vanessa commented now as they stopped to sniff a bush. "Can you imagine, though? One day, you're living your life, at home with the person you love, and the next, you're in a cage with a blanket and a concrete floor, and that person is nowhere to be found. How awful that must be. No wonder she looks so sad." Vanessa felt her eyes tear up again.

"You're not gonna cry, are you?" Amelia teased her and bumped her with a shoulder.

"No," Vanessa said, quickly pulling herself together. "How do you know Lisa?" she asked. *There you go, Martini, shift the focus.*

Amelia gave a casual shrug. "I come here sometimes. Volunteer to walk the dogs and cuddle the cats."

Vanessa stopped walking and gaped at her. "You do?"

"Why do you say it like that?" Amelia's brow furrowed. "It's not unusual."

"I mean…" Vanessa tipped her head. "It's not unusual, no, but it's unusual for you."

"Why?"

"I say this with all the love in my heart, but you are not always warm and fuzzy."

There was a beat when Vanessa was sure Amelia was going to argue the point. She even took a breath like she was going to blow up on her. Instead, she just let it out. "You're right. I'm not. At least not the past year or two."

"I'm sorry, Meels. I'm not trying to be a dick."

"S'okay. You're not." Delilah was loving the walk, so they kept going, turning around so they were following a path that led to a large barn where Junebug housed farm animals up for adoption. Amelia gazed out into the middle distance as she spoke. "I could feel myself becoming hard. Cold. Since Tammy left." She cleared her throat. "I didn't like it. So I started volunteering here. Actually..."

After a few seconds went by, Vanessa looked at her. "Actually... what?"

"Actually, I'm thinking of maybe starting a little business. Dog walking, dog sitting, that kind of thing." Amelia nibbled on her bottom lip as if she was nervous about Vanessa's reaction. She'd mentioned this idea before, but just in passing and never with any detail or follow-through. So this was big. Vanessa wanted to be positive. Supportive.

"Really? I think that's a fabulous idea." It was the truth. Amelia wasn't a huge fan of people, but she had always loved animals. As far back as Vanessa could remember, Amelia'd had a soft spot for anything with fur and four legs.

"You do?"

"Absolutely! And you can start by watching this girl when I have to stay late at school." She indicated Delilah with her eyes. "Isn't that right, Delilah?" The dog gave a quick glance up but was much more interested in a small pile of tiny brown balls. Vanessa gave her a tug. "Do not eat the rabbit poop, honey."

"Lisa said she might be able to give me referrals, too. Like, people who've adopted but work longer hours. Like you."

Vanessa heard the veil of excitement in Amelia's voice. Well, maybe not excitement exactly. A step down from it. Anticipation? Possibility? Whatever it was, she liked the effect it had on her cousin. "I think it's a great idea. The three of us should sit down and work on a business plan for you." She didn't need to specify who the three were, as she, Amelia, and Julia were always together.

Amelia nodded, and Vanessa could almost hear her brain processing the info.

"What do you think, Delilah?" Vanessa asked. The dog looked up at her, and though the sadness wasn't gone, it had receded noticeably. Vanessa squatted to hold her head in both hands and ruffle those ears.

She was rewarded with the big, wet swipe of a warm tongue, and her heart squeezed again. "You wanna come home with me? What do you think about that? Think we could be roomies?" Another swipe and Vanessa was laugh-crying before she could stop it.

"You're in love, aren't you?" Amelia asked.

"Head over heels," Vanessa said. "I admit it. Head. Over. Heels."

They rounded the corner of the building and headed back toward the parking lot, Delilah stopping at nearly every bush and flower to sniff and examine. There was a chill in the air, but Vanessa was in no hurry. She didn't have the heart to tug on the leash or speed the dog along. "It's probably been ages since she's been able to just sniff stuff, you know?" When they finally hit the parking lot, the Chapmans were just coming out the front door, and didn't that just figure? Nice timing, Universe.

"Ms. Martini!" Oliver called her name and ran toward her with all the exuberance a seven-year-old had, which was a lot. Amelia raised a hand to stop him, but it turned out to be unnecessary, as he stopped himself and his eyes went wide. "Is this your dog?" He whispered the question like he was afraid to disturb Delilah. She stood looking at him, and her tail began to wag.

"She almost is. Wanna say hi?" Vanessa squatted next to Delilah.

Oliver nodded, then approached and dropped to his knees so he was eye level with the dog. He held his hand out for her to sniff. "Like this, right? I 'member when that lady came to my old class." Vanessa guessed Miguel's class had had a visit from Junebug Farms.

"Just like that," she told him and nodded.

He petted Delilah's head gently with his little hand. "Hi," he whispered to her. "Good dog." He moved his green-eyed gaze up to her and asked, "What's his name?"

"He is a she, and her name is Delilah."

"Hi, Delilah. I'm Oliver." The two of them had a moment.

"Did you get Rudy?" Vanessa asked.

Oliver's entire face lit up as if he'd totally forgotten his reason for being there in the first place. "Yes! Wanna see him?"

Yeah, she hadn't thought that through, had she? She couldn't really say no, so she swallowed her own sigh and said, "Sure." Handing the leash to Amelia, she followed Oliver to his car. And his mom.

Amelia wasn't wrong. Grace Chapman was stupidly pretty. Her dark hair was wavy, and Vanessa wondered if it was natural or if she did something to it in the morning. It looked soft. Was it soft? A mental shake of her head and Vanessa put on a smile as Grace met her gaze with those incredible eyes. She was smaller than Vanessa—maybe five four—and Vanessa put her around thirty, if that. She wore a black pea coat, unbuttoned, and her smile seemed tired. And guarded.

"Hi, again," she said to Vanessa. "I hope he's not bothering you while you're trying to…" She indicated Amelia and Delilah, who stood a few feet away.

"Not at all," Vanessa said, waving a dismissive hand to punctuate her point.

"I wanna show her Rudy." Oliver was already crawling into the back seat and pulling the cat carrier toward the open door for Vanessa to see.

"Don't jostle him too much, honey," Grace said, placing a hand on the carrier. "Be gentle."

In response to his mother's words, Oliver went gentle by a thousand percent, moving in almost slow motion, and Vanessa rolled her lips in and bit down on them to keep from laughing. She caught Grace's eye. Grace rolled hers and shook her head with a smile, and oh my God, she was so gorgeous in the moment. Vanessa knew—just *knew*—that she'd just seen absolute genuine Grace Chapman. A glimpse of her, no barriers, no filters, no worries.

She liked it. A lot.

"Look," Oliver said, interrupting her thoughts and thank freaking God for that. He pointed at the door to the carrier and Vanessa squatted to see inside. A black-and-white cat with huge green eyes sat there, looking regal.

"Wow, he's very handsome," she said, injecting some wonder into her voice to match Oliver's. "He's so lucky he's going to live with you."

Oliver nodded. "I'm gonna take really good care of him."

"I'm sure you will." She stood up again. "And with those beautiful green eyes, he'll fit right in." Oh God. She'd said that out loud, hadn't she? A glance at Amelia's very amused raised-eyebrow face confirmed it. So did Grace's suddenly rosy cheeks.

A beat passed. Grace blinked, her face still pink, and said, "Okay, buddy, let's go. We want to give Mr. Rudy some time to get used to his new home, right?"

"Yeah!" Oliver shot a fist into the air, and it was like he punched the tension, broke it into pieces, and everybody could move again.

"Say bye to Ms. Martini." Grace smiled in Vanessa's direction, and again, it was a real smile, and Vanessa somehow knew it.

"Bye!" Oliver was already in the back of the car and buckling himself in to his booster seat.

"See you on Monday. Have fun with Rudy." She closed the car door.

"It was nice to see you," Grace said as she took steps backward around the front of her car. "Good luck with your new dog." She waved a hand in Amelia's direction again, then pulled the driver's side door open.

"Thanks." Vanessa lifted a hand, waved, and stepped back as the engine turned over.

"I guess I'm all filled up on entertainment today," Amelia said when Vanessa turned to her. "I have hit my quota. Because *that* was beyond amusing."

Vanessa covered her eyes with a hand. "I can't even believe I did that."

"What? You paid the woman a compliment. Who doesn't love a compliment?"

A groan was all Vanessa could come up with in response.

"Oh, stop. I'm sure you're not the first teacher to crush on the mom of a student." A laugh escaped through Amelia's nose.

"I don't have a crush."

Amelia's face told Vanessa she was about to do a terrible impression of her. She was not wrong, and Amelia said in a high-pitched, breathy voice, "Oh, those beautiful green eyes! He'll fit right in! Because you, too, have beautiful green eyes!"

"I hate you."

"Lies. You love me." A pause. "Not as much as you *luuuuv* Oliver's mommy, but…"

"Shut up and give me my dog."

Chapter Four

Weren't you supposed to be fresh and rested and ready to go on a Monday? Wasn't that what weekends were for? To rest you up and reset you? If so, it hadn't worked. Because Grace was exhausted, and it was only noon. Usually, if the shop was busy, it helped.

Today, it was, and it didn't.

"Did you finish that bouquet yet?" Ava Green snarked, her impatience as clear as if she'd been holding a cue card that said, *I am very impatient right now.* In her sixties, Ava Green was neither quiet nor gentle. Pretty, delicate flowers were her polar opposite, yet she'd run a flower shop very successfully since her father had passed away almost ten years ago. Or so Grace had heard. Ava didn't really share much personal info.

There were three wakes today, all starting at two, and it seemed every person who had known the dead folks had decided to send flowers to the funeral homes. Grace had spent the last four hours fashioning bouquets and sprays and bunches. Her fingers were bleeding from thorn pricks, and Ava's hovering didn't help. She clenched her jaw to keep from snarking back.

"Just about. Give me five more minutes."

"Jack's waiting." Ava managed to convey so much more than those two words, none of it positive, but Grace let it roll off. She didn't have the energy to fight with Ava today. The only other employee was Christie, a twentysomething woman who was really nice, but she only worked part-time. Grace wished for her presence right then. Hard. Squeezed her eyes shut and sent out a plea to the Universe. Shockingly, Christie did *not* magically materialize out of thin air to help with the workload. Damn it.

She finished the bouquet in its glass vase, and there was zero time to admire it. To take a moment and inhale the scents of the flowers, to rub the velvety petals between her fingers like she normally would, to send the flowers out into the world with a whispered wish to spread joy. Instead, she wrapped the bouquet in tissue, then set it in a cardboard base, wrapped the whole thing in cellophane, and brought it out the back door where Jack St. Charles, the shop's deliveryman, stood next to his minivan. It was already filled, colorful blooms visible through the back windows. Jack was retired from the Army, was never without a smile, and looked so much like Ed Asner, Grace wondered if they were long-lost twins.

"Here you go, Jack. Last one." She handed the flowers over to him as she blew a couple stray hairs out of her eyes.

"So pretty," he commented as he arranged them in with his other deliveries so they wouldn't tip. It was a complicated game of Tetris every day, but Jack was a pro. Grace didn't know how he did it. "Too bad the folks they're for don't get to enjoy 'em, you know?"

Grace nodded. "Agreed."

"You okay today, Gracie?" Jack was one of the few people in the world who she allowed to call her that, and it never failed to bring a smile to her face. She inhaled a big breath and blew it out.

"Just tired. Not sleeping great." Understatement of the year, right there. She couldn't remember the last time she'd slept more than two hours straight without waking up, her mind racing.

"Tell Ava you need a nap." Jack winked at her as he climbed into the van.

"Yes, she likes me so much that I'm sure she won't have any issues at all with me wanting to drop off to sleep during work hours."

Jack gave a snort. "*Pfft*, she likes you a lot. She's a pussycat once you get to know her. She's just real fond of her claws, too."

I've been here almost two years, how much more is there to get to know? She managed to keep the words locked in her head and, instead, smiled and waved him off.

Back in the shop, she washed her hands in the work sink and put a Band-Aid on the worst of the pokes she'd suffered. The bell on the front door jingled, and when Grace didn't hear voices, she realized the restroom door was shut, Ava likely inside. She headed out front to handle the customer.

One woman stood with her back to Grace as she scanned the flowers through the glass doors of the coolers. Blond hair in a french braid, black wool coat, cute black booties.

"Hi there, can I help you find something?" she asked. And the customer turned, and Grace's breath hitched. "Ms. Martini. Hi. What are you doing here?" She hadn't meant it to sound like that, but—hello?—she was very surprised to see her son's teacher in her place of work. And in the middle of a school day. And she wasn't the only surprised one, judging by the expression of shock tossed back at her.

"Mrs. Chapman. Oh, wow. Hi." The blue eyes were wide. "I didn't know you worked here."

"Yup. Almost two years now. And please, it's Grace. Mrs. Chapman makes me sound so old." Grace laughed through her nose. *Yeah, do that again, it's such an attractive sound.* She swallowed a groan of frustration and pretended not to wonder why it would matter if she was attractive to Ms. Martini or not.

"Grace," Ms. Martini said, then pointed at her own chest. "Vanessa."

"Hi, Vanessa."

"Hey, Grace."

A beat passed. Another and then Grace found her professionalism again. "Um, can I help you find something?"

Vanessa blinked rapidly several times, as if she'd been suddenly unfrozen. "Yeah, actually, another teacher in my building—"

"I'll take care of this," came Ava's voice, and suddenly she was standing between them, literally pushing Grace behind her. "There's another order on the counter, Grace. Could you get that going, please?"

"Sure, Mrs. Green. I'll take care of it." She gave Vanessa a shrug and stifled the desire to roll her eyes, keeping it all as good-natured as she could, and waved a little good-bye.

Though there was a large back area walled off from the shop floor, the main workspace of The Petal Pusher was open, so customers could see flowers being arranged, and she or Ava would know if there was a customer in need of assistance. Trying hard not to spy on Vanessa, she began working on a bouquet of dahlias. An unusual choice, but one Grace approved of. She loved the flower, especially those in deeper colors like reds and purples. These were a light pink, their heads almost bushy, the petals small and close together. The order called for a vase, and she decided a square one would make for a nice contrast to the very round flower heads. While she was always happy to do a mix of flowers, a request for only one type—not including a bouquet of roses, which was its own separate animal—was her favorite. Something about the symmetry, she supposed. She crisscrossed various stems with lush green leaves in the square vase until they made a nice frame of sorts, hanging over the sides of the vase until it was barely visible. Then she took the flowers and her pruning shears and went to work arranging them, the whole time straining to hear the conversation taking place in the front of the shop. While she couldn't hear a lot, she and Vanessa made eye contact three different times, and each time, Grace felt a wave of…something, low in her body. A pleasant flutter like you got when you were excited about something.

It was weird and lovely and uncomfortable and inexplicable, and Grace did her best to tamp it down, wish it away, ignore it, whatever she needed to do to not give it any validation.

Yeah, didn't work.

Vanessa walked toward her—toward the counter to pay for her flowers, Grace was sure—but for a split second, the fluttering increased in intensity as Vanessa came closer.

What the hell was that about?

Vanessa had chosen one of the prearranged bouquets from the cooler, and she and Ava chatted like they were old friends. Which maybe they were, Grace had no idea. She kept her eyes on her work and only glanced up again once Ava had said her thank-yous, and Vanessa was likely on her way out.

The eye contact again.

The pleasant flutter again.

Vanessa gave her a tight smile and was out the door.

Grace blew out a breath and didn't really get why she felt a sudden relief, as if the air had been unusually thin while Vanessa was there but went back to normal once she left.

"Looks good," Ava said, suddenly so close she made Grace jump in surprise. "What's the matter with you? Jumping around like your ass is on fire."

"Sorry," Grace said. "You startled me."

Ava grunted and grabbed up the scraps Grace had snipped off, then took them to the large garbage bin near the wall.

"So…you know Ms. Martini?" Grace didn't give her mouth permission to ask that. Apparently, she'd lost control of basic functions like speech.

"Vanessa? I've known her since she was in diapers. Went to school with her dad."

"She's my son's teacher."

"Oh yeah? She's never wanted to be anything else. Used to play school when she and her sister were little, and Vanessa was always the teacher." Something resembling a smile appeared on Ava's face. Grace did her best not to gape at such a rare sighting.

"Oliver likes her." She did not add that Ms. Martini wasn't terribly impressed with Oliver's mother.

Another grunt from Ava, and she headed to the office in the back. Enough conversation for now, apparently, and Grace smiled and gave her head a small shake as she finished up the order.

Her watch told her it was now twelve forty, and she wondered if the day would ever end.

The birthday party for Anita Cole, a fourth-grade teacher in Vanessa's small school, was short and sweet, just a cake, the flowers, and a quick gathering of well-wishers. Vanessa liked Anita a lot—when she'd been teaching fourth grade the previous year, they'd done lesson plans together—but it was her first workday away from Delilah, and she was anxious to get home.

The morning had flown by, but the afternoon had been weird. She tried not to focus on how she'd been shocked to see Grace Chapman. Since when did she work at The Petal Pusher? Vanessa had been going there for years, had known Mrs. Green since she was a kid, but she'd never noticed Grace there before.

Why did she have to be so pretty?

And why was her brain asking her such an irrelevant question? *Shut up, brain.*

Besides, it didn't matter what she looked like. At all.

Giving her head a literal shake, she finished her cake, bid her good-byes to her coworkers, and headed home. During her drive, she responded to individual texts from Amelia, Julia, and Savannah, all wanting to come by, Amelia to see her new favorite niece again and Julia and Savannah to meet Delilah, her new baby, as Savannah called her. She grinned as she used the voice command feature and told them to give her an hour and then to come on over.

She entered her house quietly, hoping to see what Delilah was up to before she noticed her new mom was home, but it didn't work. Delilah was right at the door, tail wagging gently, as Vanessa opened it, and damn if the dog didn't smile at her.

"Well, hello there, my pretty girl." Vanessa dropped everything she was holding and sat right down on the floor with her new dog. "How was your day?"

The tail picked up speed, and Delilah nuzzled into her, lay on her side between Vanessa's knees, and rolled to show her belly.

"Oh, I see how it is. I get home, and the first thing I have to do is rub your tummy?" Delilah's entire body wiggled, and Vanessa laughed. "Fine. Fine. I can do that."

And they sat there on the floor in the foyer for a good ten minutes, Vanessa rubbing Delilah's tummy and talking about her day.

"You're a very good listener," she said and bent to kiss the dog's nose. Pushing to her feet, finally, she said, "We have company coming, though, so we need to straighten up around here. You wanna go out?"

When Vanessa had purchased her little house, the fenced-in backyard had been a nice bonus, but not something she'd looked for. Now, she was thrilled to have it, as she simply opened the back door and let Delilah out, no worries about her wandering away. Apparently, every blade of grass and every fallen leaf needed to be sniffed and inspected, and it surprised Vanessa how content she was to simply stand at the window and watch. There was something relaxing about it, but after a few moments, she shook herself into action, tidying up and shoving things in drawers so the house was presentable for her cousins.

Forty-five minutes later, the doorbell rang, and Amelia entered the house without waiting for her to answer, calling, "Where's my niece? Where is she?"

"I think she recognizes your voice already," Vanessa said with a laugh as Delilah bounded from the kitchen to the front door and bounced her front feet up and down in front of Amelia.

"Of course she does. I'm her favorite aunt." Amelia took Delilah's furry black face in both hands and kissed her right between the eyes. "And we had a great w-a-l-k at lunchtime. Didn't we, Delilah? Didn't we? Yes, we did."

"Thank you for that," Vanessa said. "I was a lot less worried, knowing you were checking in on her. Everything was okay when you got here?"

"Yup. No messes in the house. She did her business on our stroll. She's a really good dog. You chose well."

"I think so, too." Vanessa stroked Delilah's silky back, then looked up at Amelia. "Wine?"

"God, yes." She followed Vanessa into the kitchen.

As she poured, she heard the front door open again, and more voices filled the house. Julia and Savannah had arrived. Vanessa pulled two more glasses out of the cupboard.

"Oh my gosh, look at you," she heard Savannah almost squeal. Then she called out, "Hi, Vanessa. You are now secondary 'cause I'm loving up your dog, and she's always going to come first. Sorry."

"I've been bumped," Vanessa said and faked a pout as she delivered wine to her guests. Savannah was literally sitting on the floor, with Delilah again on her back between Savannah's outstretched legs, getting tummy rubs and generally being spoiled. Julia was looking down at them, that stupidly love-struck smile on her face that had been there for more than three months now. Vanessa felt a quick stab of envy.

For the next hour, they sat around Vanessa's living room, Savannah never leaving the floor, even once Delilah had fallen into a sleep that had her paws moving and her ears twitching.

"It's weird to be catching up and not be at The Bar Back," Amelia pointed out. Usually when the three cousins met up to chat, it was in the back lounge area of Martini's.

"You can bring her, you know," Julia said, gesturing toward Delilah with her eyes. "As long as she stays in the back, nobody will complain. It's not like we serve food."

"Might be a nice change of pace for her," Vanessa agreed.

"Hey, how are things with your student?" Savannah asked, and Julia and Amelia both nodded. "The one we talked about. I've been meaning to text you and ask."

Grace Chapman's pretty face flashed through Vanessa's mind. "Well, I met with his mom, and it turns out, she and Oliver's dad are going through a divorce. I don't think she really thinks about how it might be affecting her son, though."

"That's the chick that was at Junebug, right?" Amelia sipped her wine.

Vanessa nodded.

"She was there when you were?" Julia asked, her eyes widening. "That's a weird coincidence."

"Right?" Amelia agreed. "I'll tell you what, though, that kid is freaking adorable."

Vanessa grinned, not at the fact that Oliver was adorable—'cause he was—but at the fact that Amelia had noticed. "He is."

"And his mom?" Amelia made a wide-eyed face and fanned herself.

"Hot?" Julia asked.

"Smokin'."

Yes, she knew Amelia had noticed that, too.

"They were adopting a cat for the kid, so maybe she *did* hear you, Ness. You think?"

As Amelia waited for her answer, Vanessa posed a question instead. "Did you guys know she works at Mrs. Green's shop?"

"The Petal Pusher?" Julia asked, and as Vanessa nodded, she squinted. "I wonder if she's the one who delivered my flowers when I opened the bar."

"Dark hair, amazing green eyes, small." Amelia described Grace. "Really, really pretty."

Julia pointed at her. "That's her. I remember her eyes."

"I went in to get flowers for a teacher's birthday," Vanessa said, grabbing back her story. "I'm standing there looking, and I turn around, and there she is, asking if she can help."

"I'd let her help me," Amelia muttered.

"I'm sorry, are you a fifteen-year-old boy?" Vanessa snapped, realizing somewhere in the back of her mind that she was protecting Grace Chapman. Not something she wanted to dwell on.

Amelia blinked at her and then glanced at the floor, and Vanessa felt awful.

"I'm sorry, Meels." She sighed, reaching out to squeeze Amelia's knee in apology. "I just…I get all weird around her, and it messes with me. When Mrs. Green came to help me instead and sent Grace to the back, I was relieved, but I'm not sure why."

"I do," Savannah said. Vanessa had learned that Savannah liked to watch and listen and absorb all the info before she gave her opinion on something. "Your worlds are colliding. You have your school world"—she held up a fist—"and your real world"—she held up the other, keeping them apart—"but now, this woman is showing up in both of them." She banged her fists together and opened her hands, mimicking an explosion. "Worlds colliding."

She was right, and Vanessa nodded. "That's exactly it."

"We usually keep our worlds separate. And there may be more than two. But whenever somebody from one shows up in another, it can mess with our schedules, our feelings, and our heads, because it's like they're out of place. They don't belong."

"It's a really weird coincidence that you met her at school, and suddenly, you're running into her everywhere." Julia sipped her wine and squinted at Vanessa. "Maybe the Universe is trying to tell you something."

"I have no idea what," Vanessa said.

"Well, if you run into her again at some random location, you'll know." Savannah shrugged, smiling.

There was a beat, and Vanessa felt a strong tug to change the subject. "Okay, let's talk about something else now." They all laughed, but Amelia's was loudest, and when Vanessa caught her eye, Amelia snapped her fingers.

"Oh! I got the name of the guy who used to own Delilah and the facility where he's living now. I'm not sure how you feel about this, but I thought we could take her to visit him if you want…" She sort of trailed off, and it was clear by her expression that she wasn't sure what Vanessa's reaction would be.

As if she completely understood the conversation, Delilah sat up and yawned widely, her long pink tongue unfurling like a party favor at a New Year's Eve shindig. Then she stood, stretched, walked over to where Vanessa sat on an overstuffed chair, and hopped up. As they all laughed, Vanessa scooted over as much as the chair would allow and made room. It wasn't nearly enough space, but Delilah made it work, folding her barrel-chested body up and settling her chin on Vanessa's thigh. Vanessa had had this dog for two and a half days, and she already couldn't imagine losing her. Her heart ached for the previous owner, and she looked over at Amelia with misty eyes.

"I think that's a great idea."

CHAPTER FIVE

Oliver never used to be cranky.

Grace tried to finger comb his hair as he dodged her and ran from the bathroom into his room where Rudy sat at the foot of the bed, watching his kid's approach. Oliver clearly gentled his demeanor, his words, his touch whenever he was with Rudy, and Grace was thankful for that. Also, kind of jealous.

Of a cat. *Seriously, Grace, get your shit together.*

She sighed. "The bus'll be here any minute, Oliver."

"The bus'll be here any minute, Oliver," he parroted back to her in a high-pitched whiny voice. But he followed her out into the living room where his coat, hat, and backpack were.

"I wish you'd be nicer to me." She didn't comment that her father would've given her a swat if she'd talked to him like that. "Don't forget we're going to see Grandma Haskins tonight." She held his coat, and he slid his arms in. She knelt in front of him to zip it, but he yanked away.

"I can do it."

She nodded, let him zip himself and put on his own hat. He *was* old enough to dress himself, she knew that, but she liked thinking he still needed her help. At least somebody would need her then.

When she turned to grab his backpack, he darted away and ran back toward his room, tossing, "Gotta say bye to Rudy!" over his shoulder. Grace stayed on her knees and hung her head, exhausted. It was fine. The kid had to say good-bye to his cat, right? Wasn't that why they'd adopted Rudy? To give Oliver something to focus on? To take care of?

She heard the rumbling sound that told her the bus was just up the street. She stood and took a few steps and peeked around the corner in the direction of his room. "Oliver! Bus!"

"'Kay!" And then a streak of little boy in boots shot past her, grabbed his backpack, and shoved his way out the door and into the snowy morning.

Grace watched through the storm door of their half of the house as he ran down their short driveway just as the bus pulled to a stop and the doors folded open. Lifting her arm, she gave a wave and the driver waved back. Nothing from Oliver as he disappeared into the bus.

"Bye, Mom. Have a great day, Mom. Love you, Mom." Catching a glimpse of herself in the mirror that hung by the door, she pointed at her reflection. "Stop it. No whining. This is how it goes. He's not a baby anymore."

In his room, she picked up his pajamas, which he'd left on the floor, as usual. Rudy lounged on the bed, watching her with his big cat eyes. She sat next to him and stroked his silky black fur. "You'll keep an eye on him, right? This snarky version of him is new. I'm not sure what to do about it."

She didn't have to leave for work for another hour, so she fed Rudy a few treats—bribes, okay—and threw a load of laundry in. She was coming up from the basement stairs when her phone rang.

"Hi, honey." Her mother. Terrific.

"Hi, Mom. What's up? I'm about to head out the door to work." Okay, not quite the truth, but not exactly a lie. She was about to head to work…in half an hour.

"What's up? That's how you answer when your mother calls?" The hurt was fake. Of course. If there was one thing Marilyn Haskins Brigman excelled at, it was making sure the topic of conversation was her.

"I'm sorry. I apologize. I'm just a little frazzled this morning." Again, not quite the truth, but not a total lie. She did have a lot to deal with.

"You always were bad at structuring your morning well."

"I'm sure I was."

"And now that Michael isn't there to help…" Her mother let the sentence dangle, and Grace could picture her disapproving expression. Pinched, with tight, slightly pursed lips and a subtle shake of the head. "I don't know what on earth you're thinking. Your generation has no idea how to work on a relationship. The first sign of trouble and you divorce."

"You're right, Mom. When your husband says he doesn't want to be married anymore, all you have to do is work a little harder. I don't know why I didn't think of that."

"Well, you don't have to get snippy with me."

Don't I, though? she almost said but knew better than to get into this kind of back-and-forth with her mother. It would go on forever, and she'd never win because her mother couldn't see beyond her own existence. Instead, she went with the tried-and-true method she'd figured out in her early twenties. "Hey, when's the next trip?" *That's it, Grace. Change the subject.* The only benefit to her mother's self-importance was that Grace had learned to use it to her advantage, to take the focus off herself and her wreck of a life. Her father had started a very successful law firm. He was quite a bit older than her mother and decided to retire when he turned sixty. Now, ten years later, he and her mother took a cruise every year, sometimes more than one, and they traveled like crazy. They were vacationing more than they were home. Her mother wasn't even sixty yet, but she'd seen more of the world than Grace could ever dream of.

For the next ten minutes, Grace made lots of sounds of agreement and said, "Uh-huh" a lot as her mother went on and on. Her parents were headed off on a cruise through the Caribbean over Christmas and New Year's Eve, and even though she hadn't spent the holidays with her parents in a very long time, knowing that maybe they had thought about it, maybe wondered if it bothered her that they were gone for those very significant days, maybe felt bad not seeing their only grandchild for Christmas, would be nice. But they never checked with her before making plans. Their life came first. Grace's dad was nearly as self-absorbed, but he loved his wife and pretty much did what she wanted without question.

"Mom, I really need to get to work, okay? How's Daddy?" Grace finally found a sliver of silence long enough for her to slip in the question as she stepped into her boots and pulled her coat from the small coat closet. The snow was coming down steadily, and she sent up a little prayer of thanks when she heard the telltale sound of somebody shoveling the front walk.

"I wish you would do something more with your life than put flowers in a vase." Her mother made a scoffing sound, and though Grace had heard the same sound, the same words, a hundred times since she'd taken the job at The Petal Pusher, it still hit its mark, still stung.

"I know, Mom. I have to go. I love you. Tell Daddy hi for me. Oliver is fine, by the way, thank you for asking." She ended the call before her mother had finished talking, and she knew she'd hear about that the next time she got a call or an email. Or even a text, as her mother was growing increasingly fond of.

With a loud exhale, she looked around the small living space. Rudy had moved to the back of the couch, so he could watch the outside world, his black tail swishing slowly back and forth like it was its own snakelike entity. Oliver's socks lay on the floor and, for some reason, reminded her she needed to pack his bag tonight as he'd go right to Mike's from school tomorrow and stay for the weekend. Grace dreaded those weekends, two days without her son.

"No time for that," she whispered to herself, giving her head a shake as she bundled up and headed out into the snowy November air.

Vanessa wasn't sure what she was expecting when she walked into Forest Hills Assisted Living. The sterile smell of antiseptic and sickness? Elderly people with blank stares sitting in wheelchairs that lined the walls? Maybe. But it was *not* the party atmosphere she walked into that Thursday night with Delilah on a leash at her side. She hadn't been there in ages, not since her great-grandma had lived there in hospice care for her last few weeks. She knew the hallway to the right took you to the wing where the residents were bedridden, and the hallway to the left took you to the small rooms and apartments where the residents needed assistance, but not twenty-four-hour care. But the colors, the feel, even the smell had all changed for the better, and Vanessa looked around in awe.

The lobby didn't look like a lobby, but rather, a giant living room. There was a fire roaring in the big stone fireplace that took up the whole of one wall. Several couches and chairs were sprinkled throughout the space, along with a round table and six chairs, all occupied by people playing cards. Vanessa couldn't tell what game they were playing, but there was a burst of sound as one elderly man threw his hands in the air while others tossed their cards into the center, shaking their heads, but with smiles on their faces.

"Can I help you?"

The voice startled Vanessa, and she turned to meet the gaze of a woman she'd put in her midforties. Tall and dark-skinned, she had an inviting smile and about a million stories swimming in her warm brown eyes. Her name tag said she was Elise Givens.

"Yes, hi, I called the other day," she said in response. "I'm, well, we're"—she held up the leash—"looking for Richard Walters? I was told—"

"Delilah!" The shout took them both by surprise as the man who'd won the card game tried to stand but ended up struggling with the chair he was in, eyes wide and focused on Vanessa and her dog.

"You found him," Elise said, and they both watched as the man fumbled with a walker and made his way to them. "I'd go help him, but he gets mad," she whispered to Vanessa. A couple other residents followed him, their eyes glowing with excitement. "We've all heard so much about the infamous Delilah. I assume this is her?"

Delilah's tail had started wagging a mile a minute when she heard her dad's voice, and now she was subtly bouncing on her front feet. Vanessa met Richard Walters in the middle of the room, and Delilah's tail swept back and forth, picked up speed.

"Oh, my girl," he said as he attempted to kneel.

"Here." Vanessa took his arm, and with Elise's help directed him to a chair. "Sit here and you can reach her."

He had to be in his late eighties, and through the lenses of his wire-rimmed glasses, his eyes were blue and watery, but bright, happy. She could see the blue veins beneath his papery skin, and he had only a handful of white hairs on his head, combed over from one side to the other. She adored him instantly.

"My girl," he said again, and Vanessa thought he might cry as Delilah snuggled her nose into his lap. When he grabbed the dog's face in both his arthritic hands and pressed his forehead to hers, she thought *she* might cry. She glanced over at Elise, and her eyes were wet as well. She shrugged as if to say, *What can you do?* and gave Vanessa a big grin.

"This was really good of you," she said to Vanessa, and Richard Walters looked up and met her eyes.

"Thank you," he said. "She's being good for you?"

Vanessa knelt down so she could pet Delilah while looking the man in the eye. "She's been great. I feel really lucky to have her." She held out a hand. "I'm Vanessa Martini. It's really nice to meet you, Mr. Walters."

He took her hand, then closed his other hand over it. "First, you call me Dick. Second, I don't know how to thank you." At that, his eyes did tear up. "I wanted to keep her so badly, but…"

"It's okay," Vanessa said. "I can't imagine how hard it was for you. But I have her now, and I promise to take the best care of her. We'll come visit you often, if you want."

"You will?" His expression registered disbelief.

"Absolutely," Vanessa said, her heart aching for this man. She couldn't imagine having to give up something she loved so much, not having a choice. "And I'll leave you my number so that if you need to see her, you can just call me."

He held her gaze for a long moment, and she felt a kinship with him, an immediate and tender affection for this man. He released her hand and went back to loving on Delilah. Two women and another man were hovering, and Vanessa sat back and just watched and listened as Dick told them about Delilah, how smart she was, what a comfort she'd been to him when his wife had passed away. In turn, they all began talking about their own pets, pets they'd lost, pets they'd left behind, pets they'd had as children. It was like being a fly on the wall, and she thought she could sit there on the floor all night, just listening to the stories and being fascinated by them.

Delilah was in her glory with all the attention, but she also seemed to understand the situation, and she would glance over at Vanessa every few minutes as if checking on her. Vanessa felt like the dog was saying, *I know this is just a visit and you're my mom now. No worries.*

This was all a great change of pace for Vanessa, given the day she'd had, and she let go of the leash and found a seat a little ways away so that Dick and his friends could pet his dog and hear his stories about her. Thanksgiving was a week away, and her students were going a little crazy in the classroom. A big difference between teaching fourth grade, as she had last year, and teaching second grade was that it was usually easier to distract second graders with art projects and stories. But they still knew a four-day weekend was coming really soon. Unruly was putting it mildly, and she was a teacher who was damn good at keeping control of her classroom.

There had been three fights today, too—she should call them arguments, not fights, since she'd put an end to them before they'd become physical—which was how she knew it was the time of year and not something more individual. She couldn't even remember what caused them. She leaned her head back in the chair and closed her eyes for a moment while the seniors loved on her dog. All she knew right then was that her students weren't the only ones ready for next week's four-day weekend.

"Ms. Martini!"

Her name had to be called a second time before she realized there was an actual child tied to the voice here in the present, and she wasn't simply flashing back on her day. Her eyes suddenly flew open because something had run into her chair, hadn't it? Several rapid blinks later, she turned her head and was face to face with one of the Rambunctious Six, as she'd mentally dubbed today's unruly students.

"Hi, Ms. Martini. What are you doing here?"

"Hi, Oliver. I could ask you the same question."

❖

"I mean, it's not the way I would have chosen, but…" Grace sighed quietly as she spoke to her grandmother, who looked at her, except not really. Eyes that used to take in everything looked at her blankly. They were still a stunning green—the color passed down to Grace and then to Oliver—but they saw very little these days. "It's the right decision. We've been in different places for a long time. This was the next logical step. Right?"

Grandma Haskins smiled a smile that said she didn't really understand but was trying, nonetheless. She patted Grace's hand, and that was enough for Grace.

"I should let you rest, Grammy." She helped her lie back, then pulled the blanket up around a body that was so shockingly small and thin, Grace couldn't think about it or she'd burst into tears. Her grandmother had always been a force. Tall and determined and sure of herself. Grace remembered how regal she used to look, standing tall in a time when women were still largely expected to be meek and small. Grandma Haskins stood out. Grace often wondered if that's why her own mother had taken a different path and married an older man who supported her—because there was no living up to her mother's example. Giving her head a little shake, she derailed that train of thought and forced her brain back to the present.

The curtains in her grandmother's room were open, but it had gone dark out long ago. Dark by dinner was not Grace's favorite time of year, nor was this early snow they'd gotten. She sighed quietly, and as she went to close out the darkness, her grandmother spoke.

"No, no. Leave them open. I like to look out at the moon."

Grace smiled. No moon was visible, but she left the curtains open anyway. Then she kissed her grandma's soft forehead and whispered, "I'll come see you again soon. I love you."

She wanted to stay longer tonight. Not sure why. Sometimes, talking through her problems with Grandma Haskins helped her to sort things out, see more clearly, even when Grandma rarely had anything of value to add. But Oliver had been restless—she couldn't blame him. How was a little boy supposed to have a conversation with somebody he didn't really know who didn't talk back? So she'd told him he could go see if Gio or Peter was around. Both were nurses, and Oliver was fascinated by men having that job. *Thanks, Mike.*

With a roll of her eyes, she slid into her coat, shouldered her purse, and headed toward the lobby, which was likely where Oliver would be, as he'd learned the names of many residents and loved to wander around among them. He was probably playing cards with Mr. Watson or asking Mrs. Davenport a million questions while she knitted.

Nodding and smiling as she passed people in the hallway, she reached the lobby and stopped in her tracks. It took her several seconds to make sense of what she was seeing. Oliver, his arms over the side of a big, overstuffed chair, hanging so his knees brushed the floor and his chin rested on the fabric of the chair before pushing himself up again, was talking to—No, it couldn't be.

But it was.

What the hell was Vanessa Martini doing here?

Before she could continue her approach, she heard her son's voice, tinged with excited disbelief as he pointed at a black and brown dog Grace only now noticed because it was surrounded by several seniors. "That's *your* dog?"

Vanessa's casual laugh was…well, it was pretty. That was the only way to describe the light, musical sound. It was pretty. *She* was pretty. No way around it. "You met her at the shelter, you goof. Don't you remember? Her name is Delilah, and yes, she's mine," she explained to Oliver. "But, see, she used to belong to Mr. Walters. He's the man sitting in the chair. When Mr. Walters got too sick to live by himself, he had to move here, and they don't allow pets here."

"Well, that's dumb," Oliver said, and Ms. Marti—err, Vanessa—ruffled his hair.

"Sometimes, it has to be that way. So Mr. Walters took Delilah to Junebug Farms, the same place you found your cat, remember?"

"Oh yeah!"

"He took her there so she could find a new home that could take care of her as well as he did before he got sick. And that's when I came along."

"And now you take care of her."

"I do. I thought, since we don't live that far away, I could bring Delilah to see Mr. Walters every now and then, so he doesn't miss her too much, see?"

Oliver was watching the dog, nodding at the words, clearly enamored. "That was real smart of you," he said, almost absently, and Grace felt herself smiling at the awe in her son's words. She appreciated the explanation Vanessa had given him, the way she'd watched his face as she spoke, seemingly to gauge his level of understanding. Before Grace could step forward, Oliver spoke again, but his voice was so soft, she had to strain to hear him. "So now Delilah has a place to live with her mommy and a place to visit with her daddy." It was almost as if he was explaining it to himself, making the connection to his own life. Grace swallowed hard.

"That's exactly right," Vanessa said. "Who's the smart one now?" And she gave him a playful nudge.

"Hey there," Grace said, jumping in at what seemed to be a good time to interrupt. "Who did you find?" she asked Oliver, then glanced at Vanessa Martini, whose smile dropped in degrees.

Oliver stood up, his face open and excited. "That's Ms. Martini's dog. Her name's Delilah." He pointed, and at the mention of her name, the dog turned and made her way toward Oliver. She wasn't a big dog, but she was bigger than anything he was used to, and he pressed himself against Grace's hip.

"Hold your hand out, sweetie," she said. "Let her smell you, remember?"

He did so, slowly. Delilah sniffed his fingertips, then gave them a lick, and he giggled like she hadn't heard since Rudy's head-bump. In the next second, he was on his knees, talking to the dog and hugging her like they were old friends, and he was so gentle that Grace felt her eyes well up. In the next moment, Delilah had led Oliver a few steps back to the cluster of seniors, and they seemed as in awe of her son as they were of the dog, even those who were already familiar with him. It was a beautiful sight.

Quickly blinking away the moisture from her eyes, she turned her attention to Vanessa because she had to say hi to the woman, right? But Vanessa beat her to it.

"I didn't expect to see you here," Vanessa said.

"I could say the same. Seems we keep ending up in the same places." Grace swallowed and felt a flutter in her stomach as she glanced at Vanessa, took in her jeans, Chucks, sweater. Completely different than her teacher look. Casual Vanessa was still incredibly pretty. Sexy, even.

Wait, what?

Her heart rate kicked up.

Ugh. Why did this woman make her so nervous?

"Oliver tells me you're visiting your grandma."

She nodded. "Yeah, she's in the other wing."

"And he…" Vanessa nodded toward Oliver while she seemed to search for the right words. "Doesn't visit her?"

All right, it was possible that Vanessa Martini wasn't judging her, but there was…like an edge to her voice. A tinge of disapproval, likely because she'd let Oliver wander on his own. Which he did often when they were here, but Elise allowed it and nobody minded, and what the hell business was it of Vanessa's anyway? She nibbled on the inside of her cheek for a beat before answering.

"He does, but my grandmother has Alzheimer's and doesn't often recognize him. Or me, for that matter. Oliver"—she gestured to her son—"time to go, honey."

Did Ms. Martini's face flush a little pink? God, she hoped so, because she could take her judgment and shove it right up her very shapely—

"I'm so sorry to hear that." Vanessa's voice had gone soft, the edge gone, and it stopped Grace's motion. She dropped her hand to her side. "I have an uncle in the early stages. It's a brutal disease."

"Well." Grace cleared her throat, the wind of insult taken out of her sails. "I'm sorry to hear that, too." Her gaze found her son, who was very busy in the middle of a group of elderly folks petting the dog. "Oliver, let's go, buddy."

A moment passed. Grace sighed quietly.

"Did you adopt that dog from Junebug Farms when we saw you that day? It's the same one you were walking, right?" Why? Why was she engaging this woman in conversation? She just wanted to get her son and get the hell out of there.

"I did and she is." Then something weird happened. Vanessa Martini's face lit right up. The shadow of disapproval floated away, replaced by a brightness. She looked almost happy as she gazed at her new dog. Clearly unaware that Grace had heard the conversation between her and Oliver, she explained, "The gentleman in the chair? He's her old owner. When he had to move in here, he couldn't bring Delilah, and he has no family, so he had to give her up. My cousin knows somebody at the shelter and got his info so I could bring her by for visits." She paused, watched the group, then turned surprisingly gentle blue eyes toward Grace and said, "He looks so happy, doesn't he?"

Grace nodded, smiled, because what the hell had just happened? How had Vanessa gone from Judgy McJudgerson to kind of warm and fuzzy in the space of three seconds? But she had. Her face now was... well. Grace wanted to reach out and touch it, run the backs of her fingers along Vanessa's cheek. Her jawline. And what the hell was that about?

The sudden thoughts spurred her into action, and she called to Oliver again.

"I'm playing with Delilah," he called back, but with that defiant tone that Grace was coming to know—and despise—because it meant he wasn't going to listen to her. Couldn't he just do what she asked? He used to be so good. Now? It was like he purposely defied her.

"Oliver, please," she said and hated the pleading, whiny sound her voice had taken on, but she couldn't help it. It was fear. And she hated that. Hated that she was afraid of him misbehaving in front of Vanessa Martini. Afraid of her opinion of her, afraid it would go lower than it already was. Which annoyed her because why did she care what Vanessa Martini thought?

"You know what?" Vanessa stood and picked up her coat. "I have to head out anyway, so why don't Delilah and I walk you guys out?" She didn't wait for a response, just slid her arms into her coat and moved forward, then picked up Delilah's leash. Grace watched as she said good-bye to the old man whose eyes were a bright azure blue and told him she'd bring the dog back again soon. Then she turned to Oliver. "Go get your coat on, and you can walk her to my car." A glance up at Grace had her adding, "If it's okay with your mom."

"Can I, Mom?" He ran to her, bouncing on the balls of his feet, looking up at her with her own eyes. "Can I walk her?"

What was she going to say? No? "Sure." She swallowed down her irritation over Vanessa being able to get Oliver to do something when she couldn't. It didn't sit well with her at all, but damn if she was going to give the woman the satisfaction of knowing that.

The three of them left together, Oliver walking on Vanessa's side rather than Grace's. Vanessa held the leash until they crossed into the parking lot, then handed it to Oliver.

"Hold it tight. She doesn't pull hard, but she tugs, and she's strong. Got it?" She slowly let go, and the smile on Oliver's face was bigger than Grace had seen in weeks. Maybe months.

"Thank you," she said to Vanessa, surprising herself when the words left her mouth. "He was about to make leaving very difficult."

"No problem. He seems to really like animals." They walked side by side comfortably, like they did it all the time. "How are things going with the cat? Rudy, was it?"

"Good memory," Grace said, impressed. "It's been good so far. It amazes me how easily they take to a litter box."

"Right? I sometimes wish dogs would do that. Save me from having to go outside in twenty-degree weather."

They chuckled politely together as they reached Grace's car. "Okay, Oliver, time to say good-bye to Delilah." And she braced and was annoyed at herself for bracing and was shocked when Oliver handed the leash to Vanessa and gave the dog a hug. He whispered something to her that Grace couldn't hear and then he stood up.

"Bye, Delilah. Be a good girl. Bye, Ms. Martini." He reached towards Grace, and she held out the key fob to her car so he could press the unlock button.

"I'll see you tomorrow, Oliver," Vanessa said. "Thanks for walking Delilah for me."

"Welcome," he called as he climbed into the back seat and his booster seat.

"It was nice to see you again." This was directed toward Grace, and she nodded and gave a tight smile because she felt weirdly off-balance around this woman in a way she couldn't explain.

"Same to you," she said, then internally rolled her eyes at such a weak response. She added, "Have a great night," in hopes of salvaging her lack of eloquence. Vanessa gave her a wave and turned away, walking her dog farther down the row of cars. Even in the light of the lampposts, she could appreciate the gentle sway of hips, the blond hair that seemed to grab the light and toss it back in Grace's direction.

Stop staring.

Giving herself a shake, she climbed into the driver's seat and started the engine. Holding tightly to the steering wheel with both hands, she wondered how a routine visit to her grandmother had ended up leaving her feeling so conflicted.

Why did Vanessa Martini stir up so many emotions in her?

Not a question she was ready to face. No, not tonight. She shifted the car into gear and had to make a conscious effort not to look over at Vanessa one more time.

No. Home. That's where they were headed. Home.

Where she could put her son to bed, pour herself a glass of wine, and soak in a hot bubble bath and think about the way those blue eyes had softened, warmed. How those hips swayed gently, and oh my God, was she crushing on her son's teacher?

Goddamn it.

CHAPTER SIX

How's this?" Vanessa stood on a barstool, holding the end of three orange, yellow, and brown streamers that had been twisted together to form a very Thanksgivingy—as Savannah had called it— color combination.

"Oh my God, what are you doing?" Savannah gasped and ran across the floor of Martini's to steady the stool. "Trying to kill yourself?"

"Your girlfriend isn't dramatic at all, Jules," Vanessa said to her cousin who was stocking the bar with bottles that would be necessary for the night's specialty cocktails. "You were right."

"Told you," Julia called back.

"Me wanting you not to fall off this very precarious stool and break your neck is not me being dramatic. Just for the record." Savannah took the ribbing easily—she always did—and continued to hold the stool steady while Vanessa fastened the streamers.

"Gonna be busy tonight," Amelia commented from where she was filling napkin holders with square bev naps in fall colors, printed with the Martini's logo. "I like that you're changing up the color scheme."

"Ness's idea," Julia said, not looking away from the bottle she was measuring.

"You gotta change with the seasons," Vanessa said, taking the hand Savannah offered and hopping off the stool. "And the holidays. It keeps people from getting bored." She exhaled and parked her hands on her hips as she took in the decorations they'd put up. "Plus, if it works on my second graders, it'll work on inebriated bar customers."

"Gotta get 'em inebriated first," Amelia pointed out.

"That's the plan," Julia said. "Though I prefer tipsy. Don't want to send people home drunk. I want to keep them happily tipsy."

"I wish I was happily tipsy," Amelia said on a dreamy sigh.

"Come back later, and I'll help with that," Julia said with a grin.

"Deal." Turning to Vanessa, Amelia asked, "And how's my favorite niece?"

"She's great," Vanessa said as she grabbed her water bottle from the bar where she'd left it. To Julia she remarked, "I love being in here when it's not open yet. I don't know why."

"Me, too," Julia said as she smiled back. "Things are going well with Delilah, then?"

"She's the best girl," Vanessa said, completely aware of the dreamy sigh quality of her voice and not caring one bit. "I can't believe I waited this long to adopt a dog."

"I kept telling you—" Amelia began.

Savannah cut her off, but gently, the way Savannah did everything. "But if she hadn't waited until when she did, she wouldn't have the exact dog she got." Turning blue eyes toward Vanessa, she raised light brows. "Right?"

"Exactly right. I think I was meant to have this girl." Vanessa rested her forearms on the bar and her chin on her hands. "I miss her already, and I've only been here for an hour."

"And she's okay at the house by herself?" Julia asked, switching to a new shelf.

"She hasn't chewed up anything that's not hers. No accidents in the house. She learned where the back door was super quick."

"When I stopped by to let her out," Amelia added, "she was sleeping on the couch."

Vanessa laughed. "You didn't tell me that. Aw, she's the cutest bug. Oh! I took her to see her former owner last night." She recalled Mr. Walters's face when he saw his dog, the way his eyes got all misty. "You should've seen it. He was this sweet old man who was so happy to see his dog." She pressed a hand to her chest and made a sappy face.

"That was so good of you," Savannah commented.

"It wasn't his fault he couldn't keep her, you know?" Vanessa let her mind replay the previous night, Mr. Walters moving as fast as he could with a walker. And then a little boy ran into the memory, and she almost gasped, making enough of a sound for Julia to turn and look at her. "And oh my God, you're not going to believe this."

"What?" Julia asked, and both Amelia and Savannah turned their attention to her.

"Oliver and his mother were there." She said it almost as if she didn't believe it herself.

Amelia did gasp from across the bar. "No freaking way."

Vanessa nodded in her direction as Julia asked, "Who's…?" She squinted at her, but Vanessa could see exactly when she remembered. "Oh, is that the kid you've been worried about? The one who's been acting out like crazy?"

A nod. "I got to the bottom of that. The cause, anyway. His parents are splitting, and I think he's just angry. Still, she could pay him a little more attention."

"Who could?" Julia asked.

"His mom." Vanessa felt a burst of energy surge through her as she sat up straight. "I mean, I'm in the lobby of Forest Hills. Ever been there? The lobby is, like, this big living room, and a whole bunch of people are there watching TV and playing cards and stuff. I'm there with Delilah, and she's visiting with Mr. Walters—whose name is Dick, by the way, but I can't bring myself to call him that—and suddenly, Oliver comes running in. All by himself."

"What was he doing there?" Amelia asked.

Vanessa shrugged. "I guess his grandmother is there?" She squinted, trying to recall what Grace Chapman had said when she'd finally come looking for her son. "Or his mom's grandmother? I don't know. But he was just running around with no supervision, all on his own. I let him pet Delilah, and he sort of hung with us until his mom found him." She didn't quite realize just how judgy she sounded until nobody made a comment. Then she dropped her head back onto her hands and sighed. "I know, I know."

"Do you realize how many times you've randomly run into this woman?" Amelia asked after a beat. Vanessa lifted her head and watched Amelia tick them off on her fingers. "You have the parent-teacher conference with her. Then she's at the shelter. Then the flower shop. And now the retirement home? In the space of—what?—two weeks?"

"Wow," Savannah said, and her eyes were bright, a hint of excitement on her face. "That's definitely the Universe telling you something."

"Yeah? What's it telling me?" Vanessa gave a quiet scoff.

"Maybe *Pay attention to the pretty girl*?" Amelia offered.

Vanessa turned toward her, made a face and said, "Really? You? The queen of doom and gloom?"

Amelia looked like she wanted to argue but shrugged instead, apparently accepting the description. "Listen, I don't know. It's just weird. That's all I'm saying."

"Weird things don't have to mean anything other than they're weird."

"This is true," Savannah agreed. "*Or...*" She drew the word out, grinned at Vanessa, and gave her a half shrug, but left it at that.

"Are we done here?" she asked after a beat or two. "I need to get home to my dog and work on my lesson plans for next week before tonight."

"We're done, yes," Julia said. "Thank you guys so much for your help. Meels? You coming back tonight, too?"

"Are you kidding? My cousin's the owner. I get to drink for free all night."

Julia snorted and held up a finger. "One. You get one free drink."

"If you're serving that cinnamon roll drink, Imma be here all night," Amelia warned with a wink. She pointed to the stool at the end of the bar nearest the cash register. "One day, that stool's gonna have my name on it."

"I'll get Savannah to start pricing nameplates," Julia said, playing along with her.

Amid laughter, they gathered up their stuff, and Vanessa took a last look around the bar at their decorating. Martini's was an interesting mix. Julia'd had a vision when she bought the place from Amelia's father: classy, upscale, a little pricey. But it had been in their family for three generations now, and in order to magically become upscale and expensive, Julia would've had to leave behind a lot of the history, the regulars, and the reputation Martini's had of being a welcoming staple in the thriving Jefferson Square area of Northwood. With Vanessa's creativity and Savannah's practicality, Julia had instead embraced all of it, every bit of what Martini's had been and what it could be, and because of that, the bar was fun, well-known, and still classy. Things like theme nights and holiday parties had become the norm, and Vanessa gave a nod of approval at the Thanksgiving decorations they'd put up.

She was looking forward to coming back tonight. There would likely be a crowd, but Vanessa knew several friends and family members who'd be there. The beauty of frequenting a bar owned by family—you were never walking into a room of strangers.

And God knew Vanessa was ready for a night out.

❖

"There was no way we were letting you wallow for the entire weekend," Janelle Fusco said as she accepted a glass of wine from Grace.

"I've been where you're standing," Courtney Miller added. "And it's way too easy to hunker down on the couch under a blanket and watch Netflix until all your friends move on with their lives and leave you behind."

The three of them stood in Grace's small duplex sipping pinot grigio in preparation for a night out.

"I appreciate you guys not giving up on me," Grace said, then took a sip of her own wine. She meant it because Courtney was right. With Oliver gone to Michael's for the weekend, Grace didn't know what to do with herself. She felt like a boat that had been unmoored, floating aimlessly in the sea with no direction or destination.

Courtney, the less serious of the two, had gone through a divorce from her husband two years earlier. "I promise not to," she said, and her face was suddenly very serious. "I had friends who gave up on me. And I blame myself mostly, but I do put a little blame on them, too. I won't do that to you." Then the shadow of seriousness faded a bit as she added, "You won't lose me in the divorce."

"Thank God." Grace remembered Courtney's split from her husband, how friends just faded away, as if they worried the divorce might be catching, contagious. Grace had stayed in contact with Courtney because, simply put, she loved her. They'd been friends for almost five years now.

"I remember when my parents split," Janelle said a little bit later as they got their coats and waited for their Uber. "It was worse back then. They'd been part of this group of couples. Four or five of them. I'm not sure my mom is friends with any of those people anymore. And two of them were bridesmaids in her wedding to my dad."

Courtney shook her head, then shifted the topic slightly. "How's Ollie?" She was the only one who called Oliver that, and it made him laugh.

"Annoyed that he couldn't take Rudy to his dad's with him." She gestured to the cat lounging on the couch and watching them with his giant green eyes. He yawned then, like they were so boring he might nap rather than keep eavesdropping. "Mike's allergic, but it's somehow my fault." She sighed. "Everything is my fault. You should hear him on the phone when he talks to Mike. His voice changes completely, and it's like he's four years old again, talking to his daddy. Then he hangs up, and he's back to being seven and snarky." Suddenly, her eyes welled with tears. "Damn it."

Courtney wrapped an arm around her shoulders and squeezed. "I know just the solution to those tears."

"You do?" Grace asked.

Courtney glanced at Janelle, who nodded in apparent agreement. "Let's get you drunk."

"You know what?" Grace said, as she sniffled and they let themselves out the door. "Normally, I would argue, but not tonight."

"No?" Janelle asked as they made their way down the front walk to their Uber.

"No. It's Saturday night. I am childless and single." She took a second or two to let that sink in, 'cause yeah. Then she gave one determined nod. "Let's get me drunk."

"Atta girl!"

They laughed as they got into the sedan.

Not quite twenty minutes later, the Uber pulled to a stop in front of Martini's, and they spilled out. The place was fairly busy, and Grace glanced at her watch, surprised to see it was barely nine o'clock. Early in bar hours.

"I knew they were remodeling this place," Grace said, recalling dropping off a flower arrangement many months before. "But I haven't actually been inside for longer than a few minutes."

"No?" Janelle asked. "I love it. It's a cool place, and they do theme nights and fun drink specials. I wonder what they have tonight."

"How about we go in and find out instead of standing out here freezing to death?" Courtney always did have great ideas.

They headed in.

Lady Gaga was singing about being born this way, and Martini's, while not exactly packed, had a healthy crowd with a festive energy. Grace, Janelle, and Courtney found one empty stool at the bar and claimed it. They'd alternate who got to sit, and since Janelle managed a clothing store and was on her feet all day, she got the stool first.

"Ladies," said the bartender, a tall, dark, and gorgeous woman whose name tag said her name was Julia. "What can I get you?"

Grace remembered delivering the flowers to her because, honestly, who could forget a face like that? "You're the owner," she said, pointing at her.

"I am." Julia nodded once, her pride clear.

"I delivered flowers way back when you first opened after your remodel. Looks amazing."

"Oh, right." Julia pointed at her. "You work at The Petal Pusher. I remember you. And thanks for the compliment. I'm happy with how we've grown."

"Good." Grace was happy for the success for some reason.

"Look, I hate to interrupt your little reunion," Janelle said, but her quirked eyebrow made it clear she was teasing, "but some of us need drinks."

Julia laughed, her husky voice making for a husky laugh. "My apologies, ma'am." She gave a slight bow. "What can I get you? Our special tonight is the Cinnamon Roll. RumChata and Kahlúa. Highly recommended."

"Three of those, please." Grace ordered before the other two had a chance to open their mouths. "First round's on me."

As Julia grabbed the ingredients for the cocktails, Grace turned to her friends. Both were looking at her. "What?"

"For somebody who had to be dragged out, you've changed your tune pretty quickly." Courtney squinted at her comically and leaned in to her personal space.

"What are you doing?" Grace laughed and leaned away from her. "Stop that."

"Looking for signs of a mask. You are clearly not the Grace Chapman I know."

The drinks were placed in front of them before Grace could respond, and if they tasted anything close to as delicious as they looked, this was going to be a very good night. They were in short rocks glasses, the liquid creamy and white, on the rocks, the rim coated with a brown powder. Grace brought it to her nose and sniffed—cinnamon. Of course. She handed her credit card to Julia, instructed her to leave the tab open, then turned to her friends and held up her glass.

"To good friends, good times, and good drinks."

They clinked glasses and all sipped.

"Oh my God," Courtney said, just as Janelle also spoke.

"Holy crap, that's good."

Grace let the creamy liquid sit on her tongue for an extra beat before finishing the sip. It was a lovely blend of richness, a little cinnamon, a little coffee, and so smooth it was like drinking flavored milk. She looked at her friends. "Oh, girls, this is gonna be trouble."

"It sure is," Janelle agreed. "Excellent."

They drank and talked and laughed and joked for a good half hour before they were ready for round two. Courtney and Janelle were debating the pros and, well, the other pros of Idris Elba, since there really were no cons to the man, and Grace turned away to lean her forearms on the bar and get Julia's attention.

The bar was one giant rectangle in the center of the room, so there were drinking customers on all sides, which Grace imagined kept the bartenders busy. There had been two when they got there, Julia and a young guy, but now a third had been added. A woman with short blond hair with a blue streak in it was shaking a martini shaker. Across from Grace, Julia was leaning forward and talking to a handful of people who looked like they were together. One of them, a darkly handsome man, met Grace's eye, then gestured to Julia, who turned and smiled at her. The moment Julia moved away so Grace could see the guy she was talking to, her heart skipped a beat. No. It skipped, like, twelve beats.

Vanessa Martini sat directly across from Grace and their eyes locked.

Even from ten feet away, it was clear how attractive she really was, and Grace hated that, wanted to stop looking, but found herself having trouble. Vanessa's light hair was in a ponytail, but a loose one, which allowed for some hair to escape and frame her face, and she tossed her head to move it out of her eyes. Her cheekbones were high, and Grace knew from experience that if she smiled, dimples would make an appearance. She wasn't smiling now, but she wasn't throwing Grace any shade either. No sign of her usual judgmental scowl. She just...looked at her.

"Ready for another round?" Julia asked, yanking Grace back to her own space.

She blinked rapidly, refocused. "Yes. Please." *I'd like seven more*, she almost said but managed not to. What the hell was Vanessa Martini doing...Wait. Martini. Martini's. How had she not made the connection?

"You know her?" Grace asked Julia, immediately horrified that she'd done so.

"Who?" Julia asked, setting down the drinks.

Well, she had to point now, didn't she? Goddamn it. Using her chin seemed less obvious—kind of—and she indicated Vanessa, who was still looking at her.

Julia glanced over her shoulder. "Vanessa? Yeah, she's my cousin. You know her?"

"She teaches my son."

"Oh, got it." It was obvious Julia wasn't picking up on any of Grace's weirdness. Or if she was, she hid it well. Either way, Grace was thankful. "I'll tell her you said hi." And Julia was off to serve another customer.

Grace picked up her glass and took a very large sip. How was it that this woman was everywhere lately? Maybe she'd had enough dealing with it on her own. Maybe it was the alcohol. Whatever. She turned back to Courtney and Janelle. "I need your opinion on something."

"You've got to be fucking kidding me."

Amelia had been in the middle of a sentence but turned at Vanessa's words. "What?" Then she followed her gaze to where Grace Chapman sat directly across the bar, chatting with Julia. "What?" she asked again.

"That's her," Vanessa said.

"That's who?" Amelia asked. "The blonde? Or one of the brunettes?"

Vanessa flinched slightly, blinked several times, and realized Amelia had no idea who she was talking about, so she turned to her cousin, feeling her eyes widen as she explained. "The brunette sitting in the middle that Julia was just talking to. *That's* my student's mom, remember? You met her at the shelter. The one I keep running into. That is Grace Chapman. And she's here. Where I am. Again."

Amelia stared at her for a moment, then looked Grace's way. "Holy shit."

Grace had finally shifted her focus to her friends, and Vanessa was grateful for that because holding eye contact with her had felt almost like a competition to see who'd turn away first. And Vanessa had felt that look. It reached into her body and headed south, down below her stomach where naughty things happened.

No. It was the alcohol. Just the alcohol. Had to be. *Had to be.* Right?

Vanessa gave her head a shake and glanced down at the half-empty

Cinnamon Roll on the bar. It was her third. Right? Was it her third? No, fourth. Maybe. It was a good thing she'd Ubered because she was very tipsy. As evidenced by the way her body reacted to seeing Grace Chapman looking at her with those eyes. All moisture went south.

Julia approached them, sliding glasses of water to both Vanessa and Amelia. "The woman across the bar says hi. You teach her son." Maybe it was the look Amelia gave Julia, but Vanessa could see the exact moment Julia put the pieces together. "Oh!" she said, then lowered her voice almost comically. "Is that *her*?" Vanessa nodded as Julia raised her eyebrows, uttered, "Wow," and headed off to wait on a customer.

"I think I forgot she was so fucking hot," Amelia said because she'd had more than a couple drinks, too.

"She is, right?" Vanessa asked.

"Super-ly. Superly?" Amelia squinted, then shrugged. "Totally."

"Are you guys drunk?" Dante Martini leaned in. He was their cousin, Julia's brother, and the sweetest guy Vanessa had ever known.

"Are you?" she asked him.

He shook his head. "One of those things was enough for me to know better." He held up his glass of water.

Vanessa grimaced, then shook her head in recognition of his intelligence. "Smart guy." She picked up the water Julia had left her and took a long drink of it.

She didn't want to think anymore about Grace Chapman or the way her body was betraying her, so she drank more water, then turned on her stool so her back was to the bar. *That oughta do it.* Her inebriated brain was no help, though, tossing her images of Grace, her dark hair down and bouncy, her black top with the neckline that left a long column of throat exposed, and those eyes.

God, I need to get laid.

She flinched at the statement. Her intoxicated brain had clearly lost its filters. True, it had been a long time now since she'd been with anyone, but she wasn't somebody who went and had casual sex with random women just to have sex. She needed to feel at least a little something.

Giving her head a shake, she did her best to sink into conversations with her cousins, not think about the woman across the bar...the very attractive and, yes, very sexy woman across the bar. One that stirred up such a confusing mix of emotions in her. Which was new. Most of the time, Vanessa was a woman who had a good handle on herself. But tonight? She had no handles. She was handleless. She downed a huge gulp of her water and tried to focus on what Dante was saying about his job. Which was really, really hard.

A glance wouldn't hurt, right? Just a quick look?

And before she could talk herself out of it—because her normally very firm voice of reason had apparently been bound, gagged, and tossed into a closet by Cinnamon Rolls—she did a quick head turn and glanced over her shoulder across the bar.

Grace was gone.

"Oh, thank God," she whispered, and even as she exhaled in relief, there was a zap of disappointment that she wanted to ignore but couldn't.

"What?" Amelia asked her.

"I said oh, thank God, it's time to use the ladies' room." Vanessa slid off her stool and gave herself a second. When Julia looked her way, she mouthed a request for more water, then made her way to the bathrooms in the back.

Okay. You're good. She felt better, walked just fine, and more relief washed through her. A quick look at her phone told her it was after midnight. No wonder she was suddenly tired. She would use the bathroom, then call an Uber and head home. Plan in place, she sidled her way through a crowd of people toward the back of the bar and chuckled to herself. To herself and at herself. *What are you, a fifteen-year-old boy with a crush? Will there be wet dreams tonight?* She was still shaking her head with a self-deprecating smile as she pushed through the door to the ladies' room.

The three stalls were empty, their doors wide open.

Grace Chapman stood at the sink.

She turned, looked at Vanessa with hooded eyes, her lips freshly glossed, and Vanessa's feet wouldn't listen to her, wouldn't stop walking. She walked right up to Grace, who had turned to face her, and then they were both walking, Vanessa forward, Grace backward, until Grace's back hit the wall, and she let go of a small gasp.

No thought. No warnings. No hesitations.

Vanessa took Grace's face in both hands and kissed her.

All of her energy, all of her thought was focused on the woman in front of her. Logic, red flags, bullhorn sirens, all of that was shut out. And the very first thing Vanessa was clear on: Grace was kissing her back. Hard. Thoroughly. She felt Grace's hands, not pushing her away, but pulling her closer, one hand tugging Vanessa's shirt toward her, the other sliding up around the back of her neck and pulling her in. Grace's lips were soft, slick from the gloss, tasted like cherries. And then mouths opened, tongues came into play, and they were no longer simply kissing. They were having a hot and super steamy make-out session in the ladies' room of her cousin's bar. Vanessa felt wonderful and horrified and super turned-on and confused and happy—

The muffled sound of the bar crowd was suddenly louder, and somewhere in the back of her mind, Vanessa realized the ladies' room door had opened, and somebody had come in. She wrenched her mouth from Grace's at the same time she felt Grace's hand push her. They stood for what was likely a second or two, but felt like a year, just staring at each other, chests heaving. Grace's eyes were wide, her cheeks flushed, and Vanessa knew hers were, too. Grace brought her fingers to her kiss-swollen lips, blinked several times, then moved around Vanessa and hurried out of the ladies' room. Vanessa followed her exit with her eyes until her gaze landed on the person who'd come in.

"I can honestly say *that* was not something I was expecting to see." Amelia was wide-eyed, her entire face registering disbelief. "Wow."

Vanessa couldn't seem to make herself move. She just stood there.

"Ness? You okay?"

Was she okay? She honestly wasn't sure. Making out in the bar bathroom with a hot chick who rubbed her the wrong way? Was she in college? Better yet, was she stuck in a romance novel? 'Cause these things didn't happen in real life. Did they?

A head shake was all she could offer Amelia. That and a shrug because she honestly *did not know* what had come over her. Her train of thought? Her careful analysis of what she'd been about to do? Yeah, none of those things existed. Her body had acted completely on impulse—a dangerous concept. Except tonight. Why? Because there was one fact that stood out. One crystal clear recollection of it all.

Grace had absolutely kissed her back.

CHAPTER SEVEN

O h, that was so stupid.
      Those five words had haunted the remainder of Grace's weekend and followed her into Monday. She could ask herself what the hell she'd been thinking, but her answer was always *No idea*. She really didn't have a clue how she'd ended up making out with her son's second-grade teacher in the bathroom of a bar, and oh my God, when she worded it like that, it sounded so much worse.

Michael had taken Oliver to school that morning, so Grace hadn't had anything to take up her time and attention. Her brain had free rein to bombard her, insult her, and toss her flashbacks.

Okay, so she didn't mind those so much because wow, was Vanessa Martini a fantastic kisser.

Stop that right now.

It was a vicious cycle that she now recognized after more than twenty-four hours. She'd remember what had happened, how she'd let it, and she'd berate herself, but then she'd remember it in more detail— the hungry, crazy sexy look in Vanessa's eyes as she crossed toward her, the feel of Vanessa's warm hands on her face, the softness of her lips, the way she somehow smelled like sunshine—and the good parts of it would make her feel all dreamy. And wet. Let's not forget that part because Jesus Christ on a bike, had Vanessa turned her on.

Stop it.

See? Her brain would bring things to a grinding halt. Although she was finding now, as she arranged a bouquet of roses and added baby's breath, that the last part of the vicious cycle—the one about how the kissing actually felt—was getting longer and longer, and her brain was letting her spend more and more time on the feel of Vanessa's slightly taller body pinning her to the bathroom wall…

Enough.

She groaned and glanced at the clock Ava had mounted to the wall. How was it possible it was only ten? She felt like she'd been there for hours and hours already.

God, this was going to be a long day.

She missed her son. She tried to focus on Oliver instead, tried to force herself to think about getting to see him when she picked him up after school. Yes, she'd have to hear about all the fun things he did with his dad, and yes, she'd be jealous—she could admit that. But it would be worth it just to have him home with her again. She felt lost without him. And she really needed something else to focus on. Like, really.

Her phone buzzed in the back pocket of her jeans. A look at the screen and her heart jumped into her throat. The school.

Of course, Ava chose that moment to glance her way. Her eyebrows went up in clear disapproval.

"It's my son's school," Grace told her in explanation, then answered.

"Mrs. Chapman?" A female voice, clipped.

"Yes, this is she."

"This is the office at Northwood Elementary. We have Oliver here in the principal's office for fighting." Grace closed her eyes as she listened. "Mr. Reynolds would like to talk to you, and we need you to come get him for the day."

All words seemed to leave Grace for a moment. Oliver was fighting? It was one thing to not share, but actual fighting? And if he was in the principal's office, it must've been bad. Too much for Ms. Martini to handle. And then her body betrayed her by flashing her a very *intimate* memory of Ms. Martini.

"Mrs. Chapman?" The impatience in the woman's voice was clear.

"Yes," she answered, her eyes locked with Ava's across the shop. "Yes, I'm here. I'll be right over." She hung up with an enormous sigh and suddenly felt so very tired.

"Trouble?" Ava asked. She'd heard enough and clearly expected it.

"Oliver got in a fight. I have to go talk to the principal." She wet her lips and swallowed the nerves the popped up as she asked, "I know there are a lot of orders today. Would it be okay if—"

"Sure. Bring him here." Ava pointed at her. "But let him know there's to be no malarkey." Her gaze moved to a small table and chair in the corner. "He can hang out there."

Grace's relief was palpable. "Thank you, Ava. I'll be back as quickly as I can."

"Well, go on then." Ava shooed her away. "These flowers aren't going to arrange themselves."

She didn't wait. She untied her apron and grabbed her coat in the same motion, didn't want to give Ava a chance to add more rules or change her mind. Purse in hand, she was out the door in less than two minutes after she'd hung up.

Parking was a little more difficult at this time of day. It was too early for lunch, so nobody had left the school property, and Grace circled twice before she found an empty spot. Then she hurried up the long walkway and through the same door she'd entered the last time she was here. Which wasn't that long ago. And was also in response to Oliver misbehaving.

What had happened to her sweet and gentle boy?

Inside the double doors, the school smelled like crayons and printer ink, this time with the slight undertone of gym socks. She entered the main office and approached the counter.

"Excuse me," she said to the woman at the desk who took her time looking up. Steel-gray hair in a tight bun with a pencil stuck through it, glasses on a chain, a puckered mouth with very red lips—the woman was a walking stereotype of School Office Lady, very much not the young, cheerful woman who was in her seat last time Grace was here. Grace almost laughed, would have if she hadn't been there for a serious reason.

"Can I help you?" the woman finally asked.

"I'm Grace Chapman. I got a call about my son, Oliver."

The woman pointed a long, bony finger at a door to Grace's left. "Mr. Reynolds is waiting for you."

Grace turned and headed toward the closed wooden door, realizing that the uncomfortable fear of entering the principal's office never really went away. She had butterflies in her stomach, her palms were sweating, and her heart rate felt like it had tripled and was now simply a jackhammer running in her chest. She swallowed hard and rapped on the door.

"Come in."

Grace pushed the door open and stepped into a fairly spacious office. Mr. Reynolds—who she'd only seen from afar at school functions—stood and gave her a smile. He was tall, maybe in his late fifties, with close-cropped graying hair and a neat goatee. He seemed welcoming, kind.

"Mrs. Chapman. Please, come in. Have a seat."

There were two chairs across from his desk, and her son sat in one of them, head bowed, feet swinging. He glanced up at her as if braced for her anger, but she gave him a sad smile as she moved in front of the chair.

"I trust you've met Ms. Martini," Mr. Reynolds said as he held his arm out to his left, and Grace followed it to Vanessa Martini, standing off to the side, her arms folded across her chest.

Grace hadn't seen her there, hadn't expected to see her, and she faltered for a second. Vanessa's cool veneer slipped, and her eyes softened for just a moment before she put her concerned teacher mask back into place.

Oh, I have certainly met Ms. Martini, was what Grace wanted to say, as a zap of electric arousal shot through her body and settled low, at the apex of her thighs. She swallowed hard and nodded instead, not trusting herself to speak right then.

"Please. Have a seat," Mr. Reynolds said again.

This time, she sat, glad for the chance to rest her suddenly wobbly knees. *Pull yourself together, Grace.* She inhaled, then asked simply, "What happened?" She looked from the principal to her son and back, as glancing over her shoulder to catch Vanessa's eye seemed somehow dangerous in that moment.

Instead of launching into the story, Mr. Reynolds turned to Oliver, and in a kind voice said, "Why don't you tell your mom what happened."

Oliver hadn't looked up from his hands since she'd sat, and he still didn't. His feet kept swinging, the chair too high for him to touch the floor, as he mumbled, "I got in a fight."

"With who?" Grace asked.

"Bash."

Sebastian, one of Oliver's good friends. "What did you fight about?" Grace appreciated that Mr. Reynolds was letting her ask the questions and Oliver tell the story without interruption.

"I told him I was at Daddy's for the weekend," he mumbled, and Grace had to lean in to hear him. "He said it was stupid that you and dad didn't live together anymore and that his mom said you didn't even try to make him stay."

Grace's eyes went wide. What seven-year-old would say that? But she'd met Kayla Kent, Sebastian's mother, on several occasions. They moved in similar circles, and she was like a walking Stepford Wife, perfect clothes, perfect house, perfect marriage. She opened her mouth to point out how ridiculous this all was, that Sebastian was clearly parroting his mother, but Oliver wasn't finished.

"I said he was wrong and told him to shut up, and then he said it must be my fault. That Daddy doesn't want to live with me anymore." His big green eyes swam as he glanced up at her for the briefest of seconds, and she knew her son well enough that she didn't need more than that glimpse to see everything going on in his little mind. Anger, hurt, regret, confusion. Then he looked back down at his hands as he whispered, "So I punched him."

"Oh, Oliver," she said and reached out to brush his hair back. He flinched but didn't lean away.

"I'm afraid he got in a good shot," Mr. Reynolds said. "Bash is gonna have one heck of a shiner, and his mother is less than happy."

"I'm sure I'll hear about it."

Mr. Reynolds folded his hands in front of him, his eyes on Oliver. "Oliver has apologized, but as I'm sure you understand, we have a zero-tolerance policy on physical violence of any kind. I have to suspend him for three days. I have no choice. Since it's Thanksgiving week and we're off on Friday anyway, he's got the week."

Grace wanted to ask if Bash had apologized for what he said, but she didn't want to be that mom. So she nodded her understanding, already trying to figure out the logistics of working while her son was home from school for half the week.

"I gave him some work to do." Vanessa spoke up for the first time, and Grace had to turn to meet her eyes. Those beautiful blue eyes. They were different today than the last time she'd seen them. Not hooded and darkened with arousal like before. Today, they were cool, though not as icy as in the beginning, and she kept her arms folded across her chest as if insulating herself from something. Someone? Grace? "It's in his backpack. He knows what needs to be done. Just have him bring it back with him next Monday."

Grace nodded, felt held by those eyes, captured, and it wasn't until Vanessa broke eye contact that Grace felt she could look elsewhere.

Stop it, she scolded herself. *This is about Oliver, and it's serious. Get yourself under control.* She felt some irritation slip in, and she grabbed for it. Anything to make her feel less adrift.

Pushing to her feet, she grabbed Oliver's backpack from the floor by the chair and handed it to him. "Okay, let's go." He slid from his chair and she put a hand on his arm. "I want you to apologize to both Mr. Reynolds and Ms. Martini."

"But I did," he whined.

Grace stepped in front of him and squatted so they were eye to eye. "Oliver." Her best mom voice right then, firm, but gentle. "I know you were upset by what Bash said, but you are never, ever to hit somebody. You know this. It is not okay. You owe these people and Bash an apology, and we're going to have a serious talk when we get home. Understand?"

Oliver's face broke into a grimace just before a sob came out, and Grace felt her heart crack in her chest just the tiniest bit. It was always like that when her child was in obvious distress. It didn't matter if he'd spilled something or committed a crime—she knew this was always how she'd feel. She had grown to understand that it was part of being a mom. His pain was her pain. Forever.

Oliver quietly apologized through his tears to both the principal and his teacher, and she led him out of the office by the hand, catching Vanessa's eye as she passed.

"I'd like to give you a call later, if that's all right," Vanessa said.

Grace gave a nod. This was certainly not the way she'd wanted— or expected—to see her again, but talking about their drunken make-out session was going to have to wait, and now she'd be anticipating a phone call for the remainder of her workday. Which meant she would be spending even more time thinking about the kiss. Replaying it in her head. Reliving it…

She shook her head as she led Oliver out of the school still holding his hand.

Terrific.

❖

That was not how Vanessa had wanted to talk to Grace Chapman the next time she saw her. In fact, part of her thought maybe they just wouldn't talk again at all. Not really what she wanted either, but she was still reeling from The Kiss. And that's how she thought of it now.

With capital letters. The Kiss. Because it had been…Well, if she was being honest, she couldn't stop thinking about it. On the one hand, she was embarrassed—horrified, really—at her own gall. She'd just walked into a ladies' bathroom, grabbed a woman by the face, and kissed the bejesus out of her. Holy hell, who did that? On the other hand, though, Grace hadn't protested. She hadn't gasped in horror. She hadn't tried to squirm away. She did the exact opposite. She'd immediately kissed Vanessa back, and that fact had stayed with Vanessa for almost two days. She'd thought about it, analyzed it, replayed it a million times. There was only one thing left to do.

Address it.

"Ugh!"

At the groan, Delilah lifted her head from the floor where she lay sprawled out in her after-dinner nap, her concern for her new person clear on her doggie face. Vanessa waved her back down.

"Sorry, sweetie. It's okay. I'm fine. Stupid, but fine." Before she could bend down from where she sat at her small kitchen table and reassure her more, her phone rang, and she glanced at the screen. Amelia.

"Still daydreaming about the hideously inappropriate kissing?"

Another groan. That seemed to be all Vanessa could do lately. "Shut up. And yes."

"Have you called her? Talked about it?"

Vanessa sighed. "No, a wrench was thrown into those gears today. Her son got in a fight, and I had to take him to the principal, and he called Grace to come in 'cause her kid is suspended for three days. It was a whole thing, and there wasn't really a time to pull her aside to say, *Hey, I know you're dealing with your kid here, but how about that kiss?*"

"I see your dilemma." A long pause.

"I have to address it, though."

"I think it's important that you do."

Vanessa took a moment to drop her forehead to the table with a thud, phone still to her ear. "I was going to call to check on Oliver anyway…" She let the sentence dangle.

"Good. Bring it up. Face to face would be better, but it's been almost forty-eight hours. You've already waited too long." She could almost see Amelia shaking her head. "You didn't call her yesterday—why?"

"Because I'm a big fat coward," Vanessa nearly wailed. And she was scared. And she was confused. And she was embarrassed. Not that she'd tell Amelia any of those things.

"Well, put your big girl pants on," was Amelia's awesome suggestion.

It actually *was* good advice, and Vanessa was still thinking about it a half hour later when she sat down with her phone and her laptop and looked up Grace's phone number. Her heart hammered in her rib cage like an angry inmate trying to get out of his jail cell. She located the number, then stared at it for a moment while she mentally prepared herself. A deep, steadying breath. Two.

She dialed.

"Hello," Grace said on the second ring, her wary tone making it clear she didn't recognize the number.

"Hi, Mrs. Chapman? It's Vanessa Martini. Oliver's teacher. I just wanted to check on Oliver, see how he's doing. And you. How you're doing. As well. Too. Um, how are you? Both? Both of you. How are both of you?" *Oh my God, stop talking. Stop talking now.* She closed her eyes, covered them with her hand. What the hell? This was not her. This was not how she did teacher things. What was wrong with her?

"Oh. Hi." Grace's tone was lined with surprise. But she seemed to pull herself together quickly. "Thanks so much for calling. Oliver is fine." A sound like a chair scraping the floor could be heard, and a second or two ticked by. When Grace spoke again, her voice was low, so Vanessa assumed she'd moved to another room in order to speak more freely. "He's just finishing his dinner, and we're going to have a serious talk after that. I'm so sorry about what happened today. It's really not like him."

"I know," Vanessa told her, torn between being annoyed at the apparent confusion in Grace's voice and wanting to help. "I spoke to his teacher last year who said he was a delight." She cleared her throat, realizing she'd already told her that the last time they talked about Oliver. She knew she needed to tread carefully here. "Listen, I'm not trying to lay any blame or tell you how to parent. I would never do that. But divorce is hard on a kid. Harder than most parents realize." She gave it a beat, and when Grace didn't interrupt or protest, she went on. "They usually try to hide how they're feeling about it—which is usually scared and/or confused about the changes in their life—because they don't want to add to the tension they already feel. So those emotions manifest themselves in other ways."

"Like fights," Grace said.

"Like fights. Sometimes, it's other things. They get quiet. They eat more. Or less. They become clingier, needier because they're afraid the remaining parent will leave, too. And sometimes, it's guilt."

"Guilt?" Clearly something Grace hadn't thought about.

"Guilt that they're the reason their parent has left. Oliver is only seven. He doesn't get the ins and outs of adult relationships quite yet. All he knows is his dad moved out."

It was quiet on the other end of the phone. For a moment, Vanessa thought maybe Grace had hung up on her. Then came a soft sniffle.

"Mrs. Chapman? Are you okay?" she asked softly.

Grace cleared her throat, apparently pulling herself together. Then she made a sound that might have been a snorted laugh. "First of all, you've had your tongue in my mouth. I think it's okay for you to call me Grace."

A pang of arousal hit Vanessa at the words even as she felt her face redden. Unexpected and strong. She swallowed.

"Second, thank you for pointing those things out to me. I'm ashamed to say that I didn't think of some of them. My parents have been together for thirty-three years, so I really don't know what he's feeling. Your guidance will help me a lot when I sit him down later."

"Well. Good." Still lost in Grace's earlier words, that was all Vanessa could manage.

Grace cleared her throat. "First, I need to recover from the verbal beating I took from Sebastian's mother."

"Ugh. Not fun." Vanessa grimaced, expecting that. Kayla Kent was not someone to be messed with. She was also the epitome of a helicopter parent, but it wasn't her place to criticize other parents to Grace, so she kept her opinions to herself.

"Not fun at all." There was a beat of silence and Vanessa could almost feel Grace gearing up for something. Then she spoke. "Also, um, about Saturday…" Grace didn't finish the sentence. Couldn't finish it? Vanessa wasn't sure.

"Yeah. That." And an embarrassed laugh bubbled up, which mortified her because this was so not funny, and she choked it back. Which made it seem like she was just making strange sounds into the phone. God, she should just hang up and never show her face again. Ever. Anywhere.

"I…" Grace cleared her throat. "I feel like I should apologize or something but…"

But?

"I also feel like I should be honest and say I was incredibly flattered. Shocked. Like, super shocked." A nervous laugh there. "But flattered because it was…" Again, she left her sentence unfinished, as if she wasn't sure what to say.

Vanessa found her voice and the English language, finally. "Nice?" Did her voice sound as pathetically hopeful as she thought it did? *God, I need to give up trying to be cool. I just cannot pull it off.*

"I was gonna say hot, but nice works, too."

Vanessa blinked. How did Grace do that? Stun her into silence? She took a moment to regroup. "What it was, was terribly inappropriate"— she nibbled her bottom lip—"and hot."

Grace laughed, thank sweet baby Jesus.

She had to toe the line, though. Own up to the fact that she'd been way out of line, given who she was to Oliver. It really was inappropriate. It didn't matter how infuriatingly sexy she thought Grace was, which she was only in that very moment coming to realize. "But seriously, I shouldn't have done that, and I'm very sorry."

"I'm not. But okay."

A gentle laugh escaped Vanessa's nose before she could stop it. Grace was…in a different mood. Not shy. Not seemingly clueless about her son's recent behavior. She was fun. A little flirty. Vanessa sat with that for a second or two before shaking her head. Hard. "Okay, so, I just wanted to check on Oliver." Ugh. She hated ending the conversation this way, but she really needed to. And then she started talking again before she even thought about it, before her brain could hit the brakes. "Listen, if you need any guidance or you have questions, just, feel free to call me, okay? This is my cell, so now you have it." God, what was she doing?

"I appreciate that more than you know. And I may take you up on that. Be careful what you offer, Ms. Martini."

And *bam*. Her underwear was damp. Just like that.

She hung up the phone and glanced down at Delilah, who had watched her from her spot on the floor during the whole call. "Okay, that did *not* go as planned. Wow."

Her house was quiet, but she felt charged. Energized. Crackling, like she'd been zapped with electricity. She sent a text to Amelia and another to Julia. She needed to talk, to analyze, to have them tell her to chill the fuck out before she bounced herself into insanity.

Responses from her cousins came three seconds apart, as both of them were in the same place, The Bar Back at Martini's.

"Wanna go for a ride, Delly?"

The dog stood, her long black tail swooshing back and forth. She got her stuff together, clipped Delilah's leash on her, and headed outside into the cold November evening.

Hopefully, her cousins would knock some sense into her.

CHAPTER EIGHT

Grace sat staring at her cell for a long time, running her index finger up and down the side of it, replaying her conversation with Vanessa. No, Ms. Martini. No, Vanessa.

Who had Grace become? That was the question at the forefront of her mind right then. She'd been flirty. Suggestive. That was not her. At all. Once the call had ended, she'd found herself a bit horrified at her own behavior. Not because Vanessa was a woman—Grace's bisexuality wasn't new or a secret—but because of who she was in their lives. She was her son's teacher. It was just…Vanessa had chosen the right word: inappropriate.

"Mom. I'm done." Oliver sat at the dining room table swinging his feet. He'd eaten his Tater Tots and most of his chicken, but a pile of green beans still sat on his plate.

"Eat some of your beans," she said.

"I don't wanna."

"Oliver."

"I don't like 'em." He swung his feet harder, now banging them into the legs of his chair.

"Eat three bites."

"No."

Grace had a very tentative hold on her patience with him right then. She put a palm on the table and leaned so she was close, but above him. Rather than raise her voice, which usually got her nowhere and filled her with shame, she spoke low and clear. "Oliver James, you are on thin ice with me today. You have already lost screen time for two days. If you want to lose more, just keep pushing me."

She heard him swallow even as he held eye contact with her. He speared a green bean with his fork and muttered, "I wish Dad was here." His tone was not sad. It was angry. And Grace felt it deep in her heart as if he'd taken his fork and stabbed her with it. She turned away, so he wouldn't see the tears in her eyes, so he wouldn't know he'd scored a direct hit.

Ava Green had allowed Oliver to hang out at the flower shop for the rest of the day today, but there was no way she'd be okay with that for two more days. "I run a flower shop, not a day care center," she'd said to Grace in no uncertain terms. Michael was traveling for business and couldn't have Oliver with him, so Grace didn't have many options left. She dialed her parents' number.

"Hey, Mom," she said when her mother picked up. "What's new?" She listened, nodded, gave the appropriate *uh-huh* when it was called for as her mother filled her in on everything she and Grace's father had been up to since the last time they'd talked. Which had only been last week, but you'd have thought it had been months the way she went on and on about dinners and movies and the Christmas cruise that was just around the corner.

"Listen, Mom, I need a favor." Grace gave herself a beat. She hated asking for help, but she didn't have many options. "What's your work schedule this week?"

"Well, I'm off until Black Friday. That's when things get crazy." She laughed because she worked part-time at the local Hallmark store. This was their busy season, and she loved it.

God, Thanksgiving was in three days, and Grace had barely thought about it. Everything was so scrambled that making plans for the holiday hadn't even been on her radar.

"Do you think you could watch Oliver tomorrow and Wednesday?"

"Is he off for the whole week?" Her mother's surprise was clear.

"Well, yes, but not because his school is. It's because he got in a fight and got suspended." She grimaced, braced herself for what was coming.

"What? What happened? Why was he fighting? Grace, honestly, what are you saying to that boy? This is because Mike moved out, you know. I keep telling your father, your generation doesn't work at it. Divorce is too easy. You just split instead of fixing the problem."

Hearing it for the seventeenth time didn't make it sting any less, and Grace's jaw started to ache from clenching it. "Mom, can you watch Oliver or not? I can't take him to work with me, and if you can't watch him, I'll have to take time off." It was her only other option, and Ava would be livid. They had so many Thanksgiving deliveries, and if

Grace took sick time this week, there was a good chance she wouldn't have a job to come back to. She needed to work.

"Of course I'll watch him." Her mother made it sound like a ridiculous question. "I love having him here—you know that."

"I know. And thank you. It'll be all day tomorrow and all day Wednesday. Is that okay?"

"Why don't you just let him stay over on Wednesday? You're coming here on Thursday for Thanksgiving, right?"

Grace swallowed her sigh. While she loved the holidays and loved going to her parents' for Thanksgiving, and it was their Christmas as well, as her parents would be gone on the cruise in a couple weeks, this was also going to be her first major holiday without Mike, and there would be other family members there. Family members with questions.

Yeah, she was dreading it.

"Okay. I'll bring him by on my way to work tomorrow. Thank you so much, Mom. Really. You're a lifesaver."

She hung up the phone, still thinking about the holiday. While it would be her first Thanksgiving since she'd started dating Mike that she'd be at her parents' without him, it wasn't really their first holiday apart. They'd drifted long ago, and even though they'd done last year's holidays together, they were already falling apart. They'd put on a front for Oliver's sake but decided in early summer that they didn't want to do that again. That's when Mike had said he'd start looking for his own place. But the whole summer had gone by and then some of the fall before he finally got his act together. Grace suspected he'd started to think about dating. Maybe more than thinking. That had been his catalyst.

He'd moved out a month ago, give or take a week, and here they were, Grace and Oliver, making the best of it. If you overlooked the fact that he'd just been suspended from school. She hadn't called Mike yet, but she'd need to. Another thing she wasn't looking forward to.

She returned to the table where Oliver sat, pushing his beans around. "Moving them around on your plate doesn't trick me into thinking you ate any," she informed him.

"I did, though! I ate three!"

It was as if exhaustion had crept up behind her and sat on her shoulders in that second. She was suddenly so tired she couldn't muster up the energy to argue with him anymore.

"Fine." She grabbed his plate. He scrambled to get out of his chair with the sudden burst of energy kids experience when they get their way, probably worried she'd change her mind and decide he should eat three more beans, but she grasped his arm. "Sit."

His face fell, but her tone was firm enough to put his butt back in his seat. He sighed, likely knowing what was coming and not looking forward to it.

"We need to talk about today."

Oliver gave the full-body groan of a seven-year-old. "We already did."

"No, just you and me." He made another sound of impatience, which tweaked Grace's nerves. "That's enough of that, young man. You'd better knock that off right now."

He had the sense to look the tiniest bit ashamed.

"Getting suspended is a big deal, Oliver. You *hit* somebody. That is not okay. I know what Sebastian said made you mad, but you cannot hit somebody just because you don't like what they say."

Oliver pouted and folded his little arms across his chest but didn't say anything. He was trying his best to remain stoic, Grace knew, but she could also see his bottom lip start to push out and his green eyes fill up.

"Sweetie," she said, softening her voice. "Daddy didn't leave you. Okay? He didn't move out because of you."

"I know," he snapped in a sudden and unexpected outburst that made her flinch. His eyes were still filled with tears, but now they were flashing. "He left because of *you*! It's your fault! I hate you!" He pushed himself off his chair, and this time, she didn't stop him as he ran to his room. She simply sat there. Mouth hanging open. Stunned.

Her son said he hated her.

And while it wasn't the first time, she knew this was just his temper. That he was seven and prone to emotional outbursts and didn't mean what he'd said, but she still felt a pain deep in her heart and felt her own eyes well up with tears.

Her son said he hated her.

❖

"There's my girl," Amelia said and immediately dropped to the floor of The Bar Back as Vanessa entered, Delilah on her leash. "Hello, baby. How are you? Are you good? Tell Aunt Amelia all about your day."

The dog was thrilled, her long black tail sweeping back and forth, easily cleaning the magazines off Julia's coffee table and onto the floor. Savannah was on the couch and watched it happen, chuckling as she shook her head.

"Sorry about that," Vanessa said with a shrug as she bent to pick them up. "That tail...I should hire her out as a cleaning assistant."

"Speaking of new jobs," Amelia said from the floor where Delilah had pushed her head into Amelia's lap. "I'm going to start up that little business I was telling you guys about. I've taken steps."

"The pet-sitting-slash-dog-walking thing?" Savannah asked, her blue eyes bright. At Amelia's nod, she clapped. "That's fantastic!"

Vanessa bent down and kissed the top of Amelia's head, then sat on the floor next to her. "I second that. Good for you." She knew Amelia had been floundering a bit, having retired early to spend time with her wife, only to have her wife leave her for somebody else.

"High five," Julia said from her spot behind the practice bar and lifted her hand into the air. Amelia did the same, and they high-fived from fifteen feet apart, like they were Jim and Pam from *The Office*. "Anybody need wine? A cocktail? Water? A Coke?" Ever the bartender, Julia looked around the room expectantly. Just because they always met in the back room of Julia's bar, that didn't mean they only drank alcohol. It had simply become the most convenient place for them to get together because Julia worked a lot and had a crazy schedule. And also owned the place.

"Can I get a Diet Coke?" Vanessa asked. "It's that time of year, and the kids are climbing the walls. They do a good enough job giving me a headache without me helping them along by having wine."

Savannah gave a chuckle and picked up her glass of white. "It's okay. I've got you covered." She raised it in a little salute.

"Aww, you're a giver," Vanessa said. Julia brought her the soda, then sat next to Savannah with a groaning sigh that said she'd been working long hours. "Tired?" she asked.

As Julia nodded, Savannah squeezed Julia's knee and answered for her. "She's been prepping. Wednesday is one of the busiest nights for bars. Did you know that?"

"The night before Thanksgiving?" Amelia asked. "That actually makes sense. Most people are off the next day, but if they're not traveling, they probably don't have to be anywhere until the afternoon. Maybe?"

"And many have Friday off, so Wednesday night is actually the beginning of a four-day weekend," Vanessa offered.

"Whatever the reason, we should have a good crowd." Julia took Savannah's glass from her hand and had a sip of her wine. "I've got three bartenders on, Terry on the door, and I hired a new barback. Got the specials down. I'm ready."

"We'll all be here, and we'll bring friends," Amelia assured her. Then she added, "Is the ladies' room all spick-and-span because Vanessa might want to make out in it again."

Silence for a beat. Two beats.

Vanessa felt all eyes turn to her. Even Delilah looked her way. One more beat and then Julia and Savannah spoke at the same time.

"Excuse me?" Julia.

"*What?*" Savannah.

Vanessa shot Amelia a death glare, to which Amelia shrugged and winked at her.

"That's why you're here, isn't it?" Amelia asked. "To talk it out?"

Goddamn it, her cousin knew her well.

"Yes, but I kinda wanted to *ease* into it…" She drew out the word and Amelia shrugged again.

"I ripped off the Band-Aid for you. You're welcome."

"Yeah, we're gonna need details." Savannah sat forward so she was perched on the edge of the couch, elbows on her knees, chin in her hands. "Spill."

Vanessa sighed. So this was how it was going to go. All right. She could do it like this. Not her first choice, but whatever. Maybe it was better that it was just out there now.

She took a deep breath, then told the whole story, reminding them of Oliver, that she'd talked to them about him before, then about Grace, then about her being at the bar with friends the previous weekend and how Vanessa had been overserved—Julia snorted at that—and how she'd thrown caution to the wind in the ladies' room.

"Oh my God." Savannah, wide-eyed, cheeks flushed. "That's so hot."

"I know," Vanessa said. Nodded. Sipped her Coke. "But wait. There's more." She turned to Amelia. "And you don't even know this part." Amelia sat up straighter and made a show of giving her full attention. She told them about Oliver getting in a fight and getting suspended and the meeting in the principal's office and her telling Grace she'd call her.

"And did you?" Savannah asked.

Vanessa nodded and drank more Coke, now wishing it was

something stronger. "I wanted to check up on Oliver, but I also thought I should apologize for Saturday." She looked from one set of eyes to the next, everyone riveted on her. "So I did. I told her what I'd done on Saturday was terribly inappropriate and that I was really sorry."

"And she said…?" Amelia looked like she was *thisclose* to grabbing Vanessa by the shoulders and shaking the rest of the story out of her.

"She said she wasn't."

A couple more seconds of silence, blinks all around, and then Savannah said, "She wasn't sorry?"

"Right." Vanessa gave one nod.

"Wait." Savannah held up a finger. "What you're saying is she said she was *not sorry* that you'd essentially kissed her face off in the bathroom of this very bar."

"That's what I'm saying. Yes."

"Hang on." Julia spoke this time. "I'd like to back this truck up for a minute." It was her turn to sit forward, perch on the edge of the couch, and put her hand on Savannah's knee. "Isn't this the same woman you were so annoyed with? The one who let her son run around the retirement home unsupervised? The one you've been so openly disapproving of?"

Vanessa groaned and bounced her body up and down from her seat on the floor like a toddler who'd been told it was time to stop playing and go to bed. "*Yes*. That's her." She hung her head.

"Wow." Julia took another swig of Savannah's wine. "I can honestly say that I did not see that coming."

Savannah, on the other hand, made a sort of humming sound as she took her wine back.

Julia turned wide eyes to her. "You *did* see it coming?"

With a shrug, Savannah said, "I mean, the lady doth protest too much…"

"The lady did protest *a lot*," Amelia added.

"No." Vanessa was firm. "No, no, no. I did not. I never thought about her that way." She looked from one face to the next, these women she trusted more than anybody, these women who knew her better than anybody. "When have you guys ever known me to lust after the parent of a student?"

Julia and Amelia looked at each other.

"I mean, there was the one woman last year," Julia said. "The news anchor."

"And the chef from the year before that," Amelia added, pointing at Julia.

"Wasn't there—"

"Okay, fine," Vanessa cut in. "Fine. But it's never gone beyond looking."

Julia and Amelia looked at each other before they both nodded. "That's true."

"Thank you." Vanessa studied the color of her Diet Coke for a second or two before she felt a hand on her shoulder and looked up into Savannah's kind eyes.

"How can we help?" she asked quietly.

Gratitude washed through Vanessa right then. This. This was why she'd come to see these women. "I'm just not sure how I feel," she said, sitting up a little taller as she searched for the best way to explain her mess of a brain to the other three. "I'm confused. That's a big one. I'm frustrated. I don't know what to do."

"Have you talked to…what's her name?" Savannah asked.

"Grace."

"Have you talked to Grace about all of it?"

Vanessa sighed. "Not really. I mean, I gave her my number and told her she could call me anytime, but I meant about Oliver. If she needed advice or anything about his situation."

Julia's lips were pursed as she nodded. "And what did she say to that. Thank you?"

"Yeah." Vanessa thought about the conversation. "That she appreciated it and…" She hesitated at the part of Grace's reply that still sat low in her body, making itself known by being sexy as hell.

"And?" Amelia prodded.

"And that I should be careful what I offer."

There was exactly one beat of silence, as she watched her cousins exchange glances before all three of them exploded at once with laughter, expressions of disbelief, and nods.

"Yeah, she's into you," Savannah said as the other two nodded their agreement.

"Definitely," Julia said.

"I mean, if the make-out session in the ladies' room wasn't clear enough for you," Amelia said with a grin, "this pretty much seals it."

"Oh my God, what do I do?" Vanessa whined the question out because the laughter and joking around her weren't making it any better. In fact, it felt worse. Yes, Grace had kissed her back in the bathroom, but that could've just been an error in judgment. A result of the alcohol. She could've regretted it and wanted to shove it into a box in the corner and leave it there forever. But today had pretty much proven that wasn't the case.

"You ask her out, dumbass," Amelia said, still laughing.

But it was Savannah who became a bit more serious first. "Is there a rule against you dating the parent of a student?" she asked.

Vanessa took a moment to think. "I'm not sure there's an official one, but I don't know that it would look great. I wouldn't want other parents to think Oliver is getting special treatment from me, you know?"

"Well, Oliver just got himself suspended," Amelia pointed out. "So I don't think that'll be a problem."

"I don't know, you guys." *What is going on with me?* The question echoed through her skull, even as her cousins were talking and laughing. Vanessa wasn't shy. She'd never had trouble going for something she'd wanted, whether it was a date or a job or whatever. She was confident and secure in herself, and asking Grace for a date shouldn't terrify her.

So how come it did?

CHAPTER NINE

The bar was packed. Vanessa was thrilled because the look on Julia's face as she stood in the back doorway to The Bar Back, hands on her hips, said *she* was thrilled. Her cousin had struggled when she'd first purchased the bar early in the year. She'd gone in with the best of intentions, but a shaky business plan. Luckily, Julia'd met Savannah, and she had Vanessa, and between the three of them, they'd put a plan on paper that included a lot of working with other local businesses to help with name recognition. Julia had implemented it all with excitement and confidence.

It was paying off.

Happy hour had officially started at four o'clock, but customers had been filing in since early afternoon, many likely bailing early from their jobs, given it was the day before a holiday weekend. Now, at nearly nine thirty, the bar was two people deep, all the tables were taken, and small groups of friends dotted the rest of the space. Julia's smile said it all as Vanessa approached her, vodka and cranberry in her hand.

"You look like a superhero standing here like that." She had to raise her voice to be heard over the music and the crowd, but she bumped Julia affectionately with her hip.

"I feel like one," Julia replied, her smile growing. "Look at all these people."

"I'm proud of you, Jules." Vanessa meant it. With all her heart. It wasn't often you got to see somebody realize their dreams, but Julia had.

"I couldn't have done it without you guys, you know." Julia dropped a kiss on Vanessa's head, then glanced at her glass. "You're not drinking one of the specials? But you're free from the kids for four whole days."

"Oh, I had one of the Nutballs." Vanessa had sampled the special—Amaretto and vodka and something else she couldn't identify. "But I'd like to remember where I am later."

Julia indicated the ladies' room with her chin. "I saw a couple of attractive women head that way if you had the itch to do some kissin'..."

"Yeah, you're hilarious," Vanessa said, shaking her head as she made her way through the crowd and back to the small slice of bar she and Amelia had managed to snag.

"Ready for a refill?" Amelia asked, holding up a hand to get the bartender's attention.

"Not yet," Vanessa replied, craning her neck to see over the crowd to the door.

"Who are you looking for?"

"You remember my friend Danika? She teaches third grade? You met her at my Halloween party last year. She and her husband should be here any minute."

Amelia nodded. "The one who told the great stories about her students, right?"

Danika had complained earlier in the day that she wanted to go out, that she and her husband had been busy with their jobs and wanted to see other humans. Vanessa finished her drink and slid the empty glass toward Amelia after all.

"Isn't that her?" Amelia asked, gesturing at the door with her eyes.

"Be right back." Vanessa began crowd surfing, which felt more like digging through an avalanche. There were way more people than she thought, and it was a hell of a mix. She sidled past a group of twentysomething girls not much younger than she was, dressed to the nines and drinking the specials, all laughing at some joke Vanessa missed. Then two couples, the guys with their arms around their partners. Five men in a group, ties loosened, sleeves rolled up, loud enough to make her guess they'd probably come after work and were very well lubricated by now. Vanessa smiled as her eyes settled on her friends. Danika was openly flirting with Terry the bouncer, and Will met Vanessa's eyes with a head shake and a grin, shrugging as if to say, *Yep, that's my wife.*

"You made it," she said as she reached them. She hooked Danika's arm. "Don't listen to her promises, Terry—she's taken."

"Doesn't mean I can't dream," Danika said and blew Terry a kiss as Vanessa pulled her away.

"Danika, meet Will. He's your husband." To Will, she said, "I'm so sorry."

Will laughed as he kissed Danika's plump cheek. "I know who she's going home with. I'm not worried."

Vanessa loved their relationship. Danika was a big talker, never quiet about any man she found attractive. But that's all it was. Talk. She was head over heels in love with Will. Honestly, she'd never met a more secure couple, and she envied them.

"You guys look fantastic," she commented. Danika's coral dress peeked out from under her black coat. Will was tall and lean, with a runner's body. He wore khakis and a purple oxford, open at the neck. "My cousin Amelia has a spot at the bar, so we can squish in there. Okay?"

As she made the comment and tugged her friends through the crowd, she scanned the bar again and her gaze was snagged. Stopped. Held.

Grace Chapman. Looking right at her.

"Holy déjà vu," she muttered as she stopped in her tracks and Danika walked into her back.

"Hello? We're walking here." A pause. Then, "Oh, who's that?"

Vanessa glanced back and saw Danika had followed her gaze and was now looking at Grace, whose attention was back on her friends. "Nobody," she said with a shake of her head.

"Mm-hmm," was all Danika said, and the way she was able to make that one simple sound into *I don't believe a word you're saying to me, and I will get the truth out of you sooner or later* was something Vanessa marveled over.

They reached Amelia, who'd been joined by Dante and one of his work buddies, and introductions were made. Drinks were ordered. Fun was had, and lots of laughter rippled through them. And Vanessa participated happily. The mood was jovial. The crowd stayed steady. The drinks flowed and the music thumped, and she caught Julia's smile from various spots around the bar, as if somebody had picked Julia up and set her back down in different places, same stance, same smile.

But Vanessa's eyes were traitors, and they continually dragged her attention back across the bar.

Where, apparently, Grace's eyes were traitors, too.

❖

Okay, Grace could admit that coming back to Martini's was her idea. She hadn't told either Janelle or Courtney about her bathroom encounter with Vanessa Martini during their last night out there, though she did think she might tell Courtney at some point. Because honestly, it had been on her mind every day and night—very much so at night—and it might be time to talk about it with somebody else. Much as it scared her.

Telling Janelle wasn't an option, as she and her husband were part of Michael's social group, too. The last thing she wanted was her almost-ex-husband to know she'd been making out with a chick in the bathroom like she was a sorority sister experimenting through college. Not because he didn't know about her sexuality—he did—but because it made her sound reckless and irresponsible. Especially if he found out it wasn't just some chick, it was Oliver's teacher. God.

But Courtney...she was divorced, and she knew, and she would get it.

So, yeah, her friends innocently agreed that they, too, liked the atmosphere of Martini's and the drink specials were killer, so they didn't object to Grace's suggestion. And now? Here they were and directly across the bar, just like last time, there *she* was. She was with a small group—a strikingly attractive opposite-sex couple—they touched a lot, so they were definitely together—the woman dark-skinned and generously curvy, the man pale-complected, tall, and lean but not skinny. Another woman that had similar facial features as Vanessa, so a sister? Cousin? Oh, wait. Yes, cousin. That was Amelia, the one she'd already met. There were also two men, one dark, one light. They all laughed and leaned into each other, clearly a group of friends, Vanessa in the center.

Why did she have to be so sexy?

The question came out of nowhere and echoed through her head so loudly that Grace almost wondered if she'd said it out loud. But when her ears refocused on the conversation, Janelle was still talking about work, so she was safe to enjoy the picture in her head of Vanessa Martini and her black shirt—a tank top?—under a pretty plaid button-down in pinks and blacks. Her blond hair was down and wavier than Grace had seen it before. She'd caught a glimpse of her laughing, and those dimples, good Lord, those dimples.

They'd addressed the kiss. Barely. And over the phone while talking about Oliver, a completely different subject. Grace had lassoed a boldness that shocked even her during that conversation, and now she wondered what Vanessa was thinking. It had been very nice of her—very *responsible teacher* of her—to call and check on Oliver, but Grace had gotten the distinct impression she'd wanted to call anyway. She'd apologized for the kiss, but Grace wondered if she was as not sorry as Grace was herself. Because she wasn't sorry at all. In fact, she was so not sorry that a large part of her wanted to simply stride across the bar, take Vanessa by the hand, tug her into a dark corner, and kiss her senseless.

"Grace? You okay?" It was Janelle, and when Grace refocused herself, both her friends were looking at her, concern on their faces.

"Oh! Yes. Yes, I'm fine. Just zoned out a bit." She picked up her Captain and Diet, flexing her fingers when she saw the slight tremor in them.

"With what you've dealt with around Oliver," Courtney said, rubbing Grace's back affectionately, "you must be exhausted. I'm glad we dragged you out again."

Grace stifled a grin. She'd played up her resistance, so her friends wouldn't suspect she actually wanted to come to Martini's. Not that they'd suspect why, but it felt like something she needed to at least *pretend* to protest. It made her feel a little better, if nothing else. Janelle excused herself to the ladies' room, and Grace seized the moment, grabbed Courtney by the sleeve, and pulled her closer.

"Okay, be cool about looking, but see the blonde directly across from us?" She said it as quietly as she could, which was louder than she'd wanted, but it was hard to hear over all the noise around them.

Courtney, bless her, looked down at her drink, then slowly and very casually looked up at the bottles on the shelves, then let her eyes wander along them until she was looking in Vanessa's direction. "In the plaid? With the dimples?"

Grace gave a quick nod.

"I see her. She's super cute. What about her? You interested?"

"This is not for Janelle's ears, okay?"

Courtney turned an invisible key in front of her closed lips and mimed tossing it over her shoulder.

"One—that's Oliver's teacher."

"The one you keep running into all over the place?"

Another nod.

"What's two?"

"Two—when we were here on Saturday, I was alone in the bathroom, and she came in, walked right up to me, and kissed me into next week."

Courtney's eyes went so wide it was comical, and she nearly choked on the mouthful of the Almond Snickerdoodle cocktail she was in the midst of swallowing. She smacked a hand flat on the bar, cleared her throat, and said loudly, "Get *out!*"

Not daring to look across the bar because doing that would ensure Vanessa knew they were talking about her, Grace said through gritted teeth, "Please don't say anything to anybody."

Courtney cocked her head. "Sweetie, I won't. I promise. But you brought it up, and you've been kinda zoned out since we got here, so I'm guessing it's been on your mind."

Grace blew out a breath, then glanced over her shoulder to see if Janelle was on her way back. "It has. It's...confusing."

"I bet. No wonder you were gone so long! I figured there was a line."

And then Janelle was back.

"Sorry it took me so long," she said, hanging her purse back under the bar. "There was a line."

It was obvious to Grace that Courtney was stifling a grin, and she shot Grace a look that said *Or she was making out with a hot blonde...* Grace rolled her lips in and bit down on them, then looked into her empty glass.

They ordered another round and kept chatting and laughing, and Grace found herself relaxing just the slightest bit, which felt good because she was only right then realizing just how tense she'd been for the past few days. She paced her drinking, though. She did not need a repeat of Saturday, and she certainly didn't want to show up hungover at her parents' the next day. Her mother had a way of smelling that kind of thing out and talking it to death. With lots of judgment and disapproval. Of course.

They talked about plans for Thanksgiving, what each of them was doing, and that's when Janelle glanced at her phone to see the time.

"Oh, girls, I have to call it a night," she said, finishing up her drink and signaling to the cute bartender—Ethan? Evan?—to ring her out. "I have twelve people at my house tomorrow, and Lord knows, my husband isn't cleaning and getting things ready while I'm here." She laughed, likely not realizing she was talking to two divorced women who might have liked to be able to affectionately complain about their partners not helping with impending company. Janelle signed her bill, hugged both Courtney and Grace, and went on her merry way.

Courtney wasted exactly zero time and turned to Grace, grabbing her hand, eyes wide with excitement. "So? Tell me more about this bathroom kissing! Wait, was it a kiss or was it making out? 'Cause there's a difference, you know."

Her excitement was fun. And contagious. And Grace couldn't help but smile, some kind of weight lifting off her just a bit at being able to actually talk it through with somebody.

"Oh, it was making out." Just the memory, just recalling that dark, hooded, sexy as hell expression on Vanessa's face as she walked right up to Grace without a second's hesitation, was enough to send flutters through her body now, send a telltale wetness into her bikinis that made her shift uncomfortably. "The weirdest part was that I not only let it happen, but I kissed her back. Like, majorly. I majorly kissed her back."

Courtney made a groaning sound and dropped her head back for a moment. "God, that's *so* sexy!"

"It really was. Sexy and confusing. But the sexy part was...God."

"Confusing because she's a girl?"

Grace scoffed. "No, not at all. She's not the first girl I've kissed. Confusing because of who she is and our previous interactions."

Courtney nodded, took a sip of her refreshed drink. "Yeah, you weren't thrilled the first time you met her. I remember you telling me."

"Not the first or the second or even the third."

"Because?"

She wanted to say *Because she's judgy* with great conviction and irritation. But lately that had faded a bit, and Grace was only realizing it right that very moment. "We didn't meet under the best circumstances."

"True. But what about now?" Courtney seemed to lean in, like she was waiting for some juicy gossip. Which she kind of was, if Grace was being honest.

She groaned and gave a little foot stomp like a twelve-year-old girl not getting her way. "She's Oliver's teacher. I really can't get involved."

"Says who?"

Grace blinked at her.

"No, really," Courtney said. "I'm asking. Is there a rule?"

"I mean..." Grace stopped. Was there a rule? "I honestly don't know. But still. She's *Oliver's teacher*."

Instead of responding, Courtney's eyes widened a bit as she closed her swizzle stick in her teeth and muttered, "Incoming."

Grace frowned. "Incoming? What does that mean? What's incoming?"

"Oliver's teacher," Courtney hissed just as somebody said, "Hi," over Grace's shoulder. She turned. Blinked.

Vanessa smiled at her and tipped her head to one side. "Hey, you." As Grace continued to search for her own voice, Vanessa turned to Courtney. "Hi there. Vanessa Martini." She held out a hand. "Teacher of Oliver."

"Courtney Miller," Courtney said, her grin huge as she shook Vanessa's hand. "Friend of Grace." Then they both turned to look at her.

"Hi," she finally managed.

"There it is," Courtney said. "I was worried for a minute."

"No, no, I'm good. Sorry about that. Was just surprised." God, what the hell? Why was she this nervous and jerky? She looked at Vanessa. "Hi," she said.

"You said that already, but I'll take it," Vanessa said, but her tone was gentle, as if she was worried about teasing Grace too hard. "Hi again. How are you?"

Grace nodded and glanced at Courtney whose facial gestures were clearly intended to telegraph *What are you doing? Talk to her!*

Grace cleared her throat and mentally willed herself to pull it together. Jesus God, she wasn't sixteen. She was a grown woman, and she knew how to talk to another grown woman. Even if that other grown woman had kissed the hell out of her not four days ago.

"I'm good," she said finally, finding her footing somehow and hoping the relief didn't show on her face. "Ready for a long weekend. How about you? Were the kids all nuts today?"

"Oh my God," Vanessa said, looking toward the ceiling. "Climbing the walls. I was so glad when the day was over." A shadow shot across her face, just for a second, and she added, "How's Oliver? Doing okay?"

Grace gave a nod. "He's spending the night with my parents since I'm going over there tomorrow." There was a beat and Courtney jumped in.

"Holy crap, look at the time." She glanced at her wrist so quickly, Vanessa probably didn't notice she wasn't wearing a watch. Grace simply raised an eyebrow at her as she sipped her drink. Courtney leaned in and kissed Grace's cheek, then whispered, "She's hot, she came over here, talk to her," in her ear. She pulled back. "So nice to meet you, Vanessa. Happy Thanksgiving, guys. See ya!" And she turned on her heel and left.

And then it was just Grace and Vanessa.

"Looks like your friends abandoned you," Vanessa said, taking Courtney's spot and leaning one arm on the bar.

"You're here."

"I am."

They looked at each other, held gazes, and did the temperature in the bar crank up about five degrees right then? Grace was pretty sure it had. Again, she willed herself to pull it together. She'd been so confident on the phone, getting all flirty with Vanessa, but now that she was in front of her, in the flesh? Grace felt like a schoolgirl. Stammering. Sweating.

She took a breath, willed herself into calm. "So," she said and turned to lean her forearms on the bar. 'Cause that was smooth. Right? Ugh. "What do you do for Thanksgiving?" Okay. Good. A safe topic.

Vanessa mimicked her position, and was that a wave of relief that zipped across her face just then? "I'll go to my mom's house in the afternoon and hang out with her so she's not alone. My sisters will show up for dinner with their husbands and kids."

This peek behind the family curtain of Vanessa Martini was super interesting, and Grace wanted to see more. "Is your dad gone?" she asked gently.

"Gone to the next town over, yeah." Vanessa laughed, but there was an edge to it.

"Oh, your parents are divorced."

"Yep."

And that shined a bit of a light on things, didn't it? "Will you see him tomorrow, too?"

The way Vanessa tipped her head from one side to the other told Grace this was a subject that she wavered on. "Not tomorrow, no. Things with my dad are, I don't know, weird? Delicate?" She shook her head. "I'm not sure how to describe it."

"When did they split?" Then she put her hand on Vanessa's forearm. "I mean, you don't have to talk about this. If I'm being nosy, just tell me to back off." She hoped the small smile helped.

"Oh no, I don't mind."

"Okay. Good." And Grace left her hand there. Just let it sit there, feeling Vanessa's warmth through the sleeve of her shirt. And Vanessa didn't move, so it must've been okay with her, right? Grace pretended leaving her hand there wasn't intentional. It was casual. Yeah, just, *Oh, I'm going to set my hand right here, okay?*

"I was thirteen, my sister Ella was ten, and my sister Izzy was eight."

"Oh, that's so young. Although"—Grace squinted—"thirteen is old enough to..." She shook her head, words escaping her.

"Old enough to know something's wrong, but too young to understand. Yeah. And eight is too young. Poor Izzy had no idea how to understand what was happening."

Grace nodded, and there was a beat or two between them, the age thing not lost on her. This was a heavy subject, especially given what she was currently going through with her own marriage and child, and suddenly, she didn't want to talk about it anymore.

"What does your mom make for Thanksgiving?" she asked, forcing herself to brighten, hoping it wasn't as obvious as it clearly was. "The usual traditional stuff? Are there things you look forward to?" It occurred to her a little late that these were probably questions Vanessa asked of her seven- and eight-year-old students, but it was too late to take them back now. She swallowed her own sigh.

Vanessa blinked and seemed to study her for a moment, as she stood straight again, removing her arm from under Grace's hand. And then it was as if she decided she'd just play along. Grace wasn't sure if she was relieved or disappointed. "She does the basics. Turkey. Stuffing. Mashed potatoes. Gravy. What about you?"

Grace nodded. "Oh yeah, the regular stuff you mentioned. Plus, my Aunt Kathy makes this sweet potato casserole that I've loved since I was a kid. With pineapple and marshmallows—"

"Marshmallows," Vanessa said at the same time, then leaned into her a bit, bumped her with a shoulder.

They laughed together, and Grace added, "The holidays are the only time I let myself have those, and sweet baby Jesus on a cracker, they're so good."

"Right?" Vanessa agreed.

Their gazes held then, and Grace marveled at the clear blue of Vanessa's eyes, the depth of them. She was blond, but her lashes and brows were darker, making the blue more intense, the color of an endless summer sky. As the silence stretched, Grace finally cleared her throat, breaking the spell. Again, she wavered between relief and disappointment.

"I should probably go," she said softly. No, she didn't want to. In fact, she had to consciously keep from inviting Vanessa back to her place. Yes, that would only complicate an already complicated situation. But also yes, it would be so incredibly hot, and she hadn't been this attracted to somebody in longer than she cared to remember. Her brain tossed her those two words, though: Oliver's teacher. And she pulled her gaze from Vanessa's, which wasn't easy and took significant effort on her part because my God, there was something about her. "I'm really glad we had a chance to talk, though." Was that a stupid thing to say? God, why was all of this so hard?

"I am, too," Vanessa said, and though Grace didn't know her well enough to gauge it, her smile seemed genuine. And then Vanessa added, "Maybe we can again. Sometime. Soonish." And the expression on her face changed to what Grace was pretty sure was the same one she herself had been wearing—uncertain, hesitant, hopeful.

"I'd like that," she replied, and something inside her told her very loudly that it was the perfect time to make her exit. She picked up her coat, and Vanessa took it from her and held it so she could easily slide her arms in. She felt Vanessa's hands on her shoulders for just a brief moment, but her entire body absorbed it. Grabbing her purse and turning to Vanessa, she said quietly, "Happy Thanksgiving." And to her own shock, she leaned in and kissed Vanessa softly on the cheek, then hurried through the crowd and out the door without looking back, feeling energized and—yes—braver than she had in a long, long time.

Outside in the November cold, her smile blossomed across her face all on its own.

CHAPTER TEN

Food, noise, wine, noise, pie, and noise.

These were the words that best described any holidays in any Martini household. People often didn't believe Vanessa when she told them she was seventy-five percent Italian because of her blond hair and blue eyes. Not that there weren't lighter-colored people in Italy, but most Americans associated being Italian with dark hair, dark eyes, and olive skin. Vanessa had the olive skin of her father, but the light hair and eyes of her mom. She was the only one of the kids who did—both her sisters were brunettes with brown eyes, and they often teased her about taking all the lighter genes and leaving them only the dark ones.

The holidays were her favorite time of year. Family was a huge part of her life, and anything that brought them together was something Vanessa relished. Even now, after they'd eaten Round One, as Izzy called it, she knew there'd be more food. More wine. More conversation.

A pull of the handle on the side of the recliner popped out the footrest, and Vanessa sighed and resolved to let the tryptophan do its thing as she relaxed and paid vague attention to the football game on the TV. She could see into the dining room where her mother sat with a glass of wine, and Rob, her boyfriend of nearly three years, brought the pies out of the kitchen, laying a hand on her shoulder when she tried to stand and help. He bent, kissed her mother on the lips, and they smiled briefly at each other before Rob went back into the kitchen. Across the table and into the living room, her mother caught her eye and winked.

Happy.

Her mom finally was that. And in love. It thrilled Vanessa to see it, given how long it had been, how much of herself her mother had given up in order to focus on her three girls after her husband left.

Vanessa didn't want to think about that right now. Her dad was with friends today. She'd called him this morning to wish him a happy Thanksgiving, and that was enough. She'd done her duty. But if she pushed thoughts of him out of her head, that made room for the other person who'd been taking up way more than her share of space since last night: Grace Chapman.

What had happened at the bar last night, exactly? Because she wasn't quite sure. She remembered locking eyes with Amelia across the bar after Grace had kissed her good-bye, leaving her standing there in complete shock. She'd had to consciously keep herself from following Grace out to the parking lot and kissing the holy hell out of her right on the sidewalk. What was that? Because it certainly wasn't Vanessa. She didn't do that. She didn't think in those crazy, throw-caution-to-the-wind terms.

Of course, her brain called her a liar by tossing her an image of her bathroom ambush, adding, *Well, maybe not unless you're intoxicated, but you definitely have it in you.*

A nudge to her foot pulled her back into the living room. Her sister Ella was looking at her.

"You're so far away today," she said gently, smiling, because that's who Ella was. "You okay?"

Jason, Ella's husband of a year, shouted at the TV, and Ella rolled her eyes good-naturedly as she put a hand on his jean-clad thigh, her attention still on Vanessa.

Vanessa nodded. "I am. Just...I don't know. Pensive?"

"I get that. You call Dad today?"

Another nod. "You?"

"This morning."

They fell quiet after that, and Vanessa knew they were probably both having the same thoughts: missing their dad, feeling bad he wasn't with them on a holiday, but loyal to their mom. It had been the story of their lives for two decades now, but somehow, it didn't seem to get a whole lot easier.

How was Grace doing today?

The question had floated around in her head on and off since she'd opened her eyes that morning. Which was annoying. And kind of sweet. And then she wondered how Oliver was doing today. She didn't know for certain, but if he'd spent the night at Grace's parents' house and Grace was going there today, it was likely that Oliver's dad would not be there. Was he okay with that? Was Grace? And why did she care?

Seriously. Why did she care?

What was it about Grace Chapman that had allowed her into Vanessa's subconscious, let her find a spot and pitch a tent and set up camp and hang the hell out?

Her fingertips touched her cheek in the exact spot where Grace had kissed her good-bye last night. Her lips had been soft. Warm. And she'd smelled like apples, and had Vanessa not been so surprised by the move, she'd have turned her head and caught Grace's mouth with her own.

And that thought had kept her wide awake, uncomfortably turned-on for much of the night, until she'd had to slide her own fingers into her underwear and find release, so she could grab at least a couple hours of sleep.

This morning, she'd needed release again.

"Dessert, everybody," Rob called from the dining room.

"Thank freaking God," Vanessa muttered as she shoved herself out of the chair, thankful for anything that would yank her train of thought in another direction. Any other direction. She'd get her mom talking about work while she shoveled pumpkin pie into her own mouth.

That oughta work.

❖

Was today over yet? Was it close?

Grace had checked her watch so many times that she'd earned herself a glare from her mother. So she'd made a game out of finding ways to be subtle about it. Thank God Aunt Kathy and Uncle Bobby were there, because she didn't think she'd survive an entire day of looks and disapproving sighs from her mother.

"How's work going, Gracie?" Aunt Kathy asked across the dinner table.

"She's still putting flowers in vases," her mother said as she passed the mashed potatoes.

"She does more than that, Marilyn." Aunt Kathy didn't snap at her sister, just said it very matter-of-factly, and Grace smothered a smile when a light shade of pink colored her mother's cheeks.

"It's going really well," Grace said, pointedly ignoring her mother. "I'm learning so much about a lot of different flowers and plants, what they need, where they come from, and what seasons they thrive in. And which flowers mean what when you send a bouquet."

"I've read that," Aunt Kathy said, her eyes widening as she nodded. "That you send certain flowers to mean true love or you're sorry or you have my sympathy."

"It's true. My boss is kind of"—Grace looked at the ceiling for the right word to accurately describe Ava Green—"rough around the edges." She laughed. "But she knows her business. It's been around for years. Her father started it. And it's clear that she loves it. It means a lot to her." She wanted to delve a little deeper, almost added *even if she is a little grouchy*, but caught herself as she remembered Oliver was sitting next to her. That's all she needed—to bring him to the shop one day and have him innocently ask Ava why she's so grouchy because that's what his mom said. It could totally happen.

Speaking of her son, he'd been quiet since she'd arrived, at least with her. Grace, of course, was still stung from him telling her he hated her. The logical person in her knew he didn't mean it, knew it was likely not the last time he'd say something like that, but the tender-hearted part of her still felt wounded, as if he'd sliced her skin open, and the wound was still fresh. Still sore and raw. He'd had a blast with Grandma and Grandpa—his toys were scattered all over the family room, and there were new pictures on the fridge—and she wished she'd been firmer in her reminder to her mother that Oliver was actually home from school for a bad reason. That he was being punished, not over for a visit on vacation. But she swallowed a sigh. It was too late now, wasn't it?

After dinner was over and Oliver was in the other room with his LEGOs, she sat at the table with her parents, aunt, and uncle, having coffee and just talking. It was the part of Thanksgiving dinner that she used to love the most. Just relaxing. Catching up. Laughing. At least, that's how it had been before her marriage began to fall apart.

As if she could see right into Grace's brain, her mother's face brightened as she asked, "What time is Michael coming to pick up Oliver?"

"Not for another hour," she said, trying to ignore the obvious cheer in her voice.

"Well, I am very much looking forward to seeing him. It's been too long." Her mother picked up her coffee cup and sipped.

Grace managed to keep her voice steady. "I'm aware that you are. Trust me."

"You're not going to see your in-laws today?"

"I'm not high on their list right now."

To the surprise of no one, her mother made no comment, no attempt to defend her daughter against the in-laws. Not that Grace expected her to, but the reality of it still stung.

"Sam, how's the golf game?" Uncle Bobby asked Grace's father, and Grace wanted to scoot around the table and kiss his bald head with gratitude for the subject change, blatant as it was.

Across the table, Aunt Kathy caught Grace's eye and gave her a wink and a smile. She smiled back.

The conversation shifted to golf and jobs, and Grace listened quietly as her parents and aunt and uncle chatted, perfectly content to be slightly on the outside. Besides, it allowed her time to let her brain wander. Which it did, of course, right over to the corner where she'd safely tucked Vanessa Martini.

She'd been beautiful last night and the differences between her two personas—second-grade teacher versus woman out for drinks with friends—were clear and interesting to Grace. Even the way she dressed, though Grace had only seen her a handful of times, showed two distinctly different styles. At school, she seemed a bit softer, with a flowy skirt or a loose, simple top. Out at the bar, it was stylish jeans that hugged her lower body in ways that made Grace flush with heat. Sweaters or shirts that were still soft and pretty, but snug and with interesting textures. Last night's top had been a ribbed Henley, the buttons dipping low to show both collarbone and a peek of cleavage, the ribbed material hugging Vanessa's breasts, the light blue of it complementing her eyes.

How were her full lips always so shiny? It was a question she'd asked herself more than once. She'd never seen Vanessa apply any gloss, yet her lips were always glistening as if they'd just gotten a fresh coat. How often did she stare at Vanessa's mouth anyway? 'Cause it was probably a lot, considering how many questions she had about it.

She felt a tiny vibration in her back pocket. Excusing herself to the bathroom was an act of self-preservation. She knew if she pulled her phone out at the table, she'd get that disapproving look from her mother—*When do I not get that look lately?*—with the pinched lips and the furrowed brow, and she just was in no mood.

Powder room door locked, she pulled out her phone, expecting a text from Courtney or Janelle wishing her a happy Thanksgiving. Or maybe even Michael with some detail about his visit with Oliver this weekend. But no. It was from none of those people.

Has the tryptophan wrestled you into a chair or couch yet?

It was from Vanessa. Out of the blue. Complete with a smiley emoji and a turkey. She felt the smile bloom across her face, and when she glanced up into the small mirror over the sink, she saw two cheeks tinted with a pretty pink.

She typed back, *No, but my mother has driven me into the powder room. #Escape*

Not allowing her brain to question the words, she added, *was just thinking about u*, and hit send before she had a chance to second-guess herself.

The little dots bounced, indicating that Vanessa was typing. They bounced. And they bounced. Then they went away, and Grace blinked at the screen until they came back and bounced some more. A year and a half later, Vanessa's text came through.

Good things, I hope. I would say I'm surprised, but been thinking about u2. That's why the very generic message... The words were followed by an emoji grimacing and gritting its emoji teeth, and it made Grace smile. She rolled around several different responses, but decided to keep it simple.

Very good things. Send.

A GIF of a cartoon dog wiping its brow came back in response, and Grace's smile grew.

And u? Thanksgiving going well? Aside from the turkey coma?

More bouncing dots, then, *It's loud! Typical. #Italian Looking forward to some quiet time this weekend.*

Grace tried to picture what it must be like to have a big, boisterous family. As an only child of parents of British descent, she was raised in a rather calm, quiet household where voices were rarely raised and manners always took priority over emotions. A memory tickled her brain, and she typed, more detailed this time. Less abbreviation because she wanted to get the story right.

I had a friend in school, Angie, and her family was Greek. She had, like, five siblings, and her grandparents lived with them and her house was always so loud. But warm and welcoming and there was always SO MUCH FOOD. She followed that with a laughing emoji, one with puffed cheeks, and one with wide, surprised eyes because that's how she'd felt at Angie's. Welcomed and fed and also shocked by the endless volume of sound. *I loved it there*, she added because it was the truth.

Sounds very much like here. I'm soooooo full.

Grace pictured Vanessa sprawled on a couch, all pretty and casual and happily stuffed, surrounded by people. She sent a smiling emoji. *Me too!* She glanced at her watch, knowing her mother was probably doing the same thing, wondering why she was in the bathroom for such a long time.

What happens now? came Vanessa's next text.

Oliver's dad is picking him up soon and taking him for the weekend. Then I'll head home. She tried not to think about how much she was torn between loving the idea of being on her own for three days and also dreading it at the same time.

Big party planned for your solo time? A winking emoji followed.

Haha, yes, a party of one, staring at walls and wondering what to do with myself till my kid is back. #Pathetic

As Vanessa's dots bounced, Grace winced at her own message, annoyed that she'd actually sent such a whiny one. But Vanessa's response surprised her.

Listen, if you don't have plans tomorrow, I am taking Delilah for a long hike in the woods over by Willow Pond Park. Wanna come with?

Grace was still reading when the next text came.

No big deal if you can't. Just an idea to keep you from bouncing off walls...

Grace liked that. She liked that Vanessa immediately gave her an out. And she realized with stark clarity as she gazed at her own reflection that she didn't need an out. Didn't want it.

That sounds great! She felt just a little bit lighter.

Yeah? Good. I'll text you tomorrow with details?

Her reflection was grinning now. She typed—*Perfect*—just as there was a rap on the door.

"Grace?" Her mother. "Everything okay?"

"Yeah, Mom, I'll be right out."

Reaching over, she gave the toilet a flush, then washed her hands to complete the whole charade. Phone returned to her back pocket, she fluffed her hair, noticing the smile was still there.

Maybe her time without Oliver wouldn't be as lonely as she'd expected.

CHAPTER ELEVEN

"W hy am I so goddamn nervous?"

Delilah looked at Vanessa in the rearview mirror from her spot in the back seat of the car, but clearly had no answers to her question.

It was a gorgeous morning for a walk, crisp and cold, but bright and sunny, the sky an amazing electric blue. There'd been a very light snowfall the night before, a dusting, really, but the coat of white gave things a clean, fresh look. It was exactly the kind of weather Vanessa loved to walk in.

Four other cars populated the parking lot, but all were empty, so she stayed in her warm SUV with the engine idling while they waited for Grace, who had texted ten minutes ago that she was on her way.

Delilah had never been in these woods with Vanessa. In this park. So, it probably didn't occur to the dog to get excited. She simply gazed out the window, fogging up the glass with her doggie breath. Then she'd move to the opposite one and do the same thing, back and forth, just calmly watching the world.

"You're a really good dog, Delilah. You know that?" She turned her head to look over her shoulder and was met with a tongue swipe. "Aww, thanks, sweetie. I love you, too." And she did. The speed with which she'd connected with Delilah amazed her. It was like they'd always been together, and she was continually sending prayers of thanks up above to whatever god might be listening.

She had zero understanding of what had gotten into her yesterday when she'd invited Grace to join her for this walk. Once they'd finished talking, she'd spent the rest of the evening second-guessing herself, going so far as to type up half a retraction of her invitation before Amelia wisely talked her out of sending it and told her she was being an idiot. Leave it to Amelia to call it like it was, right? This morning, she'd woken up nervous, but that sort of good nervous, where the butterflies in your stomach were more like anticipatory flying saucers, banging around in there, letting you know that something—fun? dangerous? wonderful?—might happen today.

With no idea what kind of car Grace drove, she watched her mirrors as one, then another, then a third pulled in. Apparently, a lot of people had decided to take a walk today. The fourth car was Grace. Vanessa's eyes locked on her in the driver's seat in a way that was almost shocking in its exactitude. Like her subconscious knew it was Grace before her eyes did. "There she is," she said unnecessarily and pushed her door open.

She leashed up Delilah and helped her out of the car as Grace crossed from her spot on the other side of the lot. Dressed in jeans, hiking boots, a deep green ski jacket, a black knit hat, and matching black mittens, she looked like she'd walked off the cover of an L.L.Bean catalog, ready to face winter in the Northeast with a smile and an unerring sense of fashion. Her green eyes were bright, and the jacket made them pop in the best of ways, her dark lashes accenting them gorgeously. Vanessa felt almost entranced by the overall picture.

"Hi there," Grace said as she reached them, then leaned down to pet Delilah. "And hello to you, sweetie pie. I would tell you that Oliver says hi, but I didn't tell him I was walking with you because if I had, he'd have thrown a fit of jealousy. But I bet he says hi anyway." She dropped a kiss on the dog's black head, and something stirred, deep and low, in Vanessa's body.

"You survived Thanksgiving," Vanessa commented as they fell into step together.

"Ugh. Barely. My mother can just…" Grace held her hands out and bent her fingers into claws, and she growled in frustration.

"In what way?" They stopped at a tree so Delilah could sniff. They smiled at a woman who passed them.

Grace inhaled a deep lungful of air and let it out slowly. "She hates that I'm getting a divorce. Thinks I didn't try hard enough. Actually, she thinks my entire generation doesn't try. Divorce is too easy. Also, she adores Michael, which makes me think she assumes the divorce is all my fault. She hasn't said that, but I can tell."

"That is…a lot," Vanessa said, and they both laughed.

"It is, right?" Grace wiped her hand across the air in front of her as if erasing it. "And I don't want to spoil this gorgeous morning and this lovely invitation to walk with you by bitching about my mom the whole time. Let's talk about something else. Tell me about your family."

They began walking again.

"Well, let's see. I think I told you I have two younger sisters. We're all pretty tight, and we're very close with my mom. She's been seeing a guy named Rob for a while now, and he treats her like a queen, so we all adore him. My dad lives about twenty minutes away, but we don't see him that often. He's divorced from the woman he left my mom for, and then he was with another woman for a few years, and now he's alone." She felt herself being tugged toward that same guilt that washed through her anytime she thought about her father and his current circumstances, how rarely they saw each other, and she envisioned herself putting on the brakes. Digging her heels in to keep from going down that path. Not today. Not with Grace by her side on such a beautiful day. She shifted and chose a different path in her head.

"Amelia and Julia are my best friends, really. It's funny that they're actually relatives, but we've all been close for years."

Grace grinned, ducking under a branch as they passed. "That's so amazing. I envy you. My family is so small. I have, like, three cousins, and they all live in different states. What made you guys so tight?"

Vanessa grinned at her. "Well, we're all gay, first of all." She paused, then looked at Grace. "I don't generally blurt out my sexual orientation to the parents of my students, but…"

"I think I'm pretty clear on your sexual orientation." Grace teased her back and gave her a playful shove with her mittened hand.

"Okay, good." Vanessa laughed. "That was always the common denominator. I'm thirty-three, Julia's thirty-eight, and Amelia's forty-eight, but the age difference never seems to matter with us. We have each other's back, always. We support each other. We will smack each other around if it's necessary, and we will cut a bitch if one of us is threatened." A chuckle there from Grace. "They are my people. I don't know what I'd do without them."

"And you all have the same dimples, I've noticed," Grace said with a grin.

"I guess we do. I never really thought about it."

They passed another couple with a yellow Lab on a leash who wanted very much to say hello, so they petted him, and he and Delilah touched noses before everybody continued on their walks.

"Let's take this path," Vanessa suggested, pointing to her right. "It's a little rougher. Is that okay?"

"I'm up for it," Grace said with a nod.

Vanessa didn't mention that it would be less populated, that she wanted a quieter walk with Grace, wanted to talk to her without feeling like every other hiker or dog walker might hear. Not that it mattered, but she was aware enough to understand that what she really wanted was to feel like she was alone with Grace. It was a desire she didn't want to analyze too much.

The new path was narrower, steeper, and their conversation stalled in favor of concentrating on their steps. Once things leveled off and Delilah decided it was a good place to do some serious sniffing, they stopped to let her. Vanessa looked at Grace and found her looking back.

"You okay with Oliver gone?"

"Nope," Grace answered without hesitation, then barked a laugh. "I feel like I'm missing a limb." She held out both arms as if to make sure they were still there. Dropping them to her sides, she said quietly, "He told me he hated me the other day." Her eyes welled up, and she indicated them with her mittens and rolled them, as if sick to death of herself, flapping her mittens to fan away the tears.

Vanessa grabbed her without thinking, pulled her into a hug, because—*hello?*—she was crying, and that wasn't a thing she could just stand there and watch happen without doing something.

"Oh my God," Grace said, her voice muffled against Vanessa's jacket. She collected herself, sniffled, and pulled back. "Sorry. I'm sorry. It's so stupid. I know kids say that and it's probably not the only time he will, but wow, did it hurt."

"Of course it did," Vanessa said. "And you know he didn't mean it, right?"

Grace nodded, looking a little chagrined now. "God, now I'm embarrassed. I'm so sorry. I didn't come here to cry on you. I came here to—" She seemed to catch herself, clamped her mouth shut.

"What did you come here to do?" Vanessa asked, her voice barely a whisper.

Time stopped. Did it? Did time stop? Because it sure felt like it. Like the air stopped moving, the leaves stilled on the trees, the birds went quiet, and even Delilah seemed to freeze in place while Grace lifted her gaze, and those deep, soulful green eyes of hers locked on Vanessa's. They stayed that way for what was probably a second or two, but somehow felt like long, slow minutes, before Grace took a step toward her, then another. She was a touch smaller than Vanessa and had to lift her chin, push up onto her toes, but she did and then her mouth was on Vanessa's. Hot. Wet. Insistent.

Grace pushed into Vanessa, took a step, and Vanessa felt the solid support of a tree trunk against her back. It allowed her to pull Grace closer, and she deepened the kiss, pushing aside the surprise at Grace's assertiveness, letting herself enjoy it instead, focusing on the feeling, the pleasure. The heat.

God, the heat.

Were they melting what little snow was left around them? Vanessa half expected the trees to start dripping on them, and her body temperature cranked up a notch, then two, then ten. Reluctantly, she pulled back so she could look Grace in the eye. Little puffs of vapor floated in the air from their ragged breaths. Grace's pupils were large, her eyes hooded, and Vanessa loved that she knew this was how Grace looked when she was turned-on. Something about having knowledge that she assumed few people did gave her a jolt of arousal.

"Well," she finally said once she'd managed to find her voice. "I guess I have my answer."

Grace flushed a pretty pink and dropped her gaze to their feet. "I mean, I didn't come here *just* to do that. But…"

"But?"

"But it's been on my mind since we texted yesterday."

Vanessa nodded.

"No—lies." Grace cleared her throat. "It's been on my mind since the last time we kissed."

Vanessa couldn't control the smile on her face. She refused to try. She also refused to let who Grace was and the complications of that overshadow what was simply a lovely moment. At least not for a while.

"Mine, too," she said honestly.

Their gazes held, and Vanessa knew Grace's goofy smile was mirrored on her face. When they heard voices in the distance, they stepped apart and resumed their walk as if by unspoken agreement. Vanessa found it comforting how they seemed to be on the same page so often. At least then. There. On that day in that park.

They were quiet for a while before Grace finally spoke. "So what do we do?"

"About what?" It took a few more steps before Vanessa realized Grace wasn't next to her, and she stopped to look back. Grace stood with her hands on her hips, head tipped to one side.

"Really?" she asked, but a smile played at her full lips.

Vanessa let go of a small laugh. "I know. I'm teasing." She waited for Grace to catch up, and they started walking again. "I guess…" She shook her head. "I haven't really thought any farther ahead than where we are."

A beat passed. Another. Then Grace said, very softly, "I'm not sure if you're with me here, but"—she wet her lips—"I'd like to see where this goes." She gestured between them with a mittened hand, then looked up, and damn it, those eyes of hers were like magnets and Vanessa was metal. Drawn in. Pulled toward her.

"Me, too," she said before she had time to think about it.

"I mean, are there rules? Is there a rule that says we can't?"

Vanessa thought about it. For about the seventy-fifth time. "Honestly, I don't think there is. Though I'm pretty sure it would be frowned upon."

Grace nodded. "Probably." They walked some more, Grace moving behind her as the path narrowed and Delilah went first. "It's not like we know what'll happen. Right?"

"Right," Vanessa tossed over her shoulder, but she heard the tone of Grace's voice, knew she was thinking the same thing that was glowing in her own brain like a neon sign. *S-E-X.* That's what would happen. The level of heat between them was too high. They were going to end up in bed. Vanessa knew it, and she was pretty sure Grace did, too.

After about forty minutes of walking, Delilah finally started to slow down, the combination of the uneven path and the fact that she was not an adolescent dog tiring her out. Vanessa and Grace had steered into safer topics, talked about lots of superficial things, from favorite foods to favorite movies, but the underlying sexual tension between them was there, clear, and so, so stupidly hot. Vanessa had unzipped her coat about halfway through the walk, worried she might melt into a puddle of goo on the hard ground. They were both silent as the path ended and spilled them back into the opening next to the parking lot.

They kept walking, and once they hit asphalt, Grace turned to her and blurted, "Have dinner with me."

Vanessa was surprised, but only because Grace had beaten her to it. "Yes."

"Good."

And they stood there. And stood there.

Vanessa swallowed and glanced down at Delilah, who was looking up at her as if to say, *Are we going now? Or are we just going to stand here in this parking lot all day?* She met Grace's eyes. "And we'll see what happens."

Grace nodded and smiled widely, and holy turn-ons, Batman, she was so fucking pretty right then—sparkling eyes, rosy cheeks, big grin. "Plan on coming over around four," she said. "We can eat, watch *It's a Wonderful Life*, whatever we feel like doing. I'll text you the address." She was bouncing slightly on her feet like an excited kid and started taking small steps backward toward her car. "Okay?"

Vanessa nodded, and her own smile was probably just as big, and did she look as excited, as thrilled as Grace did in that moment? "Okay," she said. Grace turned and walked away, and Vanessa stood there. Watching. When Grace reached her car, she turned to Vanessa and gave her a wave.

Once in her own car, engine idling and heat on, Delilah lying in the back seat, pink tongue lolling out one side, she glanced in the rearview mirror. Grace pulled out of the parking lot and drove away, and Vanessa blew out a breath, wondering if she'd been breathing at all for the past twenty minutes.

"Oh, Delilah," she said, drawing out the words on a breath. "What am I doing? Huh?"

Delilah's black ears pricked up, and she cocked her head.

"Is this a terrible idea?"

Delilah tipped her head in the opposite direction.

"Yeah, I'm not sure either." She put the car in gear and backed out of her spot, knowing she needed some advice, needed to weigh the pros and cons.

Her head was spinning, thoughts tumbling around in her brain like laundry in a dryer the whole ride home, and it didn't stop once she was inside, had shed her outerwear, and had a hot cup of coffee in her hands.

Delilah drained her water bowl, went right to her dog bed, and crashed, and for a minute, Vanessa wondered when the last time was that Delilah'd been taken on a good walk in the woods. Knowing how hampered Mr. Walters's ability to walk was, she bet it had been quite some time. The dog had already dropped a couple extra pounds since living with her.

The bright red clock on the kitchen wall said it was nearing noon.

Four hours until her date. And that's exactly what it was. A date. A dinner date. Not in a restaurant, though. At a house. Grace's house...

She picked up her phone and sent a message to her group text with Julia and Amelia. It consisted of one simple word.

Help.

❖

"You gotta do pros and cons," Amelia said. "It's the best way to see it all laid out."

Savannah was nodding and pointing at Amelia. "I think she's right. So? Let's do that." She jumped up and went to the corner of The Bar Back where Julia's desk sat and returned to the couch with a pad of paper and a pen.

"Really?" Vanessa said. She was skeptical. She could admit that. "A pros and cons list seems so cold. Analytical."

"She's the mother of a student," Amelia said to Savannah, completely ignoring Vanessa. "That's the big one." Savannah scribbled on the pad.

"True. Well, that and the whole impending divorce thing," Julia threw in from behind the practice bar where she had about eight various bottles out and was experimenting with different combinations. "She has trouble with that, too."

"Hey," Vanessa whined, feeling slightly insulted.

"What?" Amelia asked. "She's right. Your initial assessment of her was that she was getting a divorce and not paying attention to how it was affecting her kid. Plus, parent of a student is on your list of no-nos, isn't it?"

Vanessa sighed and nodded. "I don't think that now, though. About the divorce thing."

"Still." Amelia nodded at Savannah. "Put it on the list."

"How old is she?" Julia asked, slapping the top onto a martini shaker and shaking away.

Vanessa glanced down at her hands and said, "Thirty, I think."

"I'm pretty sure no women under thirty-five was also on your list of no-nos," Amelia pointed out, and Vanessa shot her a glare. Her cousin seemed to be enjoying this.

"What else was on this list?" Savannah asked, clearly curious.

"No straight girls," Julia called out.

Vanessa snorted and muttered, "She's definitely not straight."

Savannah leaned against her playfully. "Got proof of that, do you?"

"Oh yes."

"But wait." Savannah stopped jotting notes and looked from one woman to the next. "What exactly is the problem here? I mean, you're not marrying the girl. It's a date. One date. Why are we freaking out and making lists?"

Julia opened her mouth to speak, but Amelia held up a hand. "Allow me." She turned to Savannah. "Since you're still fairly new here, you don't know that our dear Vanessa tends to be a one-and-done kind of girl."

"I don't know what that means," Savannah said, glancing at Vanessa, who sighed and sat back against the couch and waved a hand at Amelia, giving her the floor.

"Well, Savannah, let me paint the picture." Amelia stood up and began to pace like she was giving a lecture.

"You don't have to enjoy it so much," Vanessa muttered.

Amelia ignored her. "While Vanessa dated here and there in college, she had trouble with anything that had the word *casual* in front of it." She made air quotes. "Casual acquaintance, casual dating, casual sex, those things don't work for Vanessa. She's not wired that way."

Savannah turned to look at her. Vanessa shrugged.

"She met a girl named Callie right out of college and fell instantly in love—ready to settle down, buy a house, and have babies. They lasted…" She looked to Vanessa. "How long?"

"Five years," Vanessa supplied.

"Five years. Suffice it to say that Callie didn't have nearly the same issues with casual things as our dear Vanessa did, and that eventually ended."

"And since her?" Savannah asked.

Another shrug from Vanessa.

"There has been nobody for a few years now," Julia finally chipped in. "Not for lack of interest," she added, and Vanessa got the feeling she was trying to soften the ache that Amelia's words had brought up.

"I mean, of course," Savannah said. Turning to Vanessa, she asked, "There are mirrors in your house, right?"

Vanessa kissed her on the cheek. "You are a doll." Turning to Julia, she pointed at Savannah and ordered, "Keep her, will you?"

"Planning on it," was Julia's reply, eyes on her bottles.

Savannah blew a kiss in Julia's direction, then held out her hands and said, "So the concern here is that if Vanessa goes on the one date with Grace, there is a danger she could fall head over heels in love, and it could get messy."

"In a nutshell, yes," Amelia confirmed, taking one of the stools at the practice bar.

"But guys…" Savannah looked from one of them to the next and finally settled her gaze on Vanessa. "I mean, isn't that life?" When not one of the three cousins responded, she went on. "We don't get to decide who we're going to fall for, right? Or when? Or how? We just do. We just…fall. That's part of the joy. The surprise. That feeling of having no control. That's the wonder of it." She blinked at them as they continued to not talk. "Oh my God, what is wrong with the Martini family?" But she punctuated it with a laugh to cushion the criticism. "Vanessa, just go. Have dinner with this woman who you are clearly attracted to. Go with an open mind and no expectations. Have dinner. Talk with her. Enjoy yourself. Maybe make out some more. And instead of trying to map out your entire possible future with her, just see what happens." She lifted her hands, palms up. "Okay?"

Vanessa let the words soak in. It was all very simple, and she was being kind of ridiculous. She knew that. She'd always known that. But seeing her parents split up had left an impression on her and had defined the kind of person she was now. She knew that, too. But knowing something and being able to fight it were two very different things, and she'd done her best to be one hundred percent sure about anything she stepped into. She didn't like surprises. Her expression must've been worrisome because Savannah laid a warm hand on her thigh.

"It's just a date."

Giving herself a little shake, she forced a smile. "You're right. You're absolutely right." And she was.

"About the making out?" Savannah winked and gave her a nudge.

"*Psh* yeah," Vanessa said and felt her cheeks heat up. "'Cause, damn."

CHAPTER TWELVE

Grace was about to set the wooden spoon down in the spoon rest when she saw it tremoring in her hand. It was slight, not a big deal, but enough so she noticed it, and it cranked her nerves up another notch. Standing in front of the stove, watching the big pot of turkey soup she'd made, she flexed her hands open and closed. Open and closed. Inhale, exhale. Inhale, exhale. Vanessa would be there any minute, and she felt like her entire body was hyped up on sugar. Or cocaine.

Rudy twined lazily between her feet, around, back through, like he hadn't a care in the world. Grace envied the damn cat, all relaxed and chill. That wasn't her. At all.

She needed to stay moving. At least for the next few minutes. That should calm her nerves a bit. She strolled the small duplex, didn't let herself actually pace because that never helped her feel less freaked out. But slow strolling did. As Rudy followed her and hopped up onto the couch to make himself comfortable, she approached the bookshelf against the wall and methodically picked up each photo of Oliver and gazed at it, focused on it, until her heart rate slowed a bit, and she started to feel like herself again.

Her invitation this morning had been brazen, not a quality she'd ever displayed before. It was ballsy. Another thing she didn't normally consider herself. She wasn't a pushover by any means. She was no shrinking violet, as her dad would say. But she also wasn't the squeaky wheel. She wasn't the person who stood up and verbalized her needs and wants. Maybe that had contributed to the end of her marriage, now that she thought about it.

She stood in the middle of the tiny living room now and looked around and let herself notice the lack of Michael. Or rather, the lack of the lack of Michael. None of his shoes or boots were on the tray near the door, but that was about it. That was the only way she could tell he was gone, at least from the downstairs, and it sort of made her wonder how long it had been that way, how long he'd had one foot so far out the door that it had taken him literally one carload of boxes and less than two hours to move out. He'd said he didn't take any of the furniture because he didn't want to disrupt Oliver's life that much, but Grace wondered if it wasn't more accurate that he wanted a clean slate, an opportunity to start fresh with a new place and new furniture and a new life. Her divorce might have been technically fresh, but the rift between her and her soon-to-be ex-husband had begun long ago. And she suspected not only was he dating, but he might actually have a new girlfriend at this point.

All these thoughts helped to ease her mind the smallest bit about this date. When she'd returned home from their walk and realized she'd actually asked her son's teacher for a date, she'd had a bit of a panic attack, but now she felt better, more at ease, having developed a different perspective for where she was in life right now. Seriously, if Michael had a new girlfriend, it was certainly acceptable for her to go on a date, wasn't it? Even if that date was Oliver's teacher. And Grace had invited her to her house.

The doorbell rang right then, and thank freaking God, because Grace was pretty sure her brain was going to swirl her into complete insanity in another minute or two.

She gave herself a full-body shake, blew out a breath, and quickly checked her hair in the small mirror in the living room as she took the seven steps to the door and pulled it open.

Vanessa was beautiful. Because of course she was. As she stood there in her white coat and comfy-looking jeans, blond hair curled around her face, and those signature Martini dimples making an appearance, there was no way of denying it. Beautiful and so incredibly sexy that Grace felt her knees go weak for a split second, and she tightened her grip on the doorjamb to keep from collapsing into a ball of arousal on the floor.

"Hey," Vanessa said, still smiling, and handed over a bottle of wine. "For you."

"You didn't have to do that," Grace said and stepped aside. "Come in. You smell amazing." Okay, so that last line slipped out, but she *did*. Like cinnamon and nutmeg and warm invitation. Vanessa turned and her smile got bigger.

"Yeah? Well, thank you." And she leaned in and gave Grace a

quick kiss on the lips before Grace even realized it was happening. Then she stepped out of her shoes and let her coat slide down her arms to reveal a waffle-weave Henley in blue-and-lavender stripes. The shirt was casual and clung to Vanessa's torso like it had been tailored to do so, tapering in around her waist and showcasing what Grace was now mentally admitting was an incredible pair of breasts. She flexed her fingers again and consciously pulled her eyes away. "This is super cute," Vanessa said as she slowly wandered into the main living area. Her voice yanked Grace out of her dream state and nudged her into action.

"Thanks. It's very small, but it's home. For now." She held up the bottle. "Shall I open?"

"Sure." Vanessa was now looking at the same framed photos Grace had been enjoying a few minutes before. "For now? Are you moving?"

The kitchen wasn't far from the living room, but there was a wall between them now, so Grace raised her voice a bit as she uncorked the wine. "Oh no, not right now. But I don't want to live in somebody else's house forever. I'd like to be able to buy something of my own in the near future. Something with a bigger yard for Oliver." She poured two glasses and returned to the living room, then indicated the couch. "Sit?"

Vanessa took the glass with a nod and they sat.

It was quiet.

They glanced at each other. And suddenly, they were both laughing.

"Okay, we're ridiculous," Vanessa said.

Grace nodded. "We really are."

Their laughter died down in tandem, but they kept their eyes on each other. It was Vanessa who finally admitted, "I'm really nervous."

"Me, too, but I don't know why."

And they laughed some more.

"Okay," Vanessa said through tears of laughter. "Okay. Here's what we're gonna do." She held up a hand and her eyebrows rose. "We're gonna breathe in…" They both did, together, big breaths that filled their lungs. "And exhale." They did it again as one, simply breathed together. Then two, three, four times until it was clear to Grace that they both felt better.

"And now a toast," Grace said and held up her glass. Vanessa followed suit. "To gratitude, turkey soup, and possibility."

Vanessa's eyes went comically wide, and her tone was one of anticipatory excitement. "Get out, are we having turkey soup?"

"We are having turkey soup."

"I may never leave."

"I'm okay with that."

There was a beat of held gazes, and Grace marveled at how she could actually feel Vanessa's eyes on her, right down to her—

"Cheers." Vanessa interrupted her naughty thoughts and touched her glass to Grace's. "I'm really glad you invited me."

"I'm really glad you came." Another moment of silently held gazes. It was weird how *not* uncomfortable Grace was looking in those blue eyes. Having them see her. Finally, she asked softly, "Hungry?"

"You'd think after how much I ate yesterday, I wouldn't be hungry for the next week, but how can one know there's turkey soup in the very next room and not want some?"

"I think we should eat it." Grace stood up and held out a hand. Vanessa grabbed it, and Grace felt the touch as if Vanessa was electrified and sent a tiny zap up Grace's arm, into her chest, and again, straight down. "Come with me."

The duplex had no formal dining room, only a small round table off to the side of the kitchen. Grace had laid it tastefully, though, opting for the nice stoneware bowls instead of the plastic ones she and Oliver usually used for soup. The napkins were linen, the salad was in a glass bowl, and all the silverware matched. She indicated a chair for Vanessa to sit, so she could serve up the soup, but instead, Vanessa set down her wine and looked past Grace to the counter, lifted her nose in the air, and sniffed.

"Oh my God, did you *bake* bread?"

Grace nodded, her smile blossoming at all of Vanessa's surprise. "I did. Just came out of the oven a few minutes ago. It's one of my favorite things to make."

"It's one of my favorite things to eat."

"Well, look at that." Grace grinned, slid a bread knife out of the block, and handed it to her. "Slice it up."

"Yes, ma'am."

They worked in tandem in the small kitchen like the perfect team. Like they'd been doing so for years in the tiny space, shoulder to shoulder, chatting about what they'd each been doing in the few hours since they'd seen each other last. It was shocking to Grace, the ease. It felt normal. It felt perfect.

It scared the hell out of her.

Once they'd finally sat down to eat, Grace felt a little more at ease.

Was it because there was a table between them now, and she wasn't caught in the weird sexual pull that Vanessa seemed to have?

"This is amazing," Vanessa said after she'd eaten several spoonfuls of soup. "Wow."

"Thank you." Grace grinned. Soup was crazy easy to make, but the compliment coming from Vanessa warmed her up from the inside, pleased her in a way she couldn't quite define.

"When does Oliver come home?" Vanessa asked as Rudy made his way into the kitchen and wound around her feet. "I bet he misses his cat."

"He does. He wanted to take Rudy with him and had a meltdown when I told him he couldn't." She remembered how mad Oliver had been at her. "Michael is allergic, but it's somehow my fault that he couldn't take the cat." She shook her head, took a sip of her wine. "You think I'd be used to that by now."

"Used to what?"

"Being the bad guy." She caught those blue eyes with her own across the table. "Did you have that when your parents split?"

"What do you mean?" Vanessa tipped her head to the side, and her eyes suddenly became guarded.

Grace studied her. This was clearly a sensitive subject for Vanessa, and though she really wanted to delve in, she wondered if maybe it was too soon. Maybe she needed it to happen a bit more organically. Not to mention, they were having such a nice time, she didn't want to ruin it. "You know what? Never mind." She waved a hand across the air in front of her. "Let's just eat and enjoy ourselves." Was that relief that zipped across Vanessa's face?

They spent the rest of dinner talking about their jobs. How Vanessa had wanted to be a teacher since she was a little kid. How Grace had a business degree but decided to stay home with Oliver when he was a baby instead of keeping her job at a large container manufacturer.

"I'd still really like to have my own business one day, but it's been on such a back burner for so long that it's kind of faded away a bit." Grace was rinsing dishes to go into the tiny dishwasher after Vanessa had been ordered to sit at the table and talk to her when she offered to help clean up. "Sometimes, life happens, and you get a curveball instead of what you were expecting and..." She shrugged.

"You should talk to my cousin Amelia. She knows all about that. She was with Tammy for years, had plans, took early retirement so they could spend time together. Little did she know, Tammy had other plans and wanted out of the marriage."

Grace felt her heart squeeze. "Oh no. That's awful." She indicated the coffee maker and raised her eyebrows in question.

Vanessa nodded her blond head. "A little cream, please."

Grace set the coffee to brewing. She could clearly see how much Vanessa cared about Amelia as she continued the story.

"It was rough on her. Still is. She's always saying how she has no desire to ever date again. Which I think will change, but for now, we let her wallow. My point, though, is that she's started her own business taking care of dogs. She walks them for people who have busy day jobs and work long hours. She will dog sit at somebody's house. That kind of thing." She shrugged. "I mean, it's a small business in the very early stages, but it's something she never expected to be doing, and she's put her heart into it. You could, too."

"I could, you're right." Grace finished wiping her hands and hung up the damp dish towel. Picking up two mugs of coffee, she indicated with a head tilt that Vanessa should follow her into the living room. Once settled on the couch, she admitted, "I didn't really give you the option *not* to watch *It's a Wonderful Life* earlier, but we don't have to."

"Here's something you don't know about me," Vanessa said, turning her body so one knee was up on the couch and she faced Grace. "I hate black-and-white movies. My mother won't even talk to me about it. Amelia calls me a movie boor."

"No worries then," Grace said, setting down the remote and doing her best to mask her disappointment. Vanessa's warm hand closed over her arm.

"You didn't let me finish." Those summer-sky eyes seemed to dance. "I hate black-and-white movies…except for *It's a Wonderful Life*. Which is amazing. The buildup. The background. The message. And have you *seen* Donna Reed? Wow."

"I mean, right?" They laughed together and Vanessa fanned herself with her hand. "Well, I have to say that while it would've been perfectly fine for you not to like old movies, and I was rethinking this whole thing because of it, you get bonus points for watching this one with me."

"Yeah?"

"Definitely."

That held gaze thing happened again right then. It was something they seemed to excel at, and Grace liked how she felt it all the way to her center. Like it was awakening feelings that had been dormant for far too long. She cleared her throat, forced herself to look at the remote, and turned on the movie, which was already fifteen minutes in.

So much washed through Grace over the next half hour as they watched. She'd seen the film dozens of times and she loved it every time, but what she loved more was watching somebody else watch it. Especially Vanessa, she realized. She might play the tough teacher, hardened against pain-in-the-ass parents, but her face now was soft. When Mr. Gower smacked George in his bad ear, Vanessa's eyes welled up. Big points right there. Big ones. During the commercial breaks, they talked, once about a commercial that made Vanessa well up again.

"Wow, I had no idea Oliver's teacher was such a sap."

"Shut up," Vanessa said but laughed and bumped against her to show she was playing. "Don't let that get around."

Grace held her hands up in surrender. "My lips are sealed. Your reputation with parents as a hard-ass shall remain intact." She lowered her voice. "Though now I know better."

"Pay no attention to the woman behind the curtain," Vanessa said with a laugh.

Grace laughed with her and then got quiet. Serious. "I like the woman behind the curtain," she said softly. Instantly, she wished she hadn't said it, gave herself a shake, and toed off her shoes, pressing her fingertips into her foot and trying to focus on something other than Vanessa's eyes on her.

"Your foot hurts?" Vanessa asked.

Grace grimaced. "I'm afraid I'm not used to walking the way you are. Plus, I could use some new boots."

Vanessa patted her thigh. "Here. Gimme." When Grace looked up at her, she was wiggling her fingers in a come-here gesture. "Gimme," she said again.

Grace grinned, turned her body so she sat against the arm of the couch, and put her socked feet in Vanessa's lap just as the movie came back on. Vanessa pulled one sock off, then the other and began what would go down in Grace's life history as the first time somebody turned her the hell on just by rubbing her feet. Vanessa alternated between pressing her fingers into different spots on her soles, massaging the sore spots into submission, and scratching lightly along her ankles. Some people might've been annoyed by that, tickled irritatingly, but not Grace. She loved to have her feet rubbed, and Michael would never do it. Of course, she'd had no idea a foot rub and wanting to rip somebody's clothes off were as closely related as they seemed to be with her. She could feel herself subtly grinding her ass into the couch cushion, trying not to be obvious about what Vanessa was doing to her. But the moment blue eyes turned and captured her gaze, Grace knew her arousal must've been clearly written on her face. And that Vanessa had read that arousal with no problem. A moment passed, the air nearly crackling with the electricity that sizzled between them.

Vanessa reached for her, grabbed the front of her shirt in her fist, and pulled Grace's face to hers.

The kiss was not gentle.

It was hard. Demanding. Exhilarating. Arousal whooshed through Grace's body like a wave, setting her blood on fire, and she grasped at Vanessa, not even sure what she was reaching for. Just…more.

When was the last time somebody had kissed her like this? Like they wanted her. Like they *wanted* her. Like there was nothing else in the world they were thinking about. Just her. Only her. How long had it been? Two years? Five? God, all she wanted to do was lose herself completely. In Vanessa's arms, in her mouth, in her touch, in the joy of being as wanted as much as you wanted that person back.

Thank freaking God she hadn't lost herself in Vanessa completely at that point, or she wouldn't have heard the key in the lock or the front door pushing open or the stomping of feet in the foyer.

Vanessa registered the noise, too, her eyes shooting open wide as she quickly pushed herself off Grace and sat up, just as, "Mom!" was called out, and suddenly, there was Oliver.

He slid out of his jacket and let it fall to the floor. His brows furrowed in confusion as he stopped and said, "Oh, hey, Ms. Martini, what are you doing here?"

Vanessa looked to Grace, still wide-eyed, and swallowed audibly as Michael came into the room and looked a lot like he wanted to ask the same question. Grace cleared her throat and fought the nearly overwhelming urge to run her hand across her lips, because how much of a dead giveaway would that be?

Standing up quickly, she thanked every god above that she and Vanessa hadn't gotten any farther than kissing, and she didn't have the telltale unbuttoned shirt or—holy hell—unfastened jeans. Putting on the immediate smile that moms had, the one that said *Don't worry, everything is just fine* even if it wasn't quite, she clapped once and reached her arms out to him. "Well, what are *you* doing here?" she asked her son, then glanced up at Michael.

"Where's Rudy?" Oliver asked instead and ran off and up the stairs to find his cat, leaving Grace standing there, arms out, hugless.

She dropped her arms, stood up, and looked at her ex-husband. "What's going on? You were supposed to have him until Sunday." Trying not to sound annoyed and exasperated was hard, since she felt both of things in a major way.

Michael was still looking at Vanessa, and it was clear he had a million questions, probably more assumptions, but also knew he didn't have a right to voice most of them. "He was complaining so much about missing the damn cat. I finally asked him if he wanted to just come home, and he said yes. What was I supposed to do?"

She sighed quietly, hyperaware that Oliver was upstairs and that sound carried in the small house. She never wanted her son to feel she didn't want him. Ever. And she was wildly frustrated that Michael didn't seem to have that same attitude. "You could've told him he'd see the cat on Sunday. That his mom is taking good care of Rudy and he's fine. That his daddy wants to spend time with him and would be really sad if he wanted to leave early."

Michael made that face. The face he always made when he knew she was right but was also totally over her telling him he was wrong. The face that said both *Here we go again* and *I don't have to listen to this*. He waved his hand dismissively with a scoff, then turned on his heel to head back to the door, Grace right behind him. Hand on the knob, he pulled the door open, then looked back and gestured vaguely toward the living room.

"And really, Grace? His teacher?" He shook his head, clearly disgusted by her decisions. "Nice." Then he was through the door, it shut behind him, and the house was silent except for Oliver's small voice, talking animatedly to his cat upstairs. Grace let her chin drop to her chest and exhaled quietly.

Back in the living room, Vanessa was on her feet, straightening her clothes, looking just this side of mortified. Because how could she not be, right?

"Well, that was fun and not at all awkward," Vanessa said, and while it seemed she tried to make it sound light, she clearly didn't feel it. Grace could tell by the way Vanessa shifted her eyes, wouldn't look right at her.

"I'm so sorry." Grace held her hands out. "He wasn't supposed to be home until—"

"Sunday. Yeah, I heard."

"I'm so sorry," Grace said again because what else could she say? She stood there, at a total loss, and dropped her arms to her sides. Shook her head.

"Look, I need to go anyway. I have Delilah at home." She made eye contact with Grace for the first time since Michael had arrived, and her expression softened just a touch. She reached out and squeezed Grace's upper arm, rubbed up and down. "We'll talk soon, okay?"

All Grace could do was nod. She walked Vanessa the three steps to the door and watched her make her way to her car. She lifted her hand in a half-hearted wave as Vanessa pulled away from the curb, then brought her fingertips to her still-burning lips, and her brain hit her with a flashback. It was intense. Sexy. Hot as hell. And as she stood there, simmering in her own arousal, she wondered what would happen next. What Vanessa was thinking. And mostly, when could they do that again?

"Mom?" The voice traveled down the stairway and shoved everything else but motherhood into the shadows.

"Yeah, honey?"

"Can I have a snack?"

With a sigh, Grace closed the front door. "Sure. Come on down. Should we make brownies?"

'Cause chocolate was as good as sex. Right?

Chapter Thirteen

"Oh my God," Vanessa muttered in relief, dropping into her chair and watching as her students filed out of her classroom at the end of Monday. The first day back after a holiday or a long weekend was always hard, and today had felt three days long.

"Did today last for, like, two weeks?" Danika walked in as if she had read Vanessa's mind and parked a hip on the edge of the desk.

"It absolutely was. It might've been a month. Wow."

"And did your kids come back with smart little mouths like mine?"

They looked at each other and said at the same time, "Freaking December."

The worst month for teachers. Well, that and June, when the school year was almost over, and half the kids completely gave up on what was left. Some of the teachers, too.

They laughed quietly together, not wanting any students that might be left in the halls to hear them.

Vanessa studied Danika for a moment, until Danika squirmed a bit. "What? Why are you looking at me like that?"

"Can I ask you a question?" Vanessa sat up straight because this was a serious subject. And she needed to talk about it with somebody who'd understand.

"No, I'm not taking questions today. Sorry."

Vanessa blinked at her.

"Oh my God, I'm kidding." Danika pushed at her with her orange heel that was the exact shade of her top. "What is wrong with you?"

"Have you—" She almost whispered the question, then looked past Danika at the open door. Got up. Crossed the room. Closed it.

"Oh, this *is* serious. Closed-door serious." Danika made a show of sitting up, sharpening her interest. "Hit me. Have I…what?"

Vanessa wet her lips. "Have you ever dated the parent of a student?"

"*Oh*," Danika said, drawing out the one syllable and widening her dark eyes. Her brows rose up toward her hairline. "Do tell." Then a little gasp and, "Is this about the girl at the bar last week?" She looked around, as if somebody else might have suddenly and magically materialized in the closed room with them, and dropped her voice to a whisper. "Was she the mom of one of your students?"

"Ugh. Yes." Vanessa wasn't sure what she'd hoped for by telling Danika. Just, someone who could relate. "You crushed on that one dad, years ago, right?"

Danika's eyes went dreamy. "God, he was *fine*." She took a beat, probably to visualize this fine man, then brought her gaze back to Vanessa. "Yeah, I did. I almost went there but never did."

"Why not? Too complicated?"

A big exhale. A shrug. "I guess? It just made me nervous. I know there's no written rule, but it just kind of is, you know?"

Vanessa could feel her shoulders drop. "Yeah. I know."

"Did you go there?"

It was Vanessa's turn to exhale a big breath. "I have come close."

"Meaning…" Danika leaned forward a bit, waiting for her to finish the thought.

"Meaning we've spent some time together."

Danika squinted at her before asking, "And what else?"

Vanessa winced. "And we made out."

"A little?"

"A lot."

"I see." Danika nodded slowly before allowing a grin to spread across her face.

Vanessa shook her head and pointed. "No. No, do not smile at me. Don't. This is not something to smile about."

Danika laughed. "Why not? I saw her. She's a hottie. And it's been a long time since you've been interested enough in anybody to make out *a lot*." She made the air quotes, still smiling.

"Yeah, well, we were interrupted. Unexpectedly and horrifyingly." She related the story of the previous Friday, told her everything from the beginning. Being overserved and making the moves at Martini's, running into her everywhere, the walk, the dinner invite, more making out—she even added that things had been heading in the direction of the bedroom as far as she was concerned Friday—Oliver and his father coming home, the father's disapproval, and Vanessa's subsequent flight. Some of it, Danika had already heard, but Vanessa told it all again, every detail, as much for herself as for Danika. For some reason, she needed to hear it all. From her own lips. In order.

When she finished, she fell back into her chair dramatically, like she'd just delivered a very important monologue in a play. Danika simply stared at her, blinking.

"Damn, girl," she finally said. "That is a freaking miniseries. Wow. I wish I'd written that. Netflix'd be calling me, right about now."

"I know." Vanessa groaned. "Tell me what to do." There was a pleading in her voice she wasn't proud of. "Help me."

"Oh, sweetie." Danika reached for her shoulder, gave it a squeeze. "I mean, like I said, there's no rule. But it could be dicey. No way around that. It could also be awesome."

There was a beat while Vanessa waited. Danika just looked at her. "That's it?" Vanessa asked as she slid her chair back and stood. Paced. "Seriously? That's not helpful. That's, like, the opposite of helpful. You are Helpful Opposite."

Danika slid off the desk and her face grew serious, which made Vanessa stop and take notice. Danika was fun. She was a woman who saw the happy, saw the joy. Her serious face was reserved for scaring students who crossed the line with her, not for her friends. Rarely for her friends. But she was using it now, and she looked Vanessa in the eye as she spoke. "Let me tell you something, Ms. Martini. Something you might not realize. You ready?"

"Should I sit back down?"

"Maybe you should."

Danika's continued seriousness dropped Vanessa's butt right back into the chair. "Okay." She swallowed.

Freaking her out a little bit with the intense eye contact, Danika said, "You deserve to be happy." That was it. Five words. Seven little syllables. A simple statement that made Vanessa's eyes well up, though she wasn't sure why. "It seems to me that you like this girl a lot. I've known you, what, three years? And not once have I heard you talk about somebody the way you talk about her, even as you're freaking out about it. Maybe give it a chance."

"Even given all the complications? The school thing. Her impending divorce. The kid."

"Honey, how many relationships you think there are that *don't* have complications? They all do. Mine does."

Vanessa scoffed. "You and Will? Please."

"Listen, I am hard to be with. And Will's got his faults. Throw in two crazy families, job stress, and a struggle to get pregnant, give it a good stir, and *voilà*, you've got a complicated relationship. See?"

Vanessa had known Danika was trying for a baby, but she'd only mentioned it in passing. This was the first she'd heard of any troubles, and she wanted to shift the topic to that, but Danika held up a finger as if she'd read her mind. Again.

"We can talk about that another time. This is about you and your worries. Needless ones, really."

"With her kid as my student?" Vanessa recalled Grace's ex's tone, his obvious displeasure over her and Grace, given that she taught their child.

"He won't be forever. Right? It's already almost December. You have him for six more months, and then he's on to the next grade, and then that worry is gone."

Vanessa let the words roll around in her head. She'd thought of that, certainly, but having it come from somebody else, somebody she trusted, made it seem more important.

"I mean, you're not proposing to the woman," Danika continued. Then she paused. "You're not, right?"

"Um, no." Vanessa grinned.

"Not yet anyway."

"Not yet." And then the weirdest thing happened. Her brain tossed her the vision of Grace in a wedding dress, walking down the aisle toward her, and Jesus, Mary, and Joseph, what was wrong with her? "I barely know her," she said aloud and with a bit more enthusiasm than was necessary, judging from the strange look Danika gave her.

"I just think you're overthinking. You don't need to."

Vanessa sighed. "Maybe you're right."

"What's happened since Friday? What does she say about it?"

Yeah, this was the part where Vanessa was a little embarrassed. A little bit less than impressed with herself. "She feels terrible. Wants to meet up again so she can apologize in person and we can talk."

"See? There you go. And when are you meeting her?"

"Well…"

Danika dropped her chin and studied Vanessa from her lowered brow. "Tell me you did not ghost that poor girl."

She hadn't. Not exactly. "I answered her. But I was probably…

um, shorter? Shorter than I needed to be." She'd accepted the apology. Of course she had. But she hadn't really reached out since. Grace had asked if she had plans for the rest of the weekend, and she'd made something up. Grace hadn't pressed. Because, seriously, why would she? Vanessa hadn't given her any reason to think she should, that it might work if she had. She'd sent a smiley face and left it at that. Looking at it now, from two days later, she couldn't blame her.

The rebuke from Danika that she had unconsciously braced for never came. Instead, her friend shrugged and shouldered her purse. "You do you, but I think she deserves a bit more from you." She said it lightly. Almost off-the-cuff. Casual. Just a statement of opinion. But Vanessa felt scolded. Not in a way that made her mad—in a way that made her feel ashamed. As if her mom had reprimanded her for bad behavior. And while she was sure that wasn't what Danika was doing, that's how it had come across.

It was probably a good thing.

Because Vanessa needed to hear it. She hadn't realized it until right then, right in that moment. She had to face it—any road forward with Grace was bound to be riddled with obstacles. Speed bumps. Potholes. But what lay at the end of that road, could it be worth the journey?

"Thanks, D," she said as Danika gave her a hug, then took her leave and headed home. She sat at her desk for several more minutes, just replaying every word exchanged with Grace since Friday. Everything Danika had just pointed out to her. And she still came back to the same questions: Could there be something wonderful beyond all the complications? And more importantly, was she willing to take the risk?

❖

December was only two days away and was the busiest month for The Petal Pusher. Grace would have guessed June because of all the weddings. Or maybe February because of Valentine's Day. But no, it was December, hands down. People sent flowers to their mothers, their grandmothers, their wives, their girlfriends, out of state friends, friends who were hard to buy Christmas gifts for…The list was endless. And it started early.

This, of course, meant that for the next twenty-six days, she would be busier than a cucumber in a women's prison. Michael had said that once, and despite its raunchiness, it made her laugh. She never said it out loud, but she thought it every so often, and right now, she grinned. Something she needed, as the pace of her job was already accelerating and wasn't going to let up for a month.

She also needed that small grin because, simply put, she was sad. There was no other way to say it. She was sad, and she had been for quite some time now. It had started a couple years ago when she'd started to realize her marriage was on its last legs. She'd found a couple things that pointed to Michael cheating on her, and she'd hardly cared—she was already that uninvested in something she'd vowed to work at until death did them part. It was insidious, the sadness. It had slid in while she wasn't paying attention. Slithered through her, passed by most of her organs, but squeezed her heart, settled in and created a soft darkness around it. When she tried to picture it in her head, that's what she saw. Her heart with a dark shadow around its outline. It made her do things like sigh for no reason. It affected her sleep and her appetite. Sometimes, she could fight the effects. Sometimes, she could let her friends drag her out for happy hour. Sometimes, she could shove it aside and make out with a beautiful woman, let herself feel wanted, desired.

But always, always, that shadow seemed to come back, like a snake that had gone hunting, and the darkness was heavy. Made her feel weighed down, made activity an effort that it never used to be.

Ava was running her ragged. She didn't really mind. Being kept busy made the time go by and kept her from wallowing. Thinking about Oliver could do that, too, but he'd been a handful for the past two days. He'd begged to come back from his dad's, yes, but once he was home, he seemed angry Michael was gone. She and Michael had an angry text thread going about how she had to deal with all their son's meltdowns and Michael got all the happy, fun times. Her ex-husband didn't know what she wanted him to do about that, and—honestly?—neither did she. But she was sad, and she was angry, and she had nowhere to put it. So she shoved it at him.

She wanted to shove some of it at Vanessa Martini, too. Grace had felt awful about Friday night, despite it not being her fault at all, and she'd apologized profusely. Vanessa had responded, but barely, and Grace just didn't have the energy to chase her.

Which was a fucking shame because they could have something. She knew it. She'd felt it. Intensely. Every conversation. Every kiss. Every touch. Every look. There was something there between them, tethering them somehow. She so wanted Vanessa to see it, to feel it as well, but it seemed like that wasn't the case. And could Grace blame her? Really? If she was honest, if she stepped back out of her own life for just a second and looked at it from the point of view of somebody else, did her life look inviting? Or did it look like a hot mess?

Grace snorted, the answer obvious, just as Ava shouted at her from the front of the store.

"Grace! Don't forget the orders for out of state!" Ava had turned over the planning calendar for the month to Grace, something that had shocked her, and was probably going to ask her about it every single day.

"On it," she called back. Organization was a strong point of hers, and this kind of planning was right up her alley. It was already after five, but she was happy to keep working. She'd arranged for Oliver to have a playdate until after dinner. Creativity would be the key this month, as many more late days were bound to happen.

Her phone buzzed in her back pocket and she grabbed it out, hoping it wasn't an issue with Oliver. She'd noticed lately that she'd started to brace whenever Oliver wasn't with her and her phone rang. Like, her body went rigid, expecting bad news.

But it wasn't bad news.

It was…was it good news?

It was a text. From Vanessa.

Grace felt her own brows climb up towards her hairline in surprise, and she put the phone back in her pocket without looking. She needed to take a breath first. If she was being honest, she'd been pretty sure Vanessa would never contact her again. She'd been very freaked out by Michael's appearance Friday night—not that Grace could blame her, it had freaked her out too—and her texts since had been abrupt. So, yeah, she'd been almost positive Vanessa was backing away, and she didn't want to think about how much that stung. It took every fiber of her being to keep her from continuing to text Vanessa, from apologizing more than she needed to, from begging her to give them a real shot. So what if her ex-husband had shown up unexpectedly? So what if she was Oliver's teacher? Why did those things matter at all if they had something that might actually be special? Maybe Vanessa didn't know that special things didn't appear every day, that you couldn't just wave them away dismissively and wait for the next special thing to come along.

She managed to work for another three and a half minutes before sighing loudly and pulling the phone back out.

Hi. I suck. I'm sorry. Can we talk?

"Wow," she said aloud. Now, that was a surprise. She thought about ignoring her. Being snarky in her response. Not responding at all. But, yeah, who was she kidding?

I'd like that. When? Where?

Was that desperate? Did she forgive her too quickly? Was she a pushover? Didn't matter. She'd already hit send. It was stupid of her to answer so fast. Now she'd be waiting for hours until—

Her phone buzzed.

Okay, maybe not hours. Maybe seconds. She picked up the phone. *Ur call. I'm flexible. #NoKids* She added a winking emoji, and Grace grinned.

Telling herself to take her time, not to jump to make a date, she forced herself to wait. Set the phone down on the table in front of her. Then the shop phone rang, and she could see Ava was on the other line, so she answered. Took an order. Wrote up the notes on the computer. The whole time she worked, she was thinking about spending time with Vanessa. Where, how, when, what it would be like to see her again after she'd left so abruptly.

Before she could get too lost in thought, her phone buzzed again, but this time, it wasn't Vanessa. It was a text from Courtney.

What's up buttercup?

Grace smiled at the familiar greeting. She grabbed her Bluetooth out of her bag, secured it in her ear, and dialed her friend. She needed a little guidance, and talking was much faster than texting. Plus, she could keep working and multitask.

Greetings finished, Grace launched right in. "I need your help."

"Hit me." It was something she'd loved about Courtney since the first time they'd met—her willingness to help a friend. She'd never let Grace down, not once.

Grace explained the situation with Vanessa. Courtney already knew about last Friday, so she filled her in on the text. "I really want to spend some time with her, but not at a bar and not when Oliver is home."

"I get that," Courtney said.

"What should I do? Take her to dinner? Not a movie 'cause we can't talk during a movie…"

"I've got it." Courtney's satisfied tone filled the line. "Take her to that pottery night we were going to this Friday. She can take my spot."

"What? What about you?"

"I've been working some crazy hours, and there's a chance I may have to go with my boss to do an out-of-town presentation this week. I was gonna bail anyway this time. It'll be a great chance for you guys to talk 'cause you'll be sitting apart from others. You can have fun with her, maybe even teach her a little if she's never done it. Plus, it could even be sexy. You can get all close and covered with clay like that movie *Ghost* with the sexy pottery wheel scene. I'll go with you next month."

She was bummed to be missing a night with Courtney. The pottery night was something they'd started doing once a month in the spring, and they had a blast. It wasn't a class—rather, it was basically akin to open swim at a pool. You could go to the community arts center, pay twenty bucks, grab a wheel and some clay, and make something. She wasn't very good, but she always had fun. It got her out of her head for a while, and now she was picturing herself there with Vanessa. Hands covered in clay. Legs spread to accommodate the wheel. Eye to eye with her while creative juices flowed...

"I'm gonna take your silence to mean you're picturing it," Courtney said and yanked Grace out of her sexy daydream.

"Totally am," she admitted with a laugh.

"So you see my point."

"I do. But are you sure?"

"Sweetie, I know you're dying to talk to this chick, especially after she flaked on you. You already have a sitter. Take advantage."

And just like that, it all clicked into place. "You're the best, Court—you know that, right?"

"I'm very aware, yes."

"Oh, good. I was hoping so." There was a muffled voice in the background, and then Courtney came back on the line.

"Crap, gotta run. I expect details!" And she clicked off before Grace could thank her again.

And now there were visions in her head. Visions of hands on pottery. Four hands. Hers and Vanessa's, molding and shaping and...

"God. Stop it." She hissed that command to herself, gave her head a good shake. But the smile stayed. She could feel it as she texted Vanessa.

I have an idea. Friday night. Do you trust me?

Was that too flirty? Too sexy? What if Vanessa wanted to tell her she didn't want to explore what they had? What if—"Oh my God, just stop." How irritating was her ability to drastically overthink things?

She sent the text, then nibbled on her bottom lip while the little gray dots bounced and bounced and bounced.

Friday it is. And yes...

Grace's grin grew. She especially liked the three little dots. They spoke of something to come. Promise. Anticipation.

My place at 6:30. I'll drive. She sent it, then laughed through her nose and added, *Wear something you don't care about.*

She could picture Vanessa all pensive, that divot that formed between her eyebrows when she was thinking hard making itself known. Finally, the response came.

Mysterious. I'll be there. And a smiley emoji with hearts around it.

Hearts.

Emoji spoke volumes.

It wasn't all better, though. She forced herself to think about that. Just because Vanessa had reached out—finally—didn't mean everything was rainbows and puppy dogs. They had some things to discuss. And Grace had no idea if Vanessa was even interested in dating her regularly. What she did know was that, the fiasco on Friday night aside, she'd never been so drawn to a person physically or emotionally for as long as she could remember. She hadn't even felt such a pull with Michael in the beginning. She'd loved him, of course. She'd wanted to be around him, absolutely. But this? This was like a magnet drawing steel. It was like a tractor beam. Some insanely strong gravitational pull. After Friday, she'd wanted to stay away. To give up. And then the text had come today, and she was steel again.

She had almost four days to think about what she wanted to say. What she wanted to wear. Where the night might lead. She hadn't planned any kind of romantic future for herself since she'd first met Michael. It felt weird, but in a good way. Weirdly good.

Of course, she also had four days to completely freak the hell out...

Chapter Fourteen

The week had dragged and flown at the same time. How was that possible? Grace didn't understand it, but it had absolutely happened that way. One minute, she couldn't believe it wasn't Friday yet. The next, she couldn't figure out how it got to be Friday already. It was possible she was losing her mind—at least, it was a possibility she considered.

December had arrived softly and quietly, on winter slippers, bringing a cold yet gentle breeze, but no snow. At least not until the weekend. The snow that had come early had melted quickly, leaving the world cold and hard. There was a storm warning for late Friday night, but it should stay clear enough for them to drive to and from the pottery place.

Michael had picked up Oliver from school and was keeping him for the weekend. *You're sure?* she had texted, likely giving away her hopes and pissing off her ex but also seriously wanting to know if he could stand up to his own son and be the parent instead of caving and doing whatever was easier on him.

Yes, I'm sure, feel free to bang our kid's teacher all night.

Grace pinched the bridge of her nose and willed the surge of anger to pass, her offense taken at the vulgarity of his words. Because fighting with Michael now would do her no good. No, snarking back at him would get her nowhere but would probably give her a pounding headache, so she tucked her phone away and finished up the last order for the day. It was only early in the month, but that was the thing about the holiday season. People sent flowers and plants and arrangements all December long. Great for business. Awful for getting a break.

Not knowing where they were going tonight was killing Vanessa, she knew, in the most fun and teasing of ways. Vanessa had texted all week, several times a day, with guesses. *Scavenger hunt? Grape stomping? Scuba diving? Scaling Everest? Haunted house?* Every guess was accompanied by either an emoji or a GIF of some wild version of her answer. Grace had been laughing all week long and was proud of herself for never giving in and telling her. She smiled as she clipped a stem and placed the last flower.

"I'm heading out, Ava," she said half an hour later, gathering her things.

Ava grunted, also working on an arrangement. She stepped back and looked at it, a beautiful mix of flowers in reds and whites, lots of lush green serving as the backdrop.

"That looks gorgeous," Grace said.

"You think so?"

"Definitely. It's rich. You picked just the right greens for the framing. It's beautiful. Nicely done."

As if Grace's words had made the final decision, Ava gave one nod and began the wrapping. "Last one for today." She glanced at Grace. "You'll be in by noon tomorrow?"

"Yes, ma'am." And she headed home.

When the doorbell rang forty-five minutes later, the tiny flutters of butterflies that had been steadily rolling through her stomach all day turned into massive birds, and for a moment, she worried they were going to send her to the bathroom to get rid of the small lunch she'd eaten. But she took in a deep, steadying breath and ordered herself to chill the fuck out as she pulled the door open.

"Hi." Vanessa stood there, looking all casual and easygoing, and it took everything Grace had not to reach out and pull her in to a hug, inhale her scent, feel her softness. "White-water rafting?"

"Hey," she said instead and stepped back. "Come on in. I'm almost ready. And no, but only because it's too cold." She breathed in as Vanessa passed her, taking in the scent of her—this time, of coconut and sunshine and warmth. It was early December and about thirty degrees out, and Vanessa smelled like the beach on a summer day in July.

"Will this work?" Vanessa asked, and when Grace closed the door and turned to look at her, she'd unzipped her jacket to reveal worn-soft jeans and a white V-neck T-shirt that looked like it would be completely see-through if it got wet. Her hair was down, wavy, begging for fingers to be run through it. Sandy brows were raised in question.

Grace tried to speak, croaked instead, then cleared her throat and tried again. "Um. Yes. Perfect." She wanted to throw in *Please zip your coat back up or we're not going anywhere* but managed to restrain herself.

"Are we going to the planetarium?"

"No, but that's a good guess. Let's add it to the list 'cause I haven't been since I was a kid." She donned her jacket, then grabbed her purse and shouldered it. "Ready?"

"Are you kidding me? I've been ready since Monday night. Are we going sledding?"

"In a T-shirt and jeans? I hope not. Brr."

"We can take my car, since I'm in the back and it's already warm, but you can drive." Vanessa tossed her the keys.

Grace got behind the wheel, made adjustments, and started the car. "How was your week?" she asked as she backed out. She knew how Vanessa's week had been, as she'd been texting with her for the past four days, but she was trying to make conversation so she could focus on the road and not on what lay underneath Vanessa's jacket. "No fights broke out in the mess hall or anything?"

Vanessa laughed. "It wasn't a bad week, given that it's December. A couple arguments between kids, but nothing out of the ordinary. Are we going up in a hot-air balloon?"

"Brr," Grace said again with a laugh as she drove.

"Swimming? Are we going swimming?"

"You know it's winter, right?"

"I wanna know," Vanessa said, bouncing in her seat like an adorable kid and patting Grace's thigh. "I can't believe I haven't guessed it yet."

That warm hand stayed on Grace's thigh, and it sent little waves of arousal through her. "Me neither, especially given your guesses have been so practical. I mean, going up to the top of the Empire State Building was *so close.*"

"Hey, it's only a six-hour drive."

A couple minutes later, they pulled into the parking lot of the Northwood Community Center, and Grace swallowed down her disappointment that the ride was over as Vanessa reclaimed her hand.

"Are we playing a pickup game of basketball?" Vanessa asked, yanking her door handle and stepping out.

"I mean, we probably could," Grace said with a half shrug. "But that wasn't my plan." She opened the back door and pulled out her tote bag but kept it fastened closed, so Vanessa couldn't see inside. "Ready?"

"God, yes."

"Let's go."

Grace loved the art room in the community center. It made her feel grounded and comfortable, the smells of clay and paint and construction paper mingling in the air and combining to smell like simple creativity. It was a huge rectangular space with easels on one side, tables in the center, six pottery wheels on the other side, a huge kiln in the corner, and shelves along one wall filled with various projects. Everything was labeled, with pieces in various stages of progress, from just started to one more coat to finished piece. She could feel Vanessa's awe as they walked through the room toward the back left where the pottery wheels were. Four people were painting. Three wheels were being used. Grace loved it here, where she could feel the weight of all her worries lift and go sit at the door until she'd finished and was ready to carry them again.

"This is amazing," Vanessa said quietly, as if concerned any volume might disturb the projects drying on the shelves. "You come here regularly?"

"Not as often as I'd like," she said, then smiled as Roland nodded at her from behind his wheel.

"Hiya, Grace. Haven't seen you in a while." He was a retired Army veteran who still wore his hair in a brush cut. His black T-shirt was stained with various colors of clay and paint, clearly not at all protected by the canvas apron tied around him, which was also spattered with color. He managed the art room three nights a week on a rotating schedule with a couple other volunteers.

"Busy time of year at work," she said, then gestured to Vanessa. "Roland, this is my friend Vanessa. We're gonna play on a wheel if that's okay."

"Nice to meet you, Vanessa." He pointed to an empty wheel with his chin. "Have at it. Clay's in the barrel."

Grace grabbed two aprons off the hooks on the wall and handed one to Vanessa. "Now, I am by no means a pro. I occasionally make a bowl that comes out nice. But I really just do this because it's relaxing and I like the way it feels in my hands. The world kind of fades away when I throw."

"Don't listen to her," Roland said over his shoulder. "She's made some nice stuff."

She felt herself blush a bit, felt Vanessa's eyes on her. "You stop it," she said teasingly to Roland. Then she turned to Vanessa—good

Lord, how was it possible the battered apron made her look even cuter? "Okay, I'll get it started, and then you'll take over. Yeah?"

Vanessa's eyes were a bit wide, and they sparkled with anticipation. Grace felt a flutter in her stomach, a tickle of arousal just looking at her. God, she was easy when it came to Vanessa. Embarrassingly so.

She grabbed a hunk of clay, set a bowl of water next to the work surface, and sat, her knees on either side of the pottery wheel. Since they weren't likely to do this on a regular basis, she wasn't worried about showing Vanessa every little nuance, just the basics.

"Okay, here's your pedal." She pointed to her foot. "That controls your speed. You don't want to go too fast. Start off slow and then sort of feel your way." The clay landed in the center of the wheel with a plop. "Wet your hands and then"—she cupped her hands around the clay as it spun—"you just shape it."

Vanessa watched with rapt attention, which made Grace happy as she let the lump of clay spin in her wet hands. Roland wasn't wrong— she had made a nice set of bowls for herself. But she had been telling the truth when she said she simply liked the relaxation, and she hoped Vanessa felt the same way. "Ready?" she asked Vanessa, who nodded with enthusiasm.

"Hell, yes."

They switched places. "Okay, get a feel for the pedal," Grace instructed. "Not too fast," she directed, when the lump started to go lopsided from speed. Once it leveled off, she said, "There you go. Now, wet your hands."

Vanessa did so and placed them on the clay. "Oh, wow. You weren't kidding. This feels so cool. The same way pizza dough does."

Grace's eyes were riveted on Vanessa's hands. The shape of them, her long fingers, tapered nails, the way they seemed to almost caress the clay. She swallowed, her brain telling her this was a great idea and also a really, really terrible one.

Vanessa played for a few minutes, getting the hang of it all, dipping her fingers in the water when instructed, then looked up at Grace. "I wanna make a bowl."

"Sure, we can do that." She instructed her how to keep it all even, to push into the center. Three times, the lump went all wonky, until they were both laughing so hard, they were crying.

"Help me," Vanessa finally pleaded.

"Okay. Scooch." And before she thought about what she was

doing, she slid a stool next to Vanessa, nudging her over a bit, and sat so their hips were side by side. It was a little awkward, but also thrilling, and she could feel the heat from Vanessa's body as well as the way her own heartbeat sped up.

Vanessa lifted her hands away from the clay as their eyes met. Held. That sizzle of electricity that Grace was beginning to understand was simply *them* shot between them. She wet her hands and put them on the clay. "Keep the wheel spinning. A little faster." When Vanessa complied, Grace said, "Now put your hands on mine. We'll make it together."

Vanessa's beautiful hands were slightly bigger than Grace's, and they covered hers completely with their warmth, their strength. Grace had to clear her throat in order to speak.

"Okay, now just feel what I'm doing."

"Oh, I feel what you're doing." Vanessa's voice was barely a whisper, likely conscious of Roland and the other people around the room, but Grace heard it, and it went straight down to the apex of her thighs and caused her muscles to tighten.

Her senses were on overload, and while she'd expected this might be a fun, maybe even a sexy experience to share, she hadn't predicted this level of sensuality. The smooth wetness of the clay, the warm strength of Vanessa's hands on top of hers, the heat of Vanessa's jean-clad thigh pressed against hers, their heads close enough to touch, their mouths breathing in the same air. She very intentionally didn't look at Vanessa. Because if she looked at Vanessa right then? It was very possible she'd simply burst into flames. Or kiss her face off. It could go either way, honestly.

Doing her best to focus on the job *at* hand and not the hands that were *on* her hands, she pressed her fingers into the center of the clay, Vanessa's fingers on top of hers. She heard Vanessa's very soft, "Oh," as the middle of the clay dipped in, and it actually started to resemble something unexpectedly and wholly sexual. It wasn't going to be a bowl. No. There was no way she could concentrate enough on evenness or form or size when she was this close to a person she'd begun to think of as walking sex, with their fingers pushing into something soft and wet and oh my God, seriously, when had she become this person? When was the last time her brain had been completely taken over by thoughts of sex? That's exactly what was happening, and she felt her body temperature crank up.

"Is it warm in here?" slipped out from between her lips before she could catch it.

"Like the inside of an oven," came Vanessa's instant reply.

And then they did look at each other. Gazes met, and Grace felt her lips part in surprise at the raw desire she saw in Vanessa's eyes.

"Come home with me," Vanessa whispered, so quietly that Grace was sure she was the only one who heard it.

"Okay," she whispered back with absolutely zero hesitation.

"Right now."

"Okay." She knew she'd hoped, deep down, that the night would end with them together, but having Vanessa suggest it made it that much sexier. "But we have to at least pretend to make a bowl."

Vanessa snorted a laugh. "Do we, though?"

Grace looked at their hands, looked at Vanessa, looked back at their hands. "You're right. Fuck it." And she closed her hands on the clay, completely destroying any semblance of a bowl they'd created.

If Roland was surprised by the short time they'd stayed, he didn't let on, just waved and nodded as they put things away, cleaned up in record time, and headed for the door, moving as fast as they could without actually sprinting from the community center.

The drive was too fast and not fast enough, and how that was possible, Grace had no clue. All she knew was that Vanessa was breaking some speed limits, and it was still taking too long to get to her house. She had her hand on Vanessa's thigh, and she squeezed it every so often.

"You know that's not helping me focus on driving, right?" Vanessa asked after one particularly firm squeeze and a slide higher up her leg.

"No?" Grace asked. "I thought maybe it would act as incentive." She squeezed again. Inched up some more.

"God, you're killing me."

"Not yet."

Vanessa's response was to groan and push the car's speed a bit higher. Four minutes later, she jerked the steering wheel to the left and pulled into the driveway of her little house. "Thank fucking God," she muttered before fisting the front of Grace's coat and hauling her closer so she could crush her mouth to Grace's. The move was shocking. And rough. And so goddamn sexy, Grace whimpered into the kiss.

"Inside." Vanessa let go of her coat, and they exited the car and headed to the side door. Delilah met them at the top of the handful of steps, all wagging tail and quiet happy woofs. Grace petted the dog and let her lick her face, before Vanessa held up one finger. "Just need to let her out. Don't go anywhere."

"No, ma'am." Grace took off her coat and draped it over a chair. She was in Vanessa's kitchen. Sky blue and pale yellow and bright and inviting, that's what it was. And she wanted to walk around, explore the house, pick up the photo frames and knickknacks, and learn what was important to Vanessa. Who was important. You could really get to know a person just by walking through their living space, and if the logical parts of her brain hadn't been completely short-circuited by the sex parts, she'd already be wandering. Instead, she stood riveted to the same spot Vanessa had left her in, her underwear wet, her lips still warm from the kiss in the car, and her entire body thrumming with anticipation. It was all she could do to keep from bouncing up and down on the balls of her feet.

How much time passed? Three minutes? An hour? Ten days? She had no idea, but Vanessa was back, Delilah strolling in after her, and she didn't stop. Didn't hesitate or seem unsure. She simply walked the ten or fifteen feet from the back door directly into Grace's personal space, looked deep into her eyes for a beat, and then treated her to another blistering kiss that Grace was pretty sure set her hair on fire.

It was the fourth time she'd kissed Vanessa. First, in the ladies' room of the bar. Second, on the walk at the park. Third, on her couch. And all three times, Grace had been in awe of how well-suited they seemed for the act of kissing. But now? Now, she was pretty sure they'd been made for this. That their mouths had been created specifically for melding and sliding along each other.

"God, I love kissing you," Vanessa whispered, as if privy to Grace's thoughts.

"I was just thinking that. That we kiss well together. It's a thing."

"It so is." Vanessa kissed her again, then grinned against her lips and added, "They should put that on dating apps."

"Oh my God, they should. *And how would you rate your kissing abilities on a scale of one to ten?*"

"You are a ten," Vanessa said.

"You're a fifty-seven," Grace countered, then pulled Vanessa's mouth back to hers so they could devour each other some more.

Another hour—or five minutes—went by before Vanessa wrenched her mouth free and whispered, "Come upstairs with me?"

"God, yes."

They kissed and walked and kissed and walked to the stairs and up them, and if asked later, Grace wouldn't be able to recall any of that trip. She was in a haze of desire and arousal and raw, primal want, and the surroundings, anything nearby, none of it mattered. All she was aware of were Vanessa's hands, Vanessa's mouth, Vanessa's tongue, and all the erotic things they were doing to her.

The room was dark, and Grace was again too preoccupied to look around, examine, learn. She did notice that it smelled lovely. Like coconut and almond and that sunny scent that was uniquely Vanessa. And then Vanessa was backing her to the bed, and her legs hit, and she sat and fell back and then Vanessa was above her, braced on her hands and kissing her more, and sweet Jesus, she thought she might die right there from too much pleasure.

Vanessa pulled away just far enough for Grace to look in her eyes, and there was something there. She could see it. Felt it way down deep inside of her, and it was more than sex. It was...Grace searched for the word, racked her brain, but the sex fog made it difficult. And then Vanessa's hands were on her shirt, tugging at it, pulling it up to expose the skin of her torso to Vanessa's exploring hands.

"You're so soft," Vanessa said, and there was a tone of wonder in her voice as she ran her flat hand up Grace's stomach to the underwire of her bra and, without a second's hesitation, pushed the fabric and wire up and over, baring her breasts, pulling a gasp from Grace's lungs. That gasp morphed into a groan when Vanessa closed her mouth over a nipple and sucked.

Oh my God. She didn't say it out loud because how cliché a thing to say was it during sex? Everybody said *oh my God.* And not five seconds later, when Vanessa switched to the other breast, the words leaked out of her, part speech, part moan, because what the hell was Vanessa doing with her tongue that was sending shockwaves from Grace's nipples straight down between her legs? It felt like zaps of electricity shooting from her breasts to her center, and her hips began to rock without her permission, lifting, searching for something solid to move against.

Vanessa freed the nipple in her mouth, but switched quickly to fingers as she gazed up at Grace, who looked back at her, and the heat between them was almost visible, like the way the sun and heat in the desert make vision wobbly and wavy.

"You're killing me," Grace said softly, using Vanessa's earlier words.

"Not yet," Vanessa replied with a wicked glint in her eye. Then she pulled Grace to a sitting position by her shirt and bra, which she quickly removed, and almost before Grace had even realized she was now topless, Vanessa was tugging at her jeans, and soon she was bottomless as well. Sitting on Vanessa's bed, propped up by her hands on the mattress behind her, she forced herself not to squirm as Vanessa looked at her and roamed over her very naked body with her eyes, stopping at intimate places, catching Grace's eye when she did, then returning to those places. Grace could feel her own wetness by simply sitting there. Never before had anyone in her life turned her on so intensely. Really, if she didn't have Vanessa's hand on her again soon…

She crooked a finger at Vanessa, summoning her closer, and Vanessa obeyed. Hands on Vanessa's sides, Grace pushed the T-shirt up, and Vanessa lifted her arms, and the shirt hit the floor. The simple white bra went next, and Grace took a moment to just look at her. To take her turn at letting her eyes roam, taking in the olive skin, the gorgeously round breasts with the brown nipples. After a moment, she moved to Vanessa's jeans. Unfastened them. Hooked her thumbs in the waistband and pushed them down, and Vanessa stepped out of them.

Grace stood and they were both naked, both the purest, most natural forms of themselves.

"You're so beautiful," Grace said on a quiet breath, and nothing had ever been truer. "God, look at you." She reached out a hand to touch a collarbone, run her fingertips along it to Vanessa's shoulder. "You have the most gorgeous skin." With a grin, she said, "You're tan in December."

Vanessa gave a small laugh through her nose. "Don't let the blond hair fool you. Lot of Italian blood in this body."

"I want this body," Grace whispered, and then felt her own eyes go wide. She swallowed and said honestly, "Apparently, my mouth is just saying everything out loud now without consulting my brain first."

Vanessa tipped her head to one side and reached for Grace. "I don't mind. It's nice to know I'm wanted."

"You are. Badly."

"Right back atcha."

And they were kissing again.

This time, though, it was different. Not teasing. Not kissing with the knowledge that they'd have to stop soon. No, this was deep, hot, wet, thorough making out because Grace was way beyond ready to have her way with this woman, and she turned and pushed, and they sort of sat-slash-fell onto the bed.

Individual steps and moments all blurred at that point, as if she was experiencing the night in flashes, sensual clips of a fever dream, gauzy and tinted blue, because being with Vanessa was almost too perfect to be anything *but* a dream.

They waged a battle that was sort of humorous to Grace, both clearly wanting to be running the show, and at the same time, wanting to be run. Grace found herself vacillating between the two, wanting nothing more than to touch Vanessa's body, skim her hands over that olive skin, dip into folds and explore hot wetness, and at the same time, wanting Vanessa above her, Vanessa's weight pressing her into the mattress, Vanessa's eyes and hands and mouth owning her body completely.

There was no shortage of dialogue, no lack of direction, and Grace was shocked by how sexually compatible they were.

"Harder."

"Do you like this?"

"Tell me."

Vanessa seemed to thrive on their whispered words, to listen raptly and put any and all guidance to excellent use, and when she finally trailed her mouth down Grace's stomach and dipped her tongue between her legs, Grace knew she had mere moments before she exploded.

Fingers of both her hands dug into Vanessa's hair as Grace lifted her bent legs, rolled them back in an attempt to give Vanessa as much access as possible, and then it hit. Like a freight train shooting through her body, her orgasm ripped a cry from her throat, and she tightened her fingers into fists as it felt like every muscle in her body contracted. Colors exploded behind her eyelids as she made sounds she'd never heard herself make before.

With no idea how long it had taken for her to come back to herself, Grace opened her eyes to find soft blue ones looking down at her.

"Wow," Vanessa said. "That was something to behold."

"Yeah? Well, that was something to *feel*, too." She swallowed, then inhaled deeply. "You're amazing. That was pure artistry."

Vanessa placed a fingertip on Grace's lips. She dutifully kissed it, and Vanessa ran it down between her breasts, then circled each one slowly. "An artist is only as good as her subject." She glanced up. "Or would you be the canvas? I'm trying to go with this metaphor but might be messing it up."

Grace laughed, then reached her hand up and touched Vanessa's gorgeous face. "I can't believe we're here. Together. Doing this."

"I can't either. I thought about this weeks ago, at the first meeting about Oliver."

Grace's eyes flew open wide. "What? You did not. You hated me that day." She gave Vanessa a playful push. Because seriously? She had felt the disdain.

"*No,*" Vanessa said. "I didn't hate you. I didn't like you, true"—that got her another shove—"but I thought you were hot."

"You *did*?"

"God, yes. I think it fueled my dislike."

Grace tipped her head from one side to the other. "I get that. I had the same thing happen with one of my sorority sisters in college."

"Yeah?" Vanessa settled on her back and pulled Grace up against her side. "Tell me."

"Her name was Addy, and she was this tall, beautiful redhead. Played tennis. Marketing major. Super popular. And I just hated her guts. I hated her perfection, how everything just fell into her lap." She wrinkled her nose as she recalled her own behavior. "I was kinda bitchy to her, and it wasn't until I accidentally walked in on her in the bathroom that I realized my issue with her."

"You were attracted to her."

"Exactly. For a long time, I thought I was jealous because I wanted to *be* her. Turns out, I just wanted her."

"Did you ever get her?"

"Sadly, no." Grace chuckled.

"Was she the first girl you had feelings for?"

"Oh God, no. I had a girlfriend in high school for almost a year. She was the first person I had sex with."

"Lucky her."

Grace felt herself blush at the compliment. "I met Michael not long after Addy and fell madly in love."

"And what happened there?"

Grace nibbled on the inside of her cheek as she traced a thumb across Vanessa's nipple, watched it harden as Vanessa's breath hitched beneath her. "Tell you what…I will give you the whole story about my failed marriage, but later. After I finish with this body. Because you kind of took over, and I didn't get to do all the exploring I wanted to."

Vanessa's swallow betrayed any attempt to look calm and cool, and Grace felt a swell of power knowing she had that effect. Without waiting for a response, she pushed herself up and rolled so she was on top of Vanessa, looking down into those eyes that had gone impossibly dark with arousal.

"My turn," she whispered.

CHAPTER FIFTEEN

Vanessa didn't have to wake up Saturday morning to let Delilah out because she was already awake. Truth was, she'd barely slept. Mostly because of all the incredible sex she'd had with the amazingly beautiful woman now sound asleep in her bed, but also because her brain wouldn't shut down. She was exhausted even now, as she crawled back under the covers in her fleece robe to sit with a mug of coffee, her body sore in places she hadn't been aware of in years, her muscles aching, her lips swollen and a little chapped, but her brain had started spinning the second she'd realized Grace had fallen asleep.

She vaguely recalled a line from a movie she'd just seen that went something like, "This just went way past complicated," and if that wasn't the damn truth, she didn't know what was.

She'd slept with the parent of one of her students.

Not cool or classy or celebrated.

And yet, the moment she'd gotten out of bed to let the dog out and feed her breakfast, she wanted nothing more than to get back in, to wake Grace up, to lose herself in Grace's body. The smells, the sounds, the softness. She remembered the whispered words between them, the coaxing, the pleading, and her body needed nothing more than those flashbacks to ratchet the level of desire up once again. How the hell was that possible? Was she a sex maniac now? Did everything take a back seat to desire?

It sure seems like it, her brain shouted as Grace rolled onto her back and stretched her arms sleepily above her head, which pulled the blanket down enough to bare her breasts.

God, those breasts.

If there was a more perfect set on the face of the earth, Vanessa hadn't seen them. And they were so sensitive, she'd learned. Whether she'd used her fingers or her mouth, or hell, her teeth, she'd pulled sounds from Grace that did nothing but crank everything higher. And suddenly, she couldn't resist. She set the mug of coffee on the nightstand, slid her body down a bit, and closed her mouth over a nipple. A soft gasp came from Grace, and Vanessa felt her fingers slide into her hair as she switched breasts, sucked, flicked, and that's all it took for Grace's hips to start rocking.

No words were spoken as Vanessa slid lower, positioned Grace's legs over her shoulders, and buried herself in the very essence of her. She was already wet, the tangy sweetness of her a wonderful start to the day, and once Vanessa slid her fingers into Grace's body, it didn't take long at all before she felt Grace's hips tense and rise up, her fingers tighten in Vanessa's hair, heard her whispered name floating on the air above them, and Vanessa held on, rode out Grace's orgasm with her.

"It's been longer than I can remember since I've had morning sex," Grace said a few moments later as she helped herself to a sip from Vanessa's mug of coffee.

"Really? Morning sex is the best. You're already warm and relaxed..." She leaned over and kissed Grace's temple. "And you are seriously the most responsive woman I've ever been with."

Grace's raised eyebrows and suddenly pink cheeks told Vanessa it was a good thing to say, and Grace snuggled closer. They were quiet for a stretch, just enjoying each other's company and watching Delilah as she chewed on a toy in her bed in the corner. "This is nice," Grace finally said, and Vanessa nodded. "Also...we've just super over-complicated things, haven't we?"

Vanessa chuckled at the similarity to the words she'd been thinking earlier. "We sure have."

"What do we do now?"

"Not a clue."

"Perfect. Glad we got that all sorted out. Good talk." Grace gave a nod and a sly grin, and the silence fell again. This time, though, it wasn't quite the companionable silence that seemed to work for them. Vanessa's brain was still whirring, and she got the impression from the way Grace's dark brows dipped slightly toward the bridge of her nose that hers might be as well.

"Big plans for your Saturday?" Vanessa asked, then almost winced at the sheer corniness of the line.

But Grace looked relieved to have something else to focus on. "I have to work for a few hours today. Gonna go in at noon. It's our busy season."

"Really? I mean, I get that Christmas is coming, but the whole month is busy?"

Grace sat up so she could meet Vanessa's gaze and there was a brightness, a spark in her eyes as she spoke. "Oh, yeah, definitely. Between mid-November and just after New Year's. Crazed. Think about it. You get deliveries from out-of-state friends for Christmas, but they don't just come the week of Christmas, right? You might get something early in the month or mid-month. Any time during December."

Vanessa nodded. "I never thought of that." She reached out and stroked some dark hair behind Grace's ear. "You're passionate when you talk about your job."

Grace lifted one shoulder. "I really do love it. Flowers and the flower business and business in general."

"Yeah?"

"It was my major in college. I think I told you that I always wanted to run a small business. Working for somebody like Ava wasn't really what I had in mind..." She laughed.

"She's a hard-ass, right?" Vanessa laughed too. "She's worked at that place since I was a kid. I think her dad started it, didn't he?"

A nod. "She's a hard-ass and we have our issues, but I can honestly say that she loves that shop. And so do I." Grace took another sip of Vanessa's coffee. "I have lots of ideas, but I have to be strategic about suggesting them because Ava is set in her ways and I wouldn't call her 'receptive to change.'" She made air quotes as she chuckled, but Vanessa could see that it frustrated her a bit.

"What time do you have to leave?" she asked. "Can I make you breakfast?"

"You want to make me breakfast?"

It was Vanessa's turn to give a half-shrug. "Yeah, 'cause you get your own coffee then and I can have mine back."

Grace pushed at her playfully, then grew more serious. "Are you busy tonight?"

"I do not currently have plans, no." Vanessa ran her fingertips up and down Grace's bare arm. "Why?"

"Because I would like to be your plans."

"Oh, really?"

"Yes, please."

"I think that can be arranged." Vanessa leaned in and kissed her softly.

"How about," Grace said, her lips just millimeters from Vanessa's, "I bring dinner and we eat here? That way, you don't have to worry about leaving Delilah."

Her heart warmed at Grace's cognizance of her dog and she nodded, rubbing her lips softly along Grace's. "I like that idea."

"Good."

And then they were kissing. Softly at first, but the urgency grew and before she realized it, Vanessa found herself on her back, Grace tugging at the tie on her robe until it fell open, baring her heated and flushed skin to Grace's eyes, her hands, her mouth…a mouth that was suddenly everywhere and all Vanessa could do was feel, rock, moan. When Grace's mouth closed on her throbbing and very, very wet center, Vanessa was pretty sure she'd lost all ability to think. Grace's fingers pressed into her and her mouth coaxed her and then she was at the precipice, teetering, and Grace gently nudged her over the edge and she was falling, floating, gloriously sated and happy…

How much time had passed?

She opened her eyes to find Grace smiling down at her, twirling a hunk of her hair around a finger. "Well, hello there," she said, her smile knowing.

"You look particularly satisfied with yourself," Vanessa teased.

"And you look particularly satisfied," Grace countered, then gave the hair a gentle tug.

A tingle ran through Vanessa's entire body, like the way a full-body shiver hits when you're anticipating something exciting. "I am," she said, and she hadn't meant to whisper it. Or to sound so damn serious when she said it. But she did both, and she wouldn't have seen the quick widening of Grace's eyes unless she'd been looking for it. "I really, really am."

Grace's eyes held hers, their gazes locked, and it felt…serious. Meaningful. Unexpected. "Well. Good. That's good. I'm glad." She wasn't stuttering, but she was definitely fumbling for the right thing to say, which Vanessa found kind of adorable.

"Were you worried?" Vanessa asked, suddenly wondering.

Cheeks flushed a deep pink. Eyes cast downward. More toying with hair. A clearing of the throat. "A little?"

Vanessa felt her own eyes go wide as she pushed herself up on an elbow. "Really? Why?"

"I mean, it's been a while since I've been with a woman." She saw Grace swallow, could almost feel her nerves.

"Grace." Vanessa put a hand on Grace's warm hip, squeezed. "You have nothing to worry about. And I mean nothing." She said the last line with a lilt in her voice and then flopped dramatically back to the bed with a huge sigh. "Seriously, did you hear me?"

Grace barked a laugh. "Oh, yes, and I think your neighbors might have too. You were very…vocal."

Vanessa's turn to flush. Heat flooded her cheeks, her neck, and hell, why not encompass her ears, too? "You should know that…" She cleared her throat. "That's unusual for me."

"It is?"

Vanessa nodded, feeling suddenly vulnerable. "Yeah. So…nothing to worry about."

"Well." Grace smiled and it grew.

"Okay, now you *really* look like you're satisfied with yourself."

Grace reached for her and wrapped her in a hug that they laughed through and Vanessa felt that acutely. The laughing. The joy. The happiness just to be with this person. It was new.

And it was scary as hell.

❖

"You're very smiley today, Gracie." Jack opened a box of doughnuts and offered her one. "It's nice to see."

"Maybe I'm smiling because there are doughnuts for my Saturday afternoon." She took a cruller, felt her mouth fill in anticipation. "Ever think of that?" She shot him a grin, took a bite, and set the doughnut down next to the Christmas arrangement she was putting the finishing touches on, adding some greenery to balance the colors.

"I actually did think of that, but you were smiling before I offered the doughnuts, so I don't think that's it." He winked at her, and it warmed her heart. Reminded her of her grandpa, the only person she knew who actually winked. Well, him and now Jack. He didn't press her, though, just gathered the deliveries and loaded his minivan up. She handed him the Christmas arrangement, all tucked into its cardboard brace so it wouldn't tip over and spill everywhere during its ride and sent him on his way.

"Thanks for the doughnut," she called as her phone rang from her back pocket. She pulled it out, hoping it was Vanessa or Oliver, then frowning at the name on her screen. She sighed, steeled herself, hit answer. "Hey, Mom, I'm working, what's up?" She didn't know why she bothered, knowing that her working wasn't going to make her mother pull up short or be extra quick. She'd tried to get her to text instead of calling, but her mother never seemed to hear that suggestion. Or more likely, she heard it, didn't care, and ignored it.

"What is going on with you?" her mother asked. Her tone was testy, which wasn't unusual, but the question was direct and vague at the same time, which was.

"What do you mean?" Grace shook her head at herself for even engaging in conversation. Ava wouldn't be happy.

"I mean that Oliver made a comment to me and I asked Michael about it and he told me you're seeing your son's teacher? And that you were…in a compromising position with her in front of Oliver? Really, Grace?"

Oh my God.

It wasn't just the judgmental tone. She was used to that from her mother. It was almost the only tone she ever got. Well, that and disapproving. But the facts she'd just spewed… "Wait, when did you talk to Oliver?"

"This morning when Michael brought him over."

"He's with you? Why? He's supposed to be with his father this weekend." Her blood was on a low simmer now.

"He had to run some errands and asked if Oliver could hang with Grandma for a few hours. Right, honey?"

She heard Oliver's "yes!" in the background and the simmer increased.

"So? Is this true?"

"Mom, you're asking me this with Oliver sitting right there, listening to everything you say?" Jesus Christ, what was wrong with her?

"Well, he obviously *knows*, Grace."

Ava peeked her head around the doorjamb and her eyebrows made a V on her face because she was clearly unhappy with the sight of Grace on her phone. Grace held up a finger at her. There was no way she was just hanging up now.

"Mom. First of all, Michael is supposed to have Oliver for the weekend. That's less than three days and he can't manage to do that without asking you to babysit? And two, what I do and who I see on my own time is nobody business. Not Michael's, not Oliver's, and *not yours.* I am working right now, and my boss is not happy with me for being on the phone, so I have to go. I love you. I'll call you later." And she hung up. She *hung up.* On her mother! She'd never done that before. She stared at the phone in her hand, then lifted her gaze to Ava and said in disbelief, "I just hung up on my mother."

"Sometimes, that's all you can do," Ava said with a shrug, then returned to the front of the shop without another word, Grace blinking after her.

Had everybody been body-snatched today? Changed out for completely different versions of themselves? What the hell?

For the rest of the afternoon, she did her best to focus on work. Ava would be in tomorrow, but told Grace not to worry about it. Honestly, Grace could use the money, but the idea of a Sunday off was lovely; she'd expected to work the whole weekend. Maybe she and Vanessa could do something before Oliver came home.

Of course, it seemed Michael was dropping him off all over the place. She wouldn't be the least bit surprised if he came home early… one of the reasons she'd suggested they do dinner at Vanessa's house. Not that she was proud to admit that. And it wasn't because she didn't want her son. Of course she did. But she wanted Michael to want him too.

Which was out of her control. She knew that. And it was hella disappointing, and she had no idea what to do about it.

"Grace."

She blinked, met Ava's gaze from across the room, her tone—and not-so-subtle eye roll—making it clear that wasn't the first time her name had been called.

"Yeah. Yeah, I'm right here. Tell me what you need."

The three Martini cousins often met up in the back of the bar on Saturday afternoons. Julia was always there, doing the books or coming up with new cocktails for the coming weeks. If Savannah hadn't grabbed a shift as a home health aid, she was often set up on the couch studying for her nursing degree. Amelia would pop by at some point and so would Vanessa. It was never an official gathering, but more often than not, they all ended up stopping in at one point or another.

That day, Vanessa entered through the back door from the parking lot. All three of the others were there, Julia behind the practice bar shaking a martini shaker, Savannah, as predicted, on the couch with textbooks and a laptop open on the coffee table, Amelia in Julia's desk chair, slowly spinning it with the toes of her shoes. Vanessa floated in, arms out from her sides like wings. She did a makeshift pirouette in the center of the room, let out a ridiculously dreamy sigh, and dropped onto the couch next to Savannah.

"I'm gonna go out on a limb here," Amelia said, "and say somebody got laid."

Vanessa sat up. "You know what? I'm not even bothered by your frat boy vocabulary."

"Yup," Amelia said with a nod. "Laid."

Savannah simply looked at her, brows raised in question.

"She is vulgar," Vanessa said. "But she is not wrong."

Savannah clapped her hands together and smiled. "Oh, yay! I'm so glad." She dropped her voice as if the others in the room couldn't hear her and wouldn't want to know the same thing. "How was it?"

Vanessa flopped dramatically back into the couch cushions.

"I'm gonna take that as an 'it was amazing, you guys,'" Julia said, pouring the contents of her shaker into a glass, then squinting at it.

"Beyond," Vanessa said. "It was beyond amazing. I'm sore in places I forgot I had."

Savannah lifted her shoulders up to her ears and gave a full-body shake. "Oh, man, I love when that happens."

"Do I make you sore in places you forgot you had, baby?" Julia asked.

"You make me sore in places I haven't even discovered yet," Savannah replied, to which Amelia made gagging sounds from her still spinning chair.

"Hey, a little sympathy for those of us who are currently *not* having sex."

"You will, Meels. Hang in there." Savannah turned back to Vanessa. "The ex didn't walk in again, did he?"

"No, thank God, but we were at my place. And..." She waited until she had all their attention. "We will be at my place again tonight. She's making me dinner and thought my house was the better idea so I wouldn't have to worry about Delilah."

"Or so the ex can't walk in on you again," Amelia pointed out.

Vanessa *had* thought about that. It wasn't like it wasn't fact. But she was so happy after their night together that she didn't want anything else coloring it. "He can't. Nope."

"And you feel better now about sleeping with the parent of your student?" Julia asked.

"I feel fine about it if I don't think about it." Vanessa clenched her teeth and grimaced. "I know, I know, it's not the best way of handling it." She said it before any of the others could.

"You think?" Amelia asked. She'd stopped spinning and now sat facing the couch. When Vanessa glanced away, Amelia added, "You know I will always take Delilah if you need me to. I love that girl. She's no trouble."

As soon as she said it, Vanessa realized that maybe the reason she had agreed so easily to Grace coming to her place was *exactly* so what happened last time couldn't happen again. She swallowed the sudden lump of dread in her throat.

There was a beat of silence in the room, then another. Finally, Savannah said softly, "Just make sure you're okay with things, yeah?"

Vanessa nodded.

"It's important." Savannah rubbed her upper arm. "*You're* important, and I think you really like this woman, so just make sure you're clear on the situation and how you really feel. Both of you."

Vanessa felt her shoulders drop as if she'd set down a heavy load, and she sighed loudly. "I know. I just…this is new. I've had some crushes on parents before. Found a few moms attractive. But this? The *actual* liking? The *actual* dating? The *actual sex*?" She shook her head. "It should feel wrong. Shouldn't it? If it's wrong, it should feel wrong. And it doesn't. It just…doesn't. It feels…amazingly *right*."

"Then carry on," Julia said cheerfully. "And taste this." She brought the cocktail she'd been working on over and handed it to Vanessa, who sipped, then winced.

"Yikes. What is that?" She handed it on to Savannah, who also sipped.

"Gah, ew, no," she said, shaking her head.

Julia sighed, took the glass, held it up in Amelia's direction.

"Those two faces tell me I don't need to taste it myself to know it's awful. Hard pass."

"Babe," Savannah said, "the creamy and the fruity just don't mix. Try chocolate or something decadent instead."

"That." Julia pointed at her. "That's why I keep you around."

"Well, that and my exceptional lovemaking skills," Savannah corrected, not looking up from her laptop.

"That, too," Julia agreed, back behind the practice bar.

"I'm gonna vomit," Amelia said.

The conversation drifted on to other things. Savannah's classes. Amelia's surprising enjoyment at creating a business plan. Julia's Christmas party reservations at the bar. Vanessa listened, smiled, laughed, and felt warm. Was she overthinking the situation with Grace? Was she under thinking it? Did it matter? If it was on her mind, it must, but was she worrying needlessly?

"That's next week, right, Ness?"

Vanessa blinked, pulled back to the present by her name, but unaware of who said it or why. "I'm sorry?"

It was Amelia and she arched an eyebrow and gave her a look before repeating her question. "Don't you have parent-teacher conferences next week?"

Vanessa shook her head. "Two weeks from Monday, actually. I have no idea why it's so late this year. I hope more people show up this time, but it's getting so close to Christmas that I'm sure people have other things to take care of."

"They still have those?" Savannah asked.

With a nod, Vanessa explained, "It's a lot easier for busy parents to email me or chat with me via FaceTime or Skype or Zoom or any other video chat platform if their kid is having a problem. But we still hold physical open houses and in-person meetings twice a year onsite. The December event gets way fewer parents than the spring one, and like I said, with the holidays and the weather... It's just one night, but I'm not expecting much. I always make sure I've got a book or a lesson plan or something to keep me busy."

"I guess Grace doesn't need to show up," Amelia said with a wink.

She laughed and pointed and agreed and didn't mention how they hadn't touched on that. How they hadn't really discussed Oliver. Or their unique situation. Or how they each felt about it. How he might feel about it. No, they'd been too busy having mind-blowing sex. She swallowed down her own shame about that. She was a teacher, for God's sake. Her students were of utmost importance, damn it. What was wrong with her?

Tonight.

Tonight, they'd talk.

CHAPTER SIXTEEN

G race loved to cook. She never minded working all day, then coming home and having to make dinner. It was her wind down from the day, her decompression time. The acts of chopping, sautéing, stirring all helped her relax, refocus her energy, and transition from workday to home life. It was one of the things Michael had been great about—he'd always checked in and offered to cook if she'd had a particularly stressful day. And she'd always thanked him and waved him off. Cooking was relaxing for her.

Vanessa's kitchen was set up nicely. Intuitively. Things were where they should be or where she'd expect to find them. "Do you cook often?" she asked now as she sautéed garlic and cherry tomatoes in a skillet, moving them around with what looked to be a well-loved wooden spoon.

Vanessa sat on her kitchen counter near the stove, glass of wine in hand, watching Grace as she worked. Grace could almost feel her eyes, and it was deliciously distracting.

"I do," Vanessa said. "My mom is a great cook, and she taught me a lot. Once my dad left, I helped her cook for my sisters."

Grace had a flash then of a teenage Oliver cooking his own meals because his mom was working and his dad was not there.

"That smells like heaven," Vanessa said, leaning closer and making a show of inhaling.

"The scent of your people," Grace said with a grin. "Is your mom Italian, too? Or just your dad? I mean, the name Martini is obviously Italian, and you have that gorgeously tan-all-year olive complexion. But the blond hair and blue eyes are throwing me off."

"You don't think there are blond Italians?" Vanessa was obviously teasing as she watched Grace over the rim of her wineglass.

Grace waved the wooden spoon in front of Vanessa. "There clearly are."

"My mom is half Italian. Her mother is. Her dad is English with light hair and eyes."

"And his recessive genes made it all the way to you. Impressive." Grace studied her. "It's a beautiful blend. You're beautiful."

Vanessa blushed fiercely, and Grace gave herself a point.

"Thank you." Vanessa leaned forward, and Grace met her lips with hers, reveling in the joys of a simple kiss from this woman.

"You're welcome," she whispered, then shook herself. "Stop distracting me, or I'm going to mess up dinner."

"So sorry. No more kisses for you."

"I didn't say that." The spoon hit the counter. Grace inserted herself between Vanessa's knees, grabbed the back of her head, and kissed the bejesus out of her. Warm lips, hot tongues, a few moans, and she pulled away, picked up the wooden spoon, and went back to cooking. Very much enjoying the look of aroused surprise on Vanessa's face, she added broth to the pan and then the chicken breasts, humming a little tune as she did so. Feeling proud of herself, she glanced up at Vanessa's face, and her breath caught in her throat at the expression there.

Vanessa's lips were still parted, glossy and full. But it was her eyes. They were hooded. Dark.

Wanting.

They held Grace as if there were actual hands on her, an actual grip, and she couldn't move as Vanessa slid off the counter and took two steps into Grace's space. A flick of the wrist and the burner turned off. Vanessa's gaze never left hers as she took the spoon from Grace's hand, set it in the pan, and walked Grace back until she hit the fridge, and then Vanessa's mouth was on hers in a hot, demanding kiss that stole all her breath and all her resolve and any kind of clear thinking.

She forgot about the chicken. She forgot about all the reasons their pairing was a bad idea. She forgot that Vanessa was her son's teacher. Everything she had, every fiber of her being, every cognizant cell in her body was hyperfocused on Vanessa. On her mouth. On her tongue. On her hands. On her smell. On the softness of her hair that Grace now had her fingers tangled in. On the way Vanessa's frame was a little broader and a little taller, and how being trapped between her and the solid fridge made her feel safe. On how Vanessa's kiss tasted like wine and promise and sex. God, she tasted like the promise of sex. How was that even possible?

There was no time to analyze that question because Vanessa's hand was under her shirt. She could feel it on her skin, her very hot skin, sliding up until it closed over her entire breast, bra and all, kneaded it. And then her bra was pushed up and suddenly both hands were on both breasts, and she had to wrench her mouth away from Vanessa's, lift her chin just to suck in some air. Vanessa took that as an invitation to launch an assault on her neck, and oh my God, how did she know that was a seriously sensitive spot? A whimper sounded, and it took a second or two for Grace to realize she'd made it. Fingers were working her nipples, and she was certain her underwear was soaked at that point, but focusing on any one thing was hard because it was all so amazing, and when was the last time she'd felt like this? When was the last time somebody had wanted her so badly, they'd stopped her from cooking just to have her right here in the kitchen?

And have her Vanessa would. Still kissing her neck, licking her throat, Vanessa tugged at the front of Grace's jeans until they were open and her hand was in them, and Grace groaned at the same time Vanessa did, when fingers hit wet.

"Oh my God, Vanessa," Grace whispered.

"You're soaked," Vanessa informed her, as if she didn't know that already, and holy hell what was she doing with her fingers?

Grace swallowed hard as her breathing became ragged and her hips started moving all on their own, picking up the rhythm that Vanessa set, and she wrapped both arms around Vanessa's neck because she could feel her orgasm barreling toward them like a runaway eighteen-wheeler, and she needed to hold on to something and—

The cry that was torn from her throat was primal. Raw. She didn't recognize it *at all* as a sound she'd ever made before. Because she hadn't. Ever. She'd only had sex with four people in her lifetime. Brian, her first boyfriend. Regina, the one and only woman she'd ever had sex with, but the one who'd helped her understand her own bisexuality. Michael. And Vanessa. Not that it was a contest, but if it was, Vanessa left the other three so far behind her, they were still in yesterday.

As her heart finally began to slow so that it wasn't in any danger of beating clear out of her chest, and she could breathe without gasping for air, she cracked one eye open. Vanessa was grinning. Widely. Still nearly holding her up because Grace's legs had gone weak when her orgasm had hit.

"You okay?" Vanessa asked, a teasing lilt in her voice.

"Did you just make me come against your refrigerator? In your kitchen? While I was in the middle of making dinner?"

"Why, yes. Yes, as a matter of fact, I believe I did." She pressed a gentle kiss to Grace's lips but pulled back before it could start anything up again. "You were gorgeous," she whispered, and Grace felt herself go into a full-body blush.

Arms still around Vanessa's neck, she wiggled her fingers into that thick blond hair and just looked into her blue eyes, inexplicably pleased that Vanessa didn't look away, holding her gaze instead. "What am I going to do with you?" she whispered back.

Vanessa let her forehead rest against Grace's as she spoke softly. "I have some ideas, but you should probably feed me first."

"Oh, I have some ideas, too, and feeding you is a good call 'cause you're gonna need your strength."

Vanessa's swallow was audible, and they both laughed and slowly let go of each other. Grace fixed her bra, then refastened her jeans, giving Vanessa a look the whole time. Vanessa's smile never left as she washed her hands, refilled her wineglass, and took her spot on the counter again.

"Sustenance," Grace said, clicking on the burner again. She pointed the wooden spoon in Vanessa's direction. "Then I have plans for you, young lady."

❖

Vanessa's phone told her it was after two in the morning. She couldn't remember the last time she'd spent the night with somebody who wasn't Grace. The whole night. She'd seen a few women over the past couple of years, but she hadn't had an actual relationship that involved staying over for the entire night since Callie, right out of college. They'd basically outgrown each other, but the relationship had left a more indelible mark on Vanessa than she'd realized, and she hadn't had anything very long-term since.

She reached behind her and set the phone back down, feeling the warmth of Grace's naked body, her back to Vanessa's front, as she snuggled back up to her. Funny how it didn't feel weird at all, sharing a bed with somebody after so long. Delilah snored softly from her dog bed in the corner, and while Vanessa had hoped to adopt a dog that would cuddle up with her, she had to admit that Grace was fitting that bill in a much more pleasing way.

They hadn't talked. Which was probably why Vanessa wasn't sound asleep like Grace currently was. They'd talked about other stuff, sure. Movies and books and dinner and then they'd been unable to keep that magnetic pull at bay and had ended up leaving all the dirty dishes in the sink because they couldn't wait any longer to undress each other.

How many orgasms had she had? Three? Four? She'd lost count, and that had never happened before. It was like Grace had a manual. A sex manual. *How to Give Vanessa Multiple Orgasms in One Night.* And she'd studied. And had gotten an A-plus on the pop quiz. They might have had things to discuss—important things—but holy hell, the sex was off-the-charts hot, and it scorched everything in its path. Important conversations included.

Amelia and Julia were not going to be happy with her, and the thought of Amelia giving her that disapproving look almost made her poke Grace awake so they could talk right now. But, as if she was privy to Vanessa's train of thought, Grace rolled over, burrowed up under her chin, entangled their legs, and sighed the sweetest, most adorable sigh of contentment Vanessa had ever heard. There was nothing she could do besides wrap her arms around this woman—who still, somehow, after all the sex and sweat, smelled amazing—and hold her close. She inhaled deeply and let it out slowly, and her brain finally let her drift off to sleep.

When a shaft of sunlight poked at her eyelids, and Vanessa gingerly opened them, they were still in the same position. She could see over Grace to the edge of the bed where Delilah stood, her chin on the mattress, her black tail wagging back and forth in anticipation of breakfast. She couldn't help but smile at the dog.

Working herself free from the winding ivy that was Grace was no easy task, but she managed to do it without waking her up. Astonishingly. Clearly, Grace was a deep sleeper.

She pulled on sweats and a long-sleeved T-shirt, instantly missing Grace's warmth, and as she glanced back at her sleeping form, she felt a tug low in her body, one that tempted her to go back to bed, to use her mouth to wake Grace up…

A glance down at the delight on her dog's face helped her fight that temptation, and she headed downstairs, Delilah hot on her heels.

It hadn't snowed the night before, but it had gotten cold, and a crunchy frost still spread across the grass of her backyard. Delilah left paw prints through it as she wandered, nose to the ground. Vanessa popped in a K-Cup for herself and made up breakfast for Delilah, warming ground beef in the microwave and then mixing it with her kibble. The scent of the coffee filled the kitchen, helping to warm up the morning nicely.

Her mornings were normally quiet, and she preferred them that way, maybe because she taught young—read: noisy—kids and knew her day would be far from silent. She wasn't sure. She just knew that she never turned on the television or even the radio until she'd had at least one cup of coffee and had just sat quietly with her thoughts.

Today's thoughts were interrupted by the gorgeously yawning woman who walked into the kitchen just then.

"Why is it so ridiculously sexy when a woman wears your clothes?" she asked as she took in Grace in the boxers and hoodie she'd clearly found in Vanessa's drawers.

"You don't mind, do you?" Grace asked as she approached. "I woke up without you and was cold." She bent and kissed Vanessa, her mouth minty fresh.

On cue, Delilah pawed at the back door, and Vanessa let her in. "Sorry about that. Somebody wanted me up."

Grace put a K-Cup into the coffee maker, then went to Delilah and squatted to her level. Vanessa watched as a little lovefest occurred between her dog and her...what was Grace? Her date? Her overnight guest? Her girlfriend?

None of those seemed right.

Though, that last one...

She watched silently as Grace placed a kiss on Delilah's big square head, then moved to the counter and doctored her coffee. Her bare legs seemed to hold Vanessa's gaze longer than anything else.

Grace's voice pulled her back to the present. "Are you ogling me?" she asked, leaning back against the counter, then crossing her legs at the ankles as she brought the cup to her lips with both hands. Her hair was up in a messy bun, and the hoodie was navy blue, one of Vanessa's favorites, and just the image of Grace standing there in her morning-after pose...It did things to Vanessa.

"God, how do you do that?" The question slipped from her lips before she could catch it.

"Do what?" Grace sipped her coffee, not moving from her very sexy position.

"Make every coherent thought fly out of my head. Except for..."

"Except for sex?"

Vanessa nodded.

Grace shrugged. "I have no idea, but you do the same thing to me."

"I mean, we have stuff to talk about, but all I can think about is—"

"Going back to bed," Grace finished.

"Yes! You must think I've got a one-track mind."

Grace's laugh was musical. Pretty. "Two things you should know. One, if your mind has only one track, then so does mine because I am having the exact same issue. And two, it's been years since somebody made me feel so desired." Her voice got quiet then. "Years. And it's really, really nice."

Vanessa got up and went to her, wrapped her arms around her, wanted to erase that expression of self-doubt right off her beautiful face. "You are very, very desired. It's kind of ridiculous, really."

"Right back atcha."

And then came the kissing.

It's what they did, and they were so fucking good at it. Vanessa could feel her brain clouding up, fogging over, obscuring the things they really needed to discuss before it all went too far. She forced herself to wrench her mouth away and was unsurprised that they were both breathless.

"Jesus Christ," she muttered, then looked toward the ceiling and added, "Sorry," to God. They stood there, in each other's arms, and just looked at one another. The eye contact was natural, comfortable, not at all intense. Like they looked in each other's eyes every day, like they were used to it, like this was how it should be.

"I don't have a ton of time," Grace whispered and then brushed her lips across Vanessa's, sending a shiver along her shoulders and down her back. "Oliver is coming home around eleven."

"Well, that's a bummer," Vanessa said, then rushed to correct herself. "Not that he's coming home, but that you can't stay longer." More featherlight kisses.

"By my calculations, we have about an hour and a half before I'll need to head out so I can shower and put on clean clothes."

"So. Ninety minutes." Vanessa made a show of looking toward the ceiling, thinking hard. "What can we do for ninety minutes?" She returned her heated gaze to Grace. "Any ideas?"

"Oh, I have lots of ideas. Lots of them. Come with me."

CHAPTER SEVENTEEN

They didn't talk.

Not much of a surprise there, Grace thought with a rueful smile as she worked on one of twenty-six arrangements she had to make today, not to mention all the walk-ins, the December weddings, and the regular array of funerals and wakes that needed to be taken care of. Business was hopping, and that was good. Kept her mind from wandering. Mostly. Okay, not really. She was still in a haze of amazing sex that she wondered if she'd ever come out of. Part of her hoped the answer to that was *N-O*.

"How was your childless weekend?" Christie asked. She was in for a few hours that afternoon, helping pack up deliveries and keeping the shop clean and presentable while Grace and Ava worked. "Did you go clubbing? Throw a party? Take a trip?"

"I am so much less exciting than you seem to think," Grace said with a laugh. "No, I read a little. Cleaned my apartment. Brushed the cat. Missed my son." Christie didn't need to know that she'd also had mind-blowing sex. So much of it that her inner thighs were still sore two days later. Deliciously so.

"I bet he was happy to see you when he got home."

Grace clipped a stem and snort-laughed. "Not really. Seems his dad has thrown discipline out the window."

Christie nodded, said, "Mm-hmm," in a way that seemed knowing. Grace looked at her, and Christie shrugged. "The guilt has started to set in, sounds like."

Brow furrowed, Grace asked, "What do you mean?"

"My dad did the same thing. When he first left, spending time with me was almost a chore. I cramped his new life as a single guy. But not long after that, it seemed like he started to feel guilty for leaving and would give me anything I wanted. I don't know what happened to make him feel like that, but I loved it. Rules didn't apply at Dad's. We ate ice cream for lunch. Stayed up way too late. Watched movies much too scary for us, and Mom had to deal with our nightmares. Going to Dad's was like a vacation for a while."

"And coming home to Mom's was boring." Grace sighed, grasping the message instantly.

"Back to rules and chores? Yup."

"He's been less than happy to be around me." Oliver had hugged his dad good-bye, and then they did a complicated handshake that they must've practiced a dozen times, and the zap of jealousy that shot through her made her flinch. He had hugged her, too, and answered all her questions, but was low-key and unenthusiastic once Michael had left. Rudy seemed to be the only source of joy for him.

"My mom had to sit my dad down eventually," Christie told her. "Laid out a schedule and rules." She stressed the last word, then chuckled. A glance at Grace and she added, "It'll be okay, Grace. He loves you."

She knew that, and she smiled gratefully at Christie. She did know that. And divorce sucked. She'd been prepared for that, but losing some of Oliver's little-kid adoration had come as a shock. She was Mom. And Mom was the hero to little kids everywhere, most of the time. Oliver would outgrow that, sure, just like every other kid in the world. But already? At seven? The thought of it depressed her more than she could put into words.

Maybe Christie was right. Maybe it was time to sit Michael down and have a discussion about their son. Seriously, what did she think? That because Michael was a good man and a good dad that things would just magically work themselves out during their split? With a quiet sigh, she admitted to herself that yes, that was pretty much exactly what she'd thought.

Stupid, stupid, stupid.

But something surprised her. Right then, right in that very moment as she stood at the table clipping stems and filling vases and contemplating greenery, it wasn't Michael she wanted to talk to. It was Vanessa.

Well, wasn't that interesting?

And unexpected. And probably not advisable. But comforting in a way she couldn't explain.

She slipped her phone out of her back pocket, staying vigilant for Ava, half expecting her to pop in right then and catch her texting. Her fingers moved quickly as she typed a simple message.

Just thinking about you...

She followed that with a flame emoji and a wink emoji and hit send before she could change her mind.

❖

December was crazy.

That was the only way to put it. Vanessa loved, loved, loved the holiday season, but it was insane. Between getting ready for Christmas, shopping, decorating, making cookies with her mom, and the nearly unhinged energy of her students, her brain often felt like the inside of a popcorn popper. Just pieces of life flipping around, banging against her skull, wanting her attention, along with dozens of other pieces. December was the best and worst month.

Clearly, it was ridiculous for Grace as well. Her work hours were long, and she came home exhausted, and it was now Thursday and they hadn't seen each other since last weekend. Much as Vanessa wanted to just pop over or invite Grace for a nightcap and a foot rub, there were complications. They were still very new, despite the electric sexual chemistry they had, so she was really cognizant of making assumptions or taking too many liberties.

And there was Oliver.

That was the big one. The big hurdle. The thing that caused all her hesitation. Because not only would a relationship with Grace raise eyebrows with Vanessa's bosses and coworkers, but how would they explain it to Oliver? How weird would it be for him to have his teacher in his house on a regular basis? And they could avoid telling him, but for how long? And what good would deceiving him do?

This had been banging around her head all week, and now it was Thursday, and she and Delilah were on their way to The Bar Back. Julia had invited her and Amelia, said she needed to run something by them, so maybe this was Vanessa's chance to think about something else for a change. It was likely a new cocktail or an event idea, but anything that wasn't about her current dating situation would be a welcome distraction.

Thursdays were pretty busy at Martini's, and it had taken much prodding—and then some begging—from Savannah, as well as the cousins, to get Julia to hire extra hands. When she first opened the bar, Vanessa's workaholic cousin had tried to run just about every aspect of it on her own. Seven days a week. She was exhausted, cranky, and almost missed out on the wonderfulness she now had with Savannah. She could still be found at the bar on Thursdays, but mostly in the back, working on orders and creating new cocktails, much less stressed and much more relaxed. Savannah could often be found curled on the couch, studying or reading a book or being a taste-tester.

When Vanessa pushed her way through the side door, Delilah in tow, it was only Julia and Amelia there, and Amelia had just arrived, as she was hanging up her coat.

"Delilah is here, the fun can start!" Amelia called out, then immediately unclipped Delilah's leash. Julia closed the door to the bar so Delilah wouldn't go wandering and cause a health code violation, but smiled down at the dog and her cousin.

"That is some impressive tail wagging, I've gotta say." Julia went back behind the practice bar.

"It's because she loves her Auntie Amelia," Amelia said in the baby voice she seemed to reserve for Delilah. "Don't you, baby? Don't you?"

Vanessa dropped onto the couch with a big sigh. "God, it feels good just to chill."

"How is Hell Month, anyway?" Julia asked with a chuckle.

"Why, it's hell, Julia, thanks for asking."

"Drinks?" Julia looked from one of them to the other. Amelia nodded, then looked Vanessa's way, silently asking if she was going to break her rule of no drinking on a school night.

"I think Hell Month calls for alcohol, don't you?" Vanessa asked. "But just one, and go easy on me. I have school tomorrow, and I need to drive home."

"You got it." Julia went to work, bottles and glasses flashing.

Vanessa watched, enthralled. "Man, Jules, you've really gotten good at that."

Julia smiled, tossed a bottle in the air and caught it, then tipped it immediately into a pour.

"Now you're just showing off."

"Clea's been teaching me." Clea was one of the first bartenders Julia had hired when she first opened, and the girl was like magic behind the bar. Julia had promoted her to bar manager several months ago. Savannah's suggestion, Vanessa knew, and an excellent one.

Drinks were handed out, and they caught up with each other's lives. Julia had six work parties booked for the holidays. Amelia's business was just getting off the ground, and she'd gotten a new client that day. They already knew Vanessa was in Hell Month.

"So, are we here to test out this cocktail?" Vanessa held up her glass, which was a blend of blackberry brandy, something fizzy—7UP?—and maybe some simple syrup, but she wasn't sure. "'Cause it's damn good. Not terribly Christmassy, though, if that's what you're going for."

"No. That's not what I'm going for, and I didn't ask you guys here for drink testing." Julia's face had gone alarmingly serious, and Vanessa blinked at her, then looked to Amelia, who looked suddenly as worried as she felt.

"Are you okay?" Vanessa asked.

Amelia was on the floor with Delilah's head in her lap. "Things are okay with the bar? With your dad? With Savannah?" It was like she was ticking off boxes, and Vanessa appreciated the organizational approach of it.

Julia smiled then. A nervous smile, but still a smile, and Vanessa felt slightly better. "All of those things are good."

"Then what's up?" Vanessa asked. "You're scaring us."

Amelia nodded, her eyes slightly wide.

"Relax, you guys." Julia moved her hands, palms down, in front of her in the universal sign for calm down. "It's nothing bad. In fact, I think it's really good. But you're my family, the most important people in the world to me, and I need your opinions." With that, she reached into her pocket and pulled out a box. A ring box.

"Oh my God," Vanessa and Amelia said at the exact same time with the exact same inflection.

Julia flipped the box open to reveal a beautifully classy diamond ring.

"Are you asking us to marry you, Jules?" Amelia asked. "'Cause that would be super weird, but you're totally cute, and you own a bar, so I might be willing to put up with the raised eyebrows…"

"When?" Vanessa asked, laughing at Amelia's words and also from the sheer joy of what Julia's actions meant.

"Christmas Eve," Julia said. "After all the family stuff and we're home by ourselves in front of the fire." Her throat moved in a swallow, and she lifted watery eyes to them. "Do you think it's too soon?" she asked, her voice so quiet it was almost a whisper. Then she sighed. "It's too soon, isn't it?"

Vanessa put a hand on Julia's wrist and waited until her gaze lifted and met hers. "Do you love her?" she asked softly, already knowing the answer, but wanting to help Julia see what she saw.

"You know I do. More than anything." Julia's unshed tears seemed on the brink of falling.

Amelia pointed at her. "Well, there's the proof right there. How many times have we seen Jules cry?" Amelia asked of Vanessa. "Four times in our entire lives?"

Vanessa grinned, nodded, and squeezed Julia's wrist. "Around that, yeah."

Amelia stood and took the few steps to sit with Vanessa and Julia. "Listen," she began, putting her hand on Vanessa's so the three of them were linked. "You know I'm not the biggest supporter of marriage right now. I'd be happy if the entire institution vanished into thin air, never to be mentioned ever again." She waited until they were both looking at her. "But if any two people in my life were meant to be married, it's you and Savannah." She cleared her throat. "I know I tell you all the time how lucky you are to have her. But what I don't often say is how lucky she is to have you."

Vanessa felt her throat tighten, and she pointed at Amelia and nodded. "Yes. That."

"You really think so?" Julia asked.

"Yes!" Vanessa and Amelia said in tandem. And then all three of them were crying and hugging, and Delilah used her nose to push at the trio, wanting in on whatever lovefest was happening.

"Savannah's gonna be so surprised," Vanessa said. "She working tonight?"

Julia shook her head and wiped the back of her hand across her cheek. "Studying. She's got a test tomorrow." She glanced down at the ring, still in her hand. "You guys think she'll like this?"

The ring was simple in its elegance. Not flashy, but not cheap. A very classy setting, gold with a diamond in the center and two small ones on either side.

"I think she's going to love it," Vanessa told her, and she knew it was the absolute truth. For a moment, she let herself feel the prick of envy, wondered what it would be like to love somebody so much you wanted to be with them until the end of time. She'd never felt that. At least not yet. Her brain instantly tossed her an image of Grace, smiling at her from the kitchen, her eyes soft, and Vanessa swallowed hard, pretending not to know how often she thought about Grace, how much she was beginning to miss not being with her.

"You guys are the best," Julia said, yanking Vanessa back to the present reality.

"I wish we could be there," Amelia said. At Julia's raised eyebrows, she added, "I mean, of course we can't be, but I wish you'd record it somehow. I'd love to see her face when you ask."

"I'll see what I can manage," Julia said, then pushed to her feet and returned to her usual spot behind the practice bar. She blew out a big breath, then looked from Vanessa to Amelia and back. "Thanks, you guys."

"Are you kidding?" Vanessa said. "We're so happy for you." She saw Amelia open her mouth, and just knew a smart-ass comment about marriage was coming, so she shot her cousin a look that basically said, *Don't you dare or I will punch you in the throat.* Amelia's mouth snapped shut, and she lifted one shoulder in a half shrug.

She'd hoped being here tonight would give her a chance to talk a bit more about her own situation with Grace because the reality was, she could feel herself slipping in deeper and deeper. Any hope of just dipping in a toe with the parent of a student was long gone, and while she was massively enjoying herself, she was still nervous. Maybe talking it through with her cousins would help. But she didn't want to steal any of the attention from Julia's news, so she laughed and nodded and kept her thoughts to herself.

She could deal with it on her own. No big deal.

She glanced up at Julia, her sparkling eyes, her flushed cheeks, her very obvious happiness, and only one thing flashed through Vanessa's mind. Just three words. Just one thought.

I want that.

Chapter Eighteen

Grace was freaking exhausted.

It had been rough the previous December as well, the flower shop taking what seemed to be endless orders, but this year was different. This year, Ava had gradually given her more responsibility, which she loved—God, the last thing she wanted to do was complain. But being on her feet for ten- or twelve-hour days, six days a week was starting to wear on her.

Luckily, this wasn't the pace all year round, and she only had to deal with it for another week and a half. She could handle that. No problem. And really, if she was being totally honest with herself, part of her loved it. The excitement, the joy when she arranged the perfect bouquet. And shockingly, she'd seen a few glances of approval from Ava. Only a few—and maybe she was just making that up—but it gave her a little boost of confidence, something she really needed, especially lately.

Her mind was a jumble, though.

It had been a week tomorrow since she'd last seen Vanessa, and she was feeling that loss more than she cared to admit. To herself, to Courtney, to anybody else. She missed Vanessa.

What she was supposed to do with that, she had no idea, because the complications were glaring.

Oliver hadn't said anything, but he likely knew something was going on. *I mean, none of his other teachers have ever been to the house for a visit*, she thought with a snort. He was a smart kid, but—hopefully—too young to understand sexuality yet. Right? Because he saw Ms. Martini at his house, that didn't mean he put two and two together and came up with *My mom's sleeping with my teacher*. Right?

Michael was the wild card, though. He'd obviously talked about the situation to her mother—something that still made her grind her teeth in anger—and Oliver had been right there when her mom was on the phone with Grace and talked so openly about it.

The solution was simple. And she knew it. She needed to sit Oliver down and have a talk with him. Be honest and upfront with him. See how he felt.

But was it too soon?

What if things with Vanessa didn't progress any farther? What if she took the time to sit Oliver down and explain the situation to him, only to end up ending things with Vanessa? What was the point of burdening him with information he might not need in a month or two?

And right there, that's when it happened. And it was unexpected. Took her completely by surprise.

The thought of not seeing Vanessa in a month or two reached into her gut, grabbed her stomach in its fist, and twisted it painfully.

Grace stopped what she was doing, pruning shears in one hand, a gorgeous red rose in the other, and blinked rapidly, absorbing what that sick feeling in her stomach might actually mean. No. Knowing what it meant.

She was good at compartmentalizing and dealing with important emotional issues on her own. Growing up with her mother, she'd really had no choice. But this felt different. Confusing. A little overwhelming. She needed a sounding board. Slipping her phone out, she sent a quick text to Courtney.

Busy tonight? My place? Need a friend...

Courtney's response made her smile. *You've got one. I'll bring the wine.*

The relief that washed through her like warm water flooding her system was a good thing. Thank freaking God. She could breathe again. Her shoulders stopped trying to be earrings. She inhaled, let it out, and focused on her job for a bit longer.

Ava must've seen how exhausted she was because she sent her home at five, waving away her insistence that she could stay until they closed at six. By six thirty, she'd grabbed Oliver from her parents—thankfully avoiding any unwanted chatter with her mom—hit the grocery store for dinner for him and munchies for her and Courtney. She was sliding pizza rolls into the oven by the time the doorbell rang, and she sent Oliver to answer it.

"I come bearing gifts," Courtney announced and presented three bottles of wine with a fun flourish and then a deep bow.

Grace laughed. "Three bottles, huh? You must think I'm in some serious trouble."

"Better to have too much and not need it, than too little and wish you had more. Words to live by, my friend."

"I can accept that," Grace said, waving vaguely around with her oven-mitted hand. "Let me get him all set. You know where the corkscrew and glasses are."

Once Oliver was sitting on the floor in front of the TV with his pizza rolls and his milk, she returned to the small table where Courtney sat, two glasses of wine in front of her. Grace had sliced up some cheese with crackers, melted some Brie, washed a bunch of grapes, and set out a bowl of Gorgonzola-stuffed olives. She picked up her glass and held it up to cheer with Courtney.

"I would normally bring white, but it's cold tonight, and red is always more my speed in the winter. Cheers." They touched glasses and took tandem sips.

Grace was just starting to learn what wines she liked, and cabernet was normally a little heavier than her usual go-to. But this one was good. A little fruity. What she thought a taster would call complex. She did what she'd learned from a wine documentary she'd watched on Netflix a while back and let the wine sit in her mouth for a moment and coat her tongue, then swallowed. Kind of amazing how much more there was to tasting something if you gave it some thought and some time.

"That's good," she said and set her glass down.

Courtney nibbled on some cheese, looking cute in jeans and a red sweater. She watched Grace as she chewed, waiting her out.

Grace sighed. She wished Oliver was in his room. She kept watch of him out of the corner of her eye as she spoke, her voice low. "I need a little guidance. A sounding board."

Courtney held her arms out to her sides. "Hit me." She used the tiny cheese knife to spread some Brie onto a cracker and popped it into her mouth. A hum of approval. When Grace still hadn't spoken, she must've decided to prod a little. "So. Are we talking the same situation? The—" She glanced at Oliver, seemingly engrossed in his show. "The same person?"

Grace nodded, the chunk of cheese she'd swallowed sitting like a rock in her stomach.

"Has it progressed?"

Grace made her eyes wide and nodded hard.

"How far?"

She widened her eyes more, pushed her head forward.

"*Oh.*" Courtney drew the syllable out, then grinned and reached out and pushed at her. "That's fantastic." When Grace didn't reply, her brow furrowed. "It's not fantastic?"

"I mean…" Another glance at Oliver. "It was. It is. It's…" She waved a hand around vaguely.

"How do you feel?"

That was the question, wasn't it? How did she feel? She gave it real, honest thought before dropping out words as if she was playing cards and snapping them down on the table one by one. "I feel… confused. Thrilled. Terrified. Wanted. Joyful. Sexy." She took a sip of her wine. "Did I mention confused and terrified? Oh! Don't let me forget guilty. That's a big one."

"Guilty? What the hell for?"

"My div—" She shot a look toward Oliver and lowered her voice to a whisper. "My divorce isn't even final yet, and I'm sleeping with somebody else."

Courtney took a deep breath. "Okay. I'm gonna drop some knowledge. Can you handle it?"

A nod.

"I don't think this will come as a surprise to you because you've already told me you suspected it. But Michael has been dating, as you know. Don't you think he's probably had sex?"

She did. She'd suspected it, though she hadn't had the courage to come out and ask him, but she knew. "Yeah."

"So what do you have to feel guilty about? I know it feels like it's too soon because of the paperwork, but, sweetie"—Courtney reached across the table and grasped Grace's forearm—"you were unhappy for a long time. The marriage has been over for a long time. You know it and I know it. And hell, Michael knows it."

Maybe she'd just needed somebody else to tell her what she already knew. Was that it? Courtney wasn't giving her a newsflash. But somehow, in some weird way, having Courtney say the things Grace already knew in her heart helped a lot. She felt a bit of the weight that had pressed down on her all day lift. And thank God, 'cause it was getting heavy.

"There's also the other issue," she said and tipped her head in Oliver's direction.

"The teacher aspect," Courtney whispered.

Grace looked at Oliver, sitting cross-legged on the floor, eating his pizza rolls like he didn't have a care in the world. As if sensing her gaze, he turned and caught her eye, waved, then refocused on the television. Her heart swelled with love, the way it always did when her son looked at her. Turning her attention back to Courtney, she said, "I don't know what to do about it. Do I tell him? Do we hide it? Do I not see her until he moves up a grade?"

"Can you stay away from her for six more months?" Courtney asked, the twinkle in her eye saying she knew the answer already.

Grace shook her head. "I don't think I can." She grimaced. "Does that make me a bad mother? It does, doesn't it. Oh God." She hung her head.

"Grace." Courtney touched her again.

It was something Grace had always liked about her. She was touchy. Physically affectionate. She touched and hugged and bumped, and Grace always felt a warmth in that. She raised her eyes, met Courtney's.

"Don't you think you deserve to be happy?" she asked softly.

That. That was a question she didn't allow herself to think about. "I'm not sure."

Courtney's eyes bugged out, and she reeled back as if Grace had poked her. "I'm sorry. You're *not sure*? Explain."

A hard swallow. "I mean, I'm a mom. That's first and foremost. My son comes first. If I put my happiness before him, that feels so selfish. And weird."

Courtney rolled her lips in and blinked at her for a moment. Grace got the impression she was searching for the best way to explain something. Finally, she said, "Okay. Listen to me. I don't have kids, so I'm not going to pretend I know what that feels like. However"—she held up a finger—"I do have a mom. A mom who's divorced. And you know what I learned from her as I was growing up?"

"Tell me." Grace topped off their wine.

"That if she was happy, her kids were happy."

Grace waited for more, and when none came, she asked, "That's it?"

"That's it."

"It's that simple?"

"It really is that simple."

"Am I overthinking?"

Courtney laughed through her nose. "No, I don't think you're overthinking. I think your concerns are valid, and it makes you a great mom for even having the worries you do. I just think you need to treat yourself the way you'd treat somebody you love. You know?" She popped a grape into her mouth.

"Oh, that's a good one. That should be embroidered on a pillow."

"Working on it. Soon as I learn to needlepoint."

They were quiet for a beat, the only sound that of the show Oliver was watching. Grace absorbed everything Courtney had said, genuinely took it in, as she turned it in her mind's eye, examining from all angles.

"So"—Courtney lowered her head so she was looking at Grace from under her lashes—"how's the sex?" she whispered.

Without saying a word, Grace slid down in her chair, let her head fall back, went boneless, and gave a small whimper. A grape boinked off her head, and she looked up just as Courtney launched another at her, laughing.

"I'm so jealous," she said.

"You should be," Grace agreed as she sat back up. "The woman is an honest-to-God dynamo. I kid you not."

"Gah. Details. Gimme. Let me live vicariously." Courtney sipped her wine. "When do you see her again?"

"Not this weekend," Grace said with a sigh. "It's too weird when I have Oliver. Plus, work is insane. I do have a parent-teacher conference on Monday, and Michael's gonna be away for work, so at least I'll get to lay eyes on her without him watching me."

"No making out at school, though. I gotta draw the line there." Courtney winked to show she was teasing.

"God, no." She would never do that. Not that the danger of getting caught didn't send a thrill through her right then, because it totally did. The excitement of the forbidden. She'd never risk it, never in a million years, but holy hell was it a turn-on to think about. Sitting on Vanessa's desk in front of her, short skirt, top unbuttoned just a little lower than it should be, wetting her lips and pretending to be all innocent and *Oh, Ms. Martini, I don't mean to be forward, but I can't help it, you're so pretty...*

"You're picturing it right now, aren't you."

"No. I'm not. Stop that." But Grace couldn't hide the mischievous grin behind the rim of her glass.

"Oh, honey," Courtney said, picking up her own wine. "You've got it bad."

CHAPTER NINETEEN

A quick glance at her phone told Vanessa it was going on seven. Darkness had settled outside the classroom windows more than two hours ago, and she gave a quiet sigh. It was the thing she hated most about this time of year, the darkness. She woke up in the dark and often went home in the dark.

"Just another week or so, and the days will start getting longer again." She whispered the comment as she sat at her desk, laptop open in front of her, and waited for the next parents to come in. She'd had quite a few already, which was a nice surprise. Only two more appointments and then the big one at seven thirty. She was both nervous and excited about it.

Grace Chapman.

Just thinking about her name made Vanessa's nerves start to buzz, dampened her underwear. What the hell had she become? What was happening to her? Had she ever felt this physically affected at the simple thought of somebody?

The answer to that was, God no. This was so brand new and wonderful and terrifying and *What the hell do I do about it?* and she knew it, but she shut it down. Because if she sat here and started thinking about-slash-analyzing-slash-flashing back to anything that had to do with her and Grace, she might seriously lose her mind. Seriously. And her coworkers would look on and *tsk*, arms folded as they stood shaking their heads and murmuring to each other how they'd known this day was coming.

Thank freaking God for the knock on her door and her next appointment.

She focused on her students, and it wasn't until she walked her seven fifteen parents out the door that she noticed Grace in the hallway with Oliver, waiting patiently for their turn.

Her stomach legit flip-flopped. Like, seriously seemed to somersault in her body, flutters and nerves and worry and joy all mixing until she had to clasp her hands together to keep from reaching out to touch Grace. Who looked absolutely gorgeous, by the way. She glowed. *Glowed.* Why? Was it seeing her, Vanessa, that made Grace look like that? Was that possible? She was dressed simply in jeans, high black boots, and a green sweater under a black leather jacket—don't even get her started on *that* fashion feature—but it was her face, her eyes. They sparkled like they contained tiny diamonds, and her smile...Vanessa swallowed hard, and for the very first time, she didn't chase the thought away before it could manifest in her head. Instead, she let it. She heard it. She felt it. She embraced it.

I am in big trouble with this woman.

She didn't care.

"Grace," she said once she'd sent the Cobens on their way. She held out a hand and Grace took it to shake, but Vanessa held on for an extra few seconds before dropping both her gaze and Grace's hand to Oliver. He stood next to his mom. Close. Too big to hold her hand, but not big enough to just go do his own thing. Not tonight, probably. Vanessa wondered if he was worried about what she'd say. Eyes back up on Grace, she said quietly, "It's really good to see you."

"Same here," Grace said but somehow conveyed much more than those two words. Vanessa could feel it, and it made her feel lighter somehow.

Allowing herself one more beat of looking at Grace, she finally held an arm out toward the classroom. "Shall we?"

With a nod, Grace and Oliver headed in, and Vanessa closed the door. She hadn't with any others, but somehow, closing the door made it feel more like she had Grace to herself. At least for the next fifteen minutes.

They all sat, Vanessa behind her desk, Grace and Oliver in chairs next to it. She had to keep up some level of professionalism, which wasn't usually a problem for her, but having Grace this close and needing to keep her distance, to not reach out, to not lay a hand on her knee as they talked, was already turning out to be much harder than she'd expected. Again, she clasped her hands together to keep them from wandering over to Grace without her brain's permission.

"How was your weekend?" she asked.

Oliver didn't answer, instead studying his hands as he swung his feet, kicking the legs of the chair.

"It was fine," Grace answered, setting her hand on his knee to stop the noise. "I worked, and Oliver got to spend time with his grandparents."

"That sounds like fun," Vanessa said, looking at Oliver.

He glanced up at her, gave a little boy shrug, and then watched his hands some more.

"Christmas is just around the corner, Oliver. Are you ready?"

That worked. His eyes, so much like his mother's it took Vanessa's breath, lit up, and he sat a little straighter. "We're seeing Santa this weekend. I need to tell him to bring my toys to my dad's."

Vanessa caught the pain as it sliced across Grace's features. Before she could ask, Grace said, "He's staying at his father's Christmas Eve. I'll get him in the early afternoon on Christmas Day."

Oh... Vanessa nodded, making a note to text Grace about that later. "Well," she said, hitting some keys on her laptop and calling up Oliver's grades, "I'm happy to say that Oliver seems to have improved his behavior quite a bit since the last time we talked about it."

"That's good news," Grace said, ruffling Oliver's hair. He leaned away, but not before she messed it up good.

"He's still got a short temper, though." She looked to him and softened her expression while adding, "And a bit of a mouth on him."

Grace shot him a look. "Yeah, he's been pushing the limits of my patience lately. I need to talk with his father." She looked pointedly back to Vanessa. "Before Friday, when he'll pick him up from school and have him for the weekend."

Vanessa could've kissed her right then. As it was, she had trouble keeping her smile under wraps as she took the clue Grace had handed her. She'd be free this weekend. She definitely had to text her later. Because it had been over a week since they'd been together, and when Vanessa flashed back on the time they'd spent, on Grace's naked body rolling and heaving and writhing with hers, all she could think was yeah, more of *that*, please.

They went over a few more things, but fifteen minutes was a really short span of time, and the loud rap on the door shouted at them that they had to be done.

All three of them stood and made their way to the door. Vanessa pulled it open just as Grace said, "I'll text you later." Then she turned and saw Vanessa's next appointment: Sebastian Kent and his mom. Kayla. Vanessa often had to struggle to remember the names of parents, but not Kayla Kent. Oh no. She made sure you remembered her.

"Well, isn't this cozy?" Kayla said, looking from Grace to Vanessa.

Grace shot Vanessa a look, clearly not knowing how Vanessa wanted her to respond.

Vanessa lifted one shoulder in forced nonchalance. "My seven thirties," she said with a smile, then gave a wave as Grace took Oliver's hand and led him away. "Come on in," she said, holding out an arm and inviting Kayla and Bash into her classroom.

"The door stays open for us?" Kayla asked, all wide-eyed innocence as she sat.

She intensely disliked this woman. Truly. Always had. Kayla had been a year ahead of Vanessa in high school and had been a walking stereotype even then: blond, pretty, head cheerleader who dated the quarterback...and a huge bully. Vanessa hadn't been on the receiving end, but she knew people who had. Kayla came from money, and she'd married money, and she never let anybody forget it. She was a walking, talking, real-life Mean Girl. Even in her thirties.

"I'd like to know if that Oliver Chapman has let loose on anybody else in the classroom since hitting my son." So, right to it then.

"*Mom*," Bash said, drawing the word out so it had three syllables, and shrank down in his seat, arms folded across his chest. "I told you he hasn't."

Vanessa felt bad for him. He and Oliver had been good friends since before they came to her class. She'd seen them around. She suspected Bash knew he'd been a little dick that day and probably deserved to get punched. He and Oliver still talked, still hung out in the same group. They maybe weren't quite as tight as they'd been, and she'd caught Bash looking wistfully Oliver's way here and there, like he wished it could be like it was, but he wasn't allowed. She would've bet a dozen doughnuts that Bash's mom forbade him to be friends with Oliver.

"Bash is right. They've been just fine."

"Well, I should hope so. There's no excuse for physical violence like that. And I sincerely hope that boy's not getting any special treatment from his teacher." Kayla didn't put air quotes around the words *special treatment*, but she might as well have, given the way she said it.

Vanessa narrowed her eyes and counted to five. "What do you

mean special treatment?" She used the same tone and inflection as she held Kayla's gaze.

Obviously not expecting to have to elaborate, Kayla took a second before tipping her head to one side. "You know. Because of your *relationship* with his mother."

What the hell?

First of all, how did she know that? Second of all, what the hell business was it of hers? Third, who had she told?

"Your silence is telling." Kayla looked at her lap, brushed some nonexistent something off her pants, and looked smug. "Word gets around, you know. Plus"—she tossed a look at the now-open door—"I have eyes."

Vanessa fought the panic that began to bubble in her stomach and resented it. Resented the sudden feelings of guilt. Resented that she now felt a little off-balance. Resented Kayla. What the hell was she doing? Vanessa had done nothing wrong. Kayla Kent had seen nothing. She was doing nothing more than gossiping, looking for Vanessa to confirm her suspicions. But still, she felt sick, had to swallow down the bile, and that pissed her off.

Hitting a few keys on the laptop, she pulled up Bash's report card and notes as if Kayla hadn't said what she'd said. 'Cause ignoring her would work. Sure.

"Bash's grades are good. He's been doing really well with his quizzes. And I'm impressed with how many books on the reading list he's checked off."

Bash really was a sweet kid, and his cheeks flushed a bright red as Vanessa spoke. She wondered how many more years it would take for him to end up like his mom. She hoped he never would, but she'd seen it happen more than once. And Kayla had a very strong personality, an air of superiority. Which she was flexing right now by giving Vanessa a look that so clearly asked *Why aren't you acknowledging what I said?*

"Overall," Vanessa went on, focusing her gaze on her student instead of his mother. "He's a really good kid. I'm happy to have him in my class." Then she turned to Kayla, schooling her features into an expression that she hoped said *Time for you to back the hell off.*

It was likely only a few seconds of them staring at each other, but it felt like a standoff. A lengthy one. And Vanessa had a quick vision of the two of them in the Old West, standing apart on a dusty street, facing each other, twitchy hands hovering just above their guns. She didn't want to draw, didn't want to shoot Kayla, but she would if forced to defend herself.

And then, just like that, the moment was over. Kayla reached down for the purse she'd set on the floor. "Good. I'm glad to hear it." She stood, looked to her son. "Ready?"

Bash nodded, sent a bashful smile Vanessa's way, and followed his mother toward the door. Vanessa stood as well and trailed behind him.

In the doorway, Kayla turned and met her gaze again. Vanessa braced because it was clear she wanted to say something more. Instead, she gave another smug smile. "Have a good night," she said.

Then they were gone.

Vanessa walked back to her desk on shaky legs because everything she'd been holding in check released right then. Her breath, her clenched jaw, her tensed muscles, her freaking adrenaline.

"Jesus Christ," she breathed out softly. The wicked smile on Kayla's face stayed with her, like it was spray-painted on her brain. Kayla Kent was talking. That was clear. If she hadn't, she would. And it would be out there. People would know. No, it wasn't anybody's business. No, she wasn't breaking any rules. No, it didn't look good.

"Jesus Christ," she said again.

CHAPTER TWENTY

Grace went to bed Monday night feeling like a blow was coming, like her body knew something bad was about to happen. When her alarm when off at O Dark Thirty—good God, when would it be light in the mornings again?—Tuesday morning, she was already awake, still with that unsettled feeling in her gut like a pit in her stomach, as she stared at her ceiling.

It was because of Kayla Kent. She knew that much. Her snide little *Isn't this cozy?* had stuck with her. Not because it had bothered her, but because it had clearly bothered Vanessa. Though she hadn't said anything, the color had drained from her face, and she'd visibly swallowed. When Grace had texted her last night, she'd been short. Not rudely so, but not terribly verbal. Said she was tired from the long day and needed sleep. Was Grace supposed to argue with that?

Now this morning, that feeling of…imbalance was a good word for it. That feeling of imbalance was still sitting square on her shoulders as she made her way downstairs and set the coffee to brewing, knowing she was going to need a gallon or two if she was to be any kind of a functioning person today.

She texted Vanessa.

Good morning, good lookin'. Sleep okay?

She sent it off, not expecting to hear back right away, given it was still early.

When three and a half hours had gone by with no response, that pit in her stomach had morphed into something much larger and much less comfortable. And the more she thought about Kayla and what she'd insinuated, the more sure she was about her source.

She took a bathroom break around eleven and, while she was in there, dialed Michael.

"Hey, what's up?" he answered. "Oliver okay?"

She wasted no time. "Did you say something to Kayla Kent about me and Oliver's teacher?"

His hesitation was all she needed to know she was right.

"My God, Michael. What were you thinking?"

"I didn't know it was a secret," he said, and she believed him. His tone seemed sincere, and she knew him well enough to know what he sounded like when he was lying. "Is it?"

"I mean…" It was Grace's turn to hesitate because she honestly didn't know. Were they a secret? She sighed. "I don't know. But Vanessa has a reputation, and it's not cool that you screwed with it. You know?"

"Maybe you shouldn't be fucking our son's teacher then."

"Okay, wow. Just…wow." She took a moment to rein in her anger, to absorb what he'd said and to wonder why. "So, wait. Is this about me and her? Or is this about me and you?" She glanced at her watch. Ava was going to kill her if she stayed in the bathroom too long, but she wasn't about to let Michael's comment slide. "Because you were seeing somebody—more than one somebody—way before I ever even thought about it."

She heard Michael exhale on the other end of the phone. "You're right," he said, his voice gone quiet. "You're right. I'm sorry. I just…" He groaned, a habit of his when he wasn't sure what to say or had to say something he didn't want to admit. "I think I was jealous."

Grace blinked, shook her head even though there was nobody around to see. "I'm sorry, you were *jealous*?"

"I'm not proud of it, Grace."

"I should hope not. 'Cause it doesn't make a ton of sense."

"I know. I guess…" More sighing and another groan and she could picture him, running his hand through his hair and sitting back in resignation. "I guess if I'm seeing somebody, it's one thing. But if you are, too, then…"

She saw it then. Got it fully. And it smacked her almost as hard as it seemed to have smacked him. "Then we're really over." She said it quietly.

"Yeah." He was just as quiet.

It felt weird. And sad. So overwhelmingly sad. Which was stupid and silly because they'd been over for a long time, and they both knew it. But as Grace sat there on the closed lid of the toilet with the phone to her ear, her eyes welled up, and the proverbial lump settled itself right in the center of her throat. "Well," she said and cleared her throat. "That came as a surprise." A gentle laugh.

"Right? For both of us, seems."

Something happened then, in that moment. In that exact minute. Grace couldn't explain exactly what it was or how it felt, but it was important. Significant. Something shifted. Something changed, and she and Michael were suddenly in different roles than before. New roles.

"Listen, I need you to be a little firmer with Oliver, okay? You have to keep to his schedule, and you have to be firm with him or he's a nightmare when I get him."

"Okay. Yeah, I just…it's so much fun when it's just him and me, and I tend to treat it like a vacation for him. I'll be better."

Grace blinked. What the hell was happening? Michael hadn't argued. Hadn't even bristled. "Okay, I'm a little weirded out right now," she said honestly.

Michael's chuckle came from deep in his throat, one of the things she loved most about him. "Same."

"Are we new people now?"

"Kinda feels like it, yeah?"

Maybe she and her ex-husband had finally became friends.

❖

"You making cookies with Aunt Monica this weekend?" Julia asked as she poked a few keys on her laptop.

Vanessa sat on the couch in The Bar Back, feet up on the coffee table, crossed at the ankles. She shook her head and set her glass of pinot grigio next to her phone. "Not until next Wednesday afternoon. I don't have a choice. We haven't been able to make our schedules work, so we're cutting it super close."

"When is school out?"

"Wednesday we have a half day."

"School in the morning, cookies at night? That's a full day for you."

Vanessa laughed through her nose. "Right?"

"And then you get the whole week between Christmas and New Year's off?"

Vanessa touched her nose with the tip of her finger.

"Savannah made cookies with my mom last weekend. You

should've seen how giddy she got. She was like a little kid." Julia looked over and smiled warmly.

"Aww, that makes me so happy."

Savannah had lost her mom more than ten years ago, and being with Julia, being embraced by Julia's huge family, had been life changing for her.

"I cannot tell you how many cookies I've eaten lately, just because she's so excited to have made them." Julia patted her stomach. Then her brow furrowed as she studied Vanessa. "You okay?"

Such a simple question with so many convoluted answers. Vanessa sighed and picked up her wine. While she adored Amelia and Savannah, there was something peaceful about it just being her and Julia that night. And Delilah, who lounged on the brand-new big round dog bed that had suddenly appeared in The Bar Back, courtesy of Aunt Julia and Aunt Savannah.

"You look like you've got a lot on your mind."

"I would call that a fair and accurate assessment, dear cousin of mine," Vanessa said.

"Wanna talk about it?" Julia closed the laptop, sat back in her chair, and crossed her ankles up on her desk. "I'm all ears."

Vanessa hadn't told anybody about Monday night. About feelings that had begun to develop for Grace or about how Kayla Kent had made vague threats because she somehow had information she thought she could scare Vanessa with. And she had. With a big gulp of wine and then a sigh of resignation, she spilled. Told Julia the whole story. Including how she'd barely texted with or talked to Grace at all since then.

Julia sat forward in her chair and braced her elbows on her knees. "How does this woman know?"

Vanessa shook her head. "No idea. Maybe Oliver said something to her son? Though I don't see how or why he'd do that."

"Do you blame Grace for it?"

"For what?"

Julia waved her open hand in a circle in front of Vanessa. "For this. You. How you're feeling about it. Your fear." Vanessa opened her mouth to protest, but Julia knew her well and stopped her in her tracks. "You absolutely *are* scared. I can see it in your eyes."

A sigh of defeat. "Fine. I am."

"Why? What are you scared of? There's no law, right? You can't get fired."

"No, but the whole thing would probably be frowned upon, you know? It doesn't look good."

"To who?"

"I don't know, anybody."

Julia tipped her head to one side. "Who cares?"

Vanessa blew out a breath. "It's my reputation, Jules. I had to work extra hard to be noticed for my work as a teacher instead of for my sexual orientation, and it sucked. This puts the focus squarely on my sexuality. You know?"

"I'll ask again—who cares?" Julia stood, went around to the practice bar, and pulled a bottle of water out of the fridge back there. As she cracked it open, she waited for Vanessa to meet her gaze before she gentled her voice and added, "'Cause it kinda sounds like this is maybe your issue."

Vanessa let a loud groan go as she flopped back against the couch. "Gah. I know!" And she did know. She'd been rolling it around in her head for nearly forty-eight hours, avoiding phone calls and answering texts from Grace with as few words as possible. Probably making her feel awful, which made Vanessa feel awful. "But I can't seem to shake it off."

"Do you want me to come over there and smack you around a little bit?" Julia offered with a grin.

"Would you? I could use it, I think."

Later that night, as she lay in bed staring at the ceiling, sleep eluding her for a third night, her phone lit up on the nightstand next to her. Grace.

Look, it's clear something's bothering you—Monday night and Kayla's comment, I'm guessing—and you don't want to talk about it with me. I can accept that. I don't like it, but I can accept it...

The dots kept bouncing, so there was more she wanted to say, and Vanessa waited in the dark, the phone held above her head.

Bouncing dots, bouncing dots.

Bracing for a long, possibly scolding paragraph—which she would totally deserve, by the way—she blinked in surprised when the text finally came.

I miss you.

That was it. No more prying. No begging her to talk. No apologies—there'd been several of them yesterday, even though Grace had nothing to apologize for, and they both knew it. Just *I miss you.* And no more dots.

Vanessa swallowed hard, and it surprised her when her eyes filled. She should respond. She should send back that she missed Grace, too. Because she did. But something kept her from doing that. Something held her tightly and wouldn't let her brain give her fingers the commands for typing. Instead, she set the phone back down on the nightstand and turned on her side, away from it, so she wouldn't see it light up if Grace texted again.

❖

Vanessa hated grocery shopping. Hated it. With a red hot passion. It's why God invented Instacart. And being in the grocery store during the last few days before Christmas? Sweet baby Jesus on a stick, no thank you. But when she'd arrived at her mother's to help make Christmas cookies the following Wednesday, she was greeted with the news that her mom was dangerously low on walnuts, a key ingredient for her thumbprint cookies.

"I need you to run to Wegmans for me," her mom had said, her face incredibly serious. "It'll be a war zone. You may need a flak jacket. Mine's in the closet if you want to borrow it."

"And a helmet," her sister Ella added. "Walnuts are in the baking aisle. You could get flattened by people trying to get to the baking soda or vanilla extract." She knocked on her own head. "Gotta protect your melon."

"You two are hilarious." Vanessa sighed, pushing her arm back into her coat before she'd gotten it all the way off. "Truly. You should take this show on the road." She shot a glare at Ella. "Why do I have to go and not her?"

"Because I was here first, and you're parked behind me in the driveway. Plus, I'm too pretty to brave such crowds."

Her mother held out a twenty-dollar bill. "Here. Get at least two bags."

Vanessa waved her away. "Ma. I can afford to buy you some walnuts." She zipped up. "If I'm not back in half an hour, send a search party."

War zone didn't begin to cover it. There were no carts outside in the cart storage spot—that's how many people were actually inside the store. Aisles were tight, folks were in a hurry, and every cashier line was open and full of waiting customers. Vanessa made it to the baking aisle without incident but had to do some fancy footwork to dance around the irritating cluster of carts left in the middle as shoppers snagged ingredients off shelves. Finally, four of the last ten or so bags of chopped walnuts in her hands, she turned to head toward the checkout and ran face-first into a rock-solid broad chest.

"Oh God, I'm so sorry," she said as she looked up into dark eyes that were vaguely familiar. She squinted at the man with the sandy hair for a moment before recognition dawned on her, and her stomach did a terrific impression of a gymnast, flipping in her body with nauseating results. "Mr. Chapman."

"Ms. Martini." He had clearly recognized her right away—after all, Vanessa thought, how often did you walk in and find another woman making out with your ex-wife? Strangely, though, his expression was almost friendly. As she went to move around him, he stopped her with one word. "Wait."

Vanessa closed her eyes for a beat before turning toward him and bracing herself, her entire body tightening in anticipation of a verbal assault. Right here in the middle of the crowded grocery store? Really, Universe? She sighed internally, accepting that maybe she had it coming and should just stand there and take it.

But no accusations came. And when she opened her eyes and met Michael Chapman's, she saw he only looked curious, like he was waiting for her to explain what she'd been waiting for. They stood that way, just looking at each other, for a few seconds before he shifted his gaze over her shoulder before coming back to her face.

"You could do worse, you know," he said, his voice low, one shoulder lifting in a half shrug.

"I'm sorry?" She shook her head. What did that mean? What was he talking about? The store? The walnuts? "Worse than…?"

"Than Grace."

Oh…

Also, odd coming from the ex, right? Vanessa found herself shocked into speechlessness. Stood there, blinking, trying to think of something to say.

"Look, I know you've been seeing her, and I also know what Kayla Kent said, and I *also* know that you've kinda stepped back."

"You seem to know a lot," Vanessa said, and God, was it hot in here? Heat suddenly flushed through her, rivulets of sweat beading and rolling down her torso under her sweater and heavy coat, and she seriously might just bake alive right there in the baking aisle. None of this was his business. Was her face red? Her ears? They felt red. Hot.

Why was he saying these things? Did he want her to explain herself? "And correct me if I'm wrong, but did you do a massive one eighty?"

"I'm sorry," he said then, and when he smiled and nodded in response to her question, she could see Oliver, as plain as day, in his features. "I did. And I don't mean to make you uncomfortable." Which he clearly knew he had, given the heat she felt in her face. With a glance around, he added, "It's not like this place isn't a zoo already. I'm getting claustrophobic. How about you?"

"Last week before Christmas. Not unexpected, right?"

"Exactly." He looked at her hands. "Walnuts, huh? For cookies?"

She nodded, then used her chin to point to the bag of flour he held. "Cookies, too?"

"Gravy," he said. "My mom used all of what she had on the cookies."

They grinned at each other, two people trying not to feel as awkward as they did, and sidled to the edge of the aisle so the other claustrophobic shoppers could get by.

"Hey, like I said, I'm not trying to make you uncomfortable here, and it's none of my business," Michael said, and the sincerity in his voice surprised her and made her listen. "Lord knows, I made enough mistakes of my own during our marriage. One thing I do know is this: us splitting up was the best thing we could've done for Oliver, even if he doesn't see that now. And another thing I know: Grace deserves better than me. I don't know if that's you, but we've been apart for a long time and kept living in the same house. The only thing that's recent is the legal aspect of it. My moving out was something that should've happened a long time ago. But I have to say…" He glanced down at his shoes, then back up to her eyes, and it was clear what he was about to say wasn't easy for him. "Grace has been different since she started seeing you. She's relaxed. Happy. Happier than I've seen her in a long time. Or she was until last week."

Vanessa swallowed, glanced down at her feet, feeling exposed and ashamed, but also super curious about what else Michael Chapman had to say. Much as she wanted to turn and run away, she made herself stay put and look him in the eye.

"That was my fault. I was out with friends, the Kents were there, and I mentioned something about Grace seeing you. I'm so sorry. That was so out of line, and as soon as I said it, I wanted to take it back." His cheeks blossomed with pink spots, and his eyes darted away, then back. "I'm really sorry about that."

Something about his chagrin paired with his obviously genuine apology snaked its way in and made Vanessa warm to him just a bit. With one nod, she said, "It's okay. I can handle the Kayla Kents of the world." And just like that, she knew she could. It was the weirdest thing, the sudden burst of confidence she got just from saying the words aloud. In an instant, she felt like she'd stood up taller, lifted her chin, puffed out her chest.

"Glad to hear it. And I mean it about Grace. She's an amazing woman. Just because she and I didn't work doesn't mean she's not. She's an amazing woman and a terrific mother, and she deserves the best." He didn't say, *So step up and be that for her,* but it was implied. Vanessa heard it as if he'd shouted it at her.

"She's pretty incredible," Vanessa said, and she meant it.

"Well, I'd better get this flour to my mother before she and Oliver send out a search party."

Vanessa's laugh was genuine. "I told my mom to send one for me if I wasn't back in thirty minutes."

"How much time do you have left?"

A glance at her phone. "About six."

They both laughed together, then stopped, and there was a beat of awkward. "You take care of yourself, Ms. Martini. Okay?"

She smiled at him, inexplicably feeling different than she had when she'd walked in. Braver somehow. Stronger. "Merry Christmas, Mr. Chapman."

The smile stayed for her entire drive to her mom's.

CHAPTER TWENTY-ONE

G race was cracking.

She could feel it. Like she was some antique piece of sculpture or the foundation of an old building that just couldn't hold up the weight anymore.

And she resented it. She resented the hell out of it.

Christmas had always been her favorite time of year. She knew that wasn't a revelation. Lots of people loved the holidays. Tons of people loved Christmas. But for Grace, it had always meant an easing. Of the rules. The requirement to please her parents. It all loosened just a bit. She could even get her mom to laugh and joke around during Christmas—a shockingly difficult thing to do at any other time of year. And once she'd been married? Once she'd had Oliver? Her love of Christmas doubled. Tripled. Multiplied by hundreds. Her husband and her son only intensified her joy.

This year, she'd spend Christmas Eve without either of them.

The thought alone was crushing.

How had she let herself be talked into giving up her son on Christmas Eve? She was so pissed off at herself for allowing it to happen, but she'd had him on Thanksgiving, and it was only fair to let Michael have him for part of Christmas. But she didn't think it through. She didn't make the connection that he'd have Santa with Michael. Sure, she'd make sure Santa stopped at her place, too, but...She shook her head. Once Oliver had heard he was spending Christmas Eve at Michael's, he was so excited that it wasn't like she could change her mind about it. She had to force a smile and pretend to be excited for him, even though she was sure she could feel her heart cracking in her chest.

Maybe that was the cracking she felt. Not her entire being. Only her heart.

It was Thursday evening. Tomorrow was Christmas Eve, and Saturday was Christmas. She was finishing up at work, cleaning up her mess. Jack had left an hour ago with the last of the flower deliveries for Christmas. Ava might have been a demanding boss at times, but she wouldn't dream of making her tiny staff work on Christmas Eve.

"You okay, Grace?" As if conjured, Ava appeared in the doorway, her face showing concern. "You seem, I don't know, a little off."

Grace sighed, then was horrified to feel her eyes well up. Ava's eyes went wide, her discomfort as clear as if she wore a printed T-shirt announcing *I'm so uncomfortable right now.* That, of course, made Grace laugh through her impending tears, and she waved her hand through the air as if erasing it.

"I'm fine. I'm good. A little stressed, I think."

Ava nodded, her sigh of likely relief audible. "I get that. The holidays are a lot. But I thank you for the good work you did. Appreciated." She slipped an envelope onto the counter. It had Grace's name on it in Ava's block-letter handwriting. "Merry Christmas, Grace." A dip of her head, and she turned and was gone, leaving Grace to lock up like normal.

Her phone buzzed a text as she grabbed the envelope—her Christmas bonus—and slid it into her purse. She wanted to go pick up Oliver from her mother's as soon as she could, as her parents needed to head off for their flight and cruise. She had him tonight and tomorrow until three, and then he was off to Michael's. She wanted to spend as much time as she could with him until then.

The text was from Vanessa.

That stopped her in her tracks.

Working late?

It was random and innocuous, and it pissed Grace off instantly. They'd barely spoken since the parent-teacher conference and Kayla Kent's snide I-know-your-secret remarks that clearly freaked Vanessa the hell out and sent her running for the hills. Grace knew she'd needed to cut her some slack, and she had, but Vanessa had taken that slack and run with it. She'd run so far that she'd run right away from Grace and whatever it was they might've been starting. And maybe that was for the best, but it had truly sucked. They'd had so much fun, such a great connection, but apparently not so great that the threat of starting a rumor couldn't sever it easily. Grace had offered time and space and Vanessa had taken it and then some.

And now, here she was, randomly texting her on a Thursday at seven. She sighed, texted back, because she couldn't not. But she kept it short. Impersonal.

Yep. Last day before the holiday weekend.

She grabbed her coat and slid it on, zipped it up, turned the lights out in the back of the store. Ava had already locked up the front, so Grace let herself out the back and locked it behind her.

"Hi."

Grace jumped at the voice, then pressed a hand to her forehead as she willed her heart to leave her throat and go back down into her chest where it belonged. She glared at Vanessa, who stood against Grace's car, ankles crossed, arms folded, apparently waiting for her. "Jesus Christ, you scared me."

"I'm sorry," Vanessa said with a wince. "I'm not trying to be a creepy stalker."

"No?" Grace raised her brows and gave her a look.

Vanessa looked down at herself. "Doing a good impression of one, though, huh?"

"Yep." She pulled out her keys, hit the button. The lights flashed and the car beeped, and Vanessa stood.

"Okay," Vanessa said. "The *yep*s are a pretty good indicator that you're irritated with me. And I get it."

Grace stopped with her hand on her door handle. She got it? Really? This oughta be good. She rolled her lips in for a beat, then shifted her gaze to Vanessa. Okay. She'd hear her out.

It took Vanessa a second or two to realize Grace was giving her a shot, but she took it, pushed herself away from the car, and stood, hands out. "Okay. Look. You were right. Kayla Kent freaked me the fuck out with her veiled threats. I don't know why. I don't scare easily. I never have. But girls like her…" She looked off toward the dark sky like she was looking for the right explanation. "They've always made me feel less-than. Less than them. Less than good. Less than who I know myself to be. I don't know if you can understand what that's like."

Grace knew all too well what that was like. If Vanessa knew her mother, she'd get that. So she had empathy. She did understand. Unfortunately, her coping skills were at an all-time low right then, and she was mad at the world, and letting Vanessa off the hook or easing this whole thing for her wasn't on her to-do list for the day. She was too busy with other things. Too mad. Too hurt.

"That's it? That's the whole reason you went practically radio silent for more than a week?" She pointed at Vanessa with her keys, felt her anger go from a simmer to a low boil. "Because you were worried people might find out you were seeing me? How do you think that makes me feel? On top of the crazy hours I've been working. On top of my mother's analysis of my parenting skills? On top of not having my son this year on Christmas morning?" Her voice caught at the last one, and she let go of a small growl because no, she was not going to cry in front of Vanessa. "I don't understand why you couldn't call, could barely text, and left me twisting in the wind for something that had very little to do with me. I have enough stress in my life right now, Vanessa—" Her eyes welled up, goddamn it, and that only fueled her anger. "I have felt so much judgment from everybody around me, and I am *so sick* of it. Judgment from you initially for my crappy parenting." Vanessa opened her mouth to protest, but Grace gave her a look that shut her right up, her mouth snapping closed. "Judgment from my mother because I divorced a man I no longer love. Judgment from Ava for not arranging flowers fast enough, despite the emails and Yelp reviews we've gotten from tons of happy customers. Judgment from my seven-year-old son who thinks that his father's moving out is *my* fault. And judgment from *fucking* Kayla Kent who thinks that who I sleep with is somehow her business, and seriously, who gives a shit what she thinks?" She was at a full rolling boil now, words tumbling out of her loudly, uncontrolled, as if they had fed-up destructive little lives of their own. "I know we weren't exclusive or even officially dating, but we had sex, Vanessa. Maybe that doesn't mean a lot to you, but it's huge for me. *Huge.* And after our rocky start, I really thought we had something. I thought we had a connection. Something real. Something worth exploring." She dropped her hand to her side and felt like the wind had instantly gone from her sails, the fire in her belly suddenly extinguished by exhaustion, as if she'd just used up the very last bit of energy she had for the day. She inhaled and blew it out. "I guess I was the only one, though."

"No. You weren't." Vanessa shook her head. "You weren't the only one." Her voice was firm, certain, but Grace couldn't. She just couldn't.

"You sure let me feel like I was." She pulled her car door open with the sigh of somebody who was, quite simply, *done.* "I have to go get my son."

❖

Christmas Eve with the Martinis was like nothing else on earth. And yes, Vanessa would say that, being a Martini, but it was true. Callie was the only girlfriend she'd ever brought home for Christmas Eve, and that was years ago. She'd been in awe of the Italian Christmas Eve festivities the entire time. Literally—walked around the house, sat at the dinner table, played board games in the living room, the whole time with her mouth slightly agape.

The Martini family had become too big for everybody to gather in one place, but various members went to various homes for dinner. Vanessa's father had four brothers and a sister, and despite their divorce, Vanessa's mother was still considered very much a part of the Martini family. This year, Vanessa's mom was cooking Christmas Eve dinner for Julia's parents and her family, which was the biggest of the bunch— Julia had four brothers, each of them married or with significant others, and her brother John had two boys of his own.

"A lot of damn people," Vanessa muttered as she parked on the street, her parents' driveway already full.

Entering the house, three bottles of wine and a bag of presents in hand, was like walking into a restaurant or a bar, the din of many conversations creating a steady hum. Amelia was there—her father lived in Florida for most of the year, which left her alone. She waved to Vanessa from the corner of the living room where she was conversing with Vanessa's sister, Izzy.

The whole house smelled amazing, both Vanessa's mom and Aunt Anna, Julia's mom, buzzing around the kitchen like worker bees, getting everything ready. The smell of sauce—tomatoes, garlic, fresh basil—was like another person in the room, the loudest one, but also the most perfect, and Vanessa inhaled deeply, the scent encompassing love and family and tradition and Christmas all at once. Julia's father stood at one end of the kitchen island, electric knife in his hand, carving a massive turkey. Because yes, it was somehow necessary to have both pasta *and* meat and potatoes. Every year, Vanessa told her mother to do herself a favor and cut her work in half by serving one or the other. And every year, instead of taking something away from the menu, she added something new. This year, it was stuffed endive. Vanessa could see the breadcrumb-topped pan sitting on the stove.

The only thing missing from this family portrait was her father, who was across town having dinner with his friends, who had him over on holidays. And even though it had been years, even as an adult with a fairly clear understanding of life, Vanessa still felt the loss of him.

Julia stood against the wall, glass of wine in hand, eyes abnormally wide, and Vanessa saw a good opportunity to think about something else.

"You look like you're going to faint," Vanessa said quietly, once she'd had her own wine in hand and sidled up next to her. "Are you all right?"

Julia gave a weak smile and took a huge gulp of her wine. "Just nervous as hell."

"That's right! Oh my God, I'd forgotten that it's"—she lowered her voice to a whisper—"proposal night."

Julia looked at her like she was about to hurl up everything in her stomach.

"My advice?" Vanessa said, taking the glass from her. "Don't get drunk. Nobody wants to be proposed to by a drunk chick."

"Oh. Good call." Lots of nodding. "You're right. Thanks."

It was cute, her stoic, put-together cousin being so worried. Vanessa didn't share that worry, though. She knew how perfect Julia and Savannah were together. They were forever. Solid. Anybody looking in from the outside could see that. They were each other's people. She'd never had that. Not really. She'd never looked at anybody and thought, *I can see me with her for the rest of my life. She's my person.*

Well. Not before Grace.

No, she hadn't said that about Grace, hadn't thought it, hadn't allowed herself to, except…she did now. Was it envy, knowing that Julia was proposing to Savannah tonight? Maybe. Was it residual guilt and wonder left over from her chat with Grace the night before? Very possibly. She couldn't get the expression of disappointment on Grace's face out of her head. If anything was going to make her feel awful, it was that look. It was that let-down tone in her voice. Grace had stood up for herself. She hadn't let Vanessa get away with being a coward. She'd called her on her behavior, and that was something. Vanessa couldn't remember the last time she'd met a woman who'd matched her, gone toe-to-toe, and not only did it make her reevaluate things, it had been a huge turn-on, that unexpected confidence. She'd disappointed Grace in a big way, and that had sat with her for nearly twenty-four hours, hanging around her neck like some kind of albatross, going with her everywhere today.

She'd texted Grace several times. Kept it light, but also mixed in some apologies, a few pleas. It might have seemed like she was trying to wear Grace down. And that's because she was. Persistence, she'd told herself. *You've told her how sorry you are, now show her.*

That was the plan, anyway.

Because she had to get her back. Had to. The thought had punched her in the gut the night before as Grace had driven away. Something about that moment, the car pulling away, the taillights fading into the night, something reached in and took Vanessa's heart in its fist and *squeezed.* Squeezed until she thought she'd never be able to breathe again.

"I know why Jules looks like she's going to throw up, but why are you scowling?" Amelia was suddenly standing next to her. "There's no scowling on Christmas."

Vanessa hadn't told anybody about what had happened the night before, about her ambushing of Grace, about Grace leaving her standing in the parking lot of The Petal Pusher all by herself. And she knew why. She was embarrassed. Ashamed. She also hadn't been to The Bar Back since she'd told Julia and Amelia what had gone down at the parent-teacher conference, and it was for the same reason. She was ashamed of her behavior. And she should've been.

She spilled the whole thing to her cousins. Every last detail. And the more she talked, the more ashamed she felt. And the more she talked, the more she wanted to see Grace.

"You are *such* an idiot," Amelia said, and if she was pretending to be annoyed with Vanessa, she did a great job of it.

"Helpful," Vanessa said, lifting her glass in salute. "Thanks."

"I'm fucking serious," Amelia said, lowering her voice enough so that only Vanessa and Julia could hear the curse. "You meet this woman, you jump to conclusions about her, but she proves you wrong. You start to really like her, you sleep with her, and it's like fireworks and perfection, but somebody says something that you find vaguely threatening—which is nobody's issue but yours, by the way—and you run away with your tail between your legs and hide under the couch. And now, what? You've changed your mind, but she's not having it, and we're all supposed to feel sorry for you? Please." Her sarcastic snort might as well have been a slap, and Vanessa blinked at her, stunned by her anger.

"Wow. Ouch." She turned to Julia for support.

"Don't look at me," Julia said, shaking her head. "She's right. You fucked this up good."

The three of them stood there, Julia looking off into the kitchen, Amelia looking right at her as if daring her to argue. And just like that, her shoulders dropped. She sighed, and she cast her gaze down to her glass as her eyes filled, and she tried to swallow down the lump in her throat. They were right. Goddamn it. They were absolutely right.

Taking a moment to collect herself, she brought her watery attention back up to Amelia, who was still looking at her, though her glare had eased up a touch. A tone of pleading in her voice, Vanessa asked simply and quietly, "What do I do?"

CHAPTER TWENTY-TWO

The sleep aid Grace had taken the night before Christmas hadn't really done a whole lot. She'd learned throughout life that her churning brain was much stronger than any herb or drug, but she liked to try every now and then, see if she could catch it off guard. Or maybe find some newfangled miracle pill.

Not today, though.

It was Christmas morning, and a glance at her phone told her it was six seventeen. Early, but later than she'd expected. Her phone buzzed a text, and she was surprised to see it was from Michael. It was a photo of Oliver, still in his *Avengers* pajamas, standing next to a small Christmas tree, the base of it bulging with toys and gifts.

Up at the ass-crack of dawn, as usual. And four laughing emoji, a Santa, and a tree. Then another text. *Merry Christmas, Grace. See you at 12.*

Well.

That was unexpected. And nice. And her eyes welled up and she didn't even fight the tears. It was her first Christmas morning since Oliver had been born that she'd been away from him. If that wasn't a reason to cry, she didn't know what was, so she let herself, let the tears flow.

Rudy had taken to curling up on her bed next to her in the night, and now, as she cried it out, he shifted his position so that he was closer to her. He curled up again, this time, his warm body leaning against her hip as if offering his kitty comfort and sympathy. Which made her cry harder, but at least she was able to lay her hand on his soft fur, feel the presence of another living being, so she wasn't completely alone on Christmas morning.

Reaching for a tissue from the box on her nightstand, she shook herself back into shape. After all, she was going to have to get used to this kind of thing. This was what happened when you divorced and you had kids—you lost half their important moments to the other parent. It was only fair, she understood that. Didn't make it suck any less.

It was an effort to drag herself out of bed, but she did it and headed directly into the shower. Another change. In the past, she'd put on her fun Christmas jammies and head downstairs to make coffee and maybe pancakes or waffles, plus mimosas for her and Michael, while they waited for Oliver to wake up. Today, she showered, dressed in jeans and a fun sweater with an elf on the front, then headed down to make herself some coffee and get Oliver's Santa gifts set up under the tree. They'd told him Santa would stop at both houses, which he seemed to quickly understand meant he'd get more presents. He was no dummy, her kid.

Michael sent her periodic texts, even called so that she could wish Oliver a merry Christmas, despite his preoccupation with his new stuff and his very clear groan that told her she was interrupting his time with it.

She was putting the finishing touches on the display when her doorbell rang. A quick glance at the clock on the shelf said it was only nine forty-five. They hadn't shown up this early, had they?

An expectant smile on her face and a Merry Christmas ready on the tip of her tongue, she pulled the door open and felt her own eyes go wide.

There at her front door, a travel mug in one hand and a foil-covered plate in the other, Santa hat on her head, stood Vanessa Martini.

"Merry Christmas," she said with a huge smile, and if Grace looked carefully, she could see the uncertainty.

"Hi," Grace said back, not bothering to hide her surprise. And surprised, she was. "Merry Christmas to you, too. What are you doing here?"

"Well, you said on Thursday that you didn't have Oliver this morning, which I took to mean you'd be alone, and so I wanted to stop by and make sure you weren't. At least for a moment, in case you don't want me to come in." She grimaced. "Which I totally get."

It *was* Christmas. And it *was* cold. And Vanessa *did* look stupidly cute in her Santa hat and hopeful smile. She stepped aside. "Come on in."

Rudy sat along the back of the couch and watched this new houseguest enter, his feline expression very clearly intensely unimpressed, and Grace wanted to kiss his furry face. At least somebody had her back.

Vanessa stayed in the entryway. "While I'm sure you have things planned, I wanted to bring you something." She handed over the travel mug, and when their fingers touched, Grace was sure she felt a slight tremble in Vanessa's. "This is coffee, but not just any coffee. It's my special Christmas blend. A little cinnamon, a little nutmeg, a little eggnog." She swallowed audibly. "If you hate it, that's cool. Some people don't like eggnog."

"I do. Thank you."

Vanessa held up the plate. "This is an assortment of cookies that my mom and I made. Not sure if you have your own, but...here." She handed it over. "Christmas needs cookies, and I know firsthand that Oliver has a sweet tooth."

"He does. Thank you," Grace said again and set the plate on the small end table. The coffee smelled heavenly, though she didn't want to admit it.

There was a beat of awkward silence, and they stood face to face, Vanessa shifting her weight and wiping her palms down the thighs of her jeans. If she'd been a child, she'd be bouncing on the balls of her feet. "So," she said, "I had a whole speech planned. I rehearsed it a million times, right up until I pulled in the driveway, but now that I'm standing here in front of you, and you look"—she shook her head, swallowed—"so freaking beautiful, it just seems so...stupid and insignificant. Just let me say that I heard you. Okay? On Thursday. I heard you. I heard everything you said. You were so right. About all of it. And I want you to know how very sorry I am. I was an asshole. I was selfish. I was weak. And the majority of the time, I'm not any of those things, I swear to God."

Grace nodded. It was clear Vanessa was flying by the seat of her pants, and she kind of loved the whole gesture of showing up at her door on Christmas morning with cookies and coffee. Yeah, she scored big points for that. Not that Grace would tell her so. Yet.

"And if you're so inclined, after you have Christmas with your son and you get to relax a bit, I'd love it if we could sit down and talk. Grab some coffee. Or a drink. Just the two of us. Because the fact of the matter is you were right. When you said you thought we connected?

That we have something…I think you said *worth exploring*? Yeah. I feel that, too. I've felt it for a long time now, and I'm so sorry I got scared and was a…" She shook her head like she was having trouble finding what she wanted to say. "A cotton-headed—"

Grace cut her off with a hand, rolled her lips in, flared her nostrils in an attempt not to smile. "I'm sorry, were you about to quote *Elf* at me?"

And then Vanessa blushed. Hard. Deeply. Until her face was pretty completely red. It was adorable, Grace had to admit it.

Vanessa lifted a shoulder. "Seemed appropriate. What with it being Christmas and everything." She cleared her throat, clearly not sure whether Grace thought it was funny or ridiculous. "So. I'm gonna go, but…I'll text you?" She phrased it as a question, and Grace liked that, liked that she didn't just assume.

She let her hang for a second or two before giving her a nod. "Yes. Text me."

"Okay. I will. Cool."

They stood there for a beat before Vanessa seemed to jolt herself into action, pulling her coat tighter and securing her hat. Then, without warning, she leaned forward and kissed Grace on the cheek. Her lips were soft and warm, and Grace's eyes drifted shut before she realized it and blinked them open again.

"Merry Christmas, Grace." And without waiting for her response—maybe worried she wouldn't get one—she turned quickly and let herself out the door.

Grace stood there and watched as she got into her car, started the engine, and backed out. Once in the street, Vanessa waved a now-mittened hand and drove away, and Grace stayed standing there for a long time, her brain a jumble of confusion, irritation, and huge piles of joy.

Well. She hadn't seen that coming.

❖

The next week left Grace in a whirlwind of thoughts and emotions and frankly—and unexpectedly—super turned-on.

Vanessa was wooing her. A good old-fashioned courting. That's what was happening.

Grace had never really been courted before. She'd known Michael for almost a year before they'd started dating, so there was no period of getting-to-know-you—they already did. So this was new. And, Grace had to admit, it didn't suck.

Vanessa, who was off for the week, took her for coffee two days after Christmas, Monday, during Grace's lunch break. She was back to work at The Petal Pusher, but the chaos had eased, and they'd have a couple quiet weeks before the Valentine's Day rush would hit. Vanessa had apologized once again for being an idiot, and Grace had told her she forgave her and there was no need to say she was sorry anymore. Vanessa gave one nod, and that had been that for the sorrys.

They talked. A lot.

About stupid stuff. About superficial stuff. About family. About television.

They went to dinner on Wednesday while Oliver stayed with Michael's parents for the night.

They talked. A lot.

About books. About their college experiences. About sexuality in general and in particular to each of them.

Vanessa drove her home, told her she'd had a great time, kissed her cheek, and left.

On Thursday morning, Vanessa stopped by the flower shop to drop off coffee and a doughnut. Grace knew she'd blushed. Ava had raised an eyebrow. Vanessa had kissed her on the cheek, told her to have a great day, and left.

They texted. A lot.

Grace wasn't sure what to make of the whole thing, but she knew she was flattered. She was impressed. She'd gotten to know so much more about Vanessa and had shared way more than she'd expected to. Maybe there was something to be said for this whole wooing thing, huh?

Friday at The Petal Pusher was quiet. A gentle snow fell outside the front window. Only she and Ava were working. Grace had arranged four bouquets and sent Jack off with them. After lunch, she'd sat down behind the counter to look at orders and also to do a little internet research, see what new trends were on the way.

When the bell tinkled and she looked up from her computer, she felt her smile blossom across her face like the sun coming out after a summer rain. It was out of her control when she saw Vanessa, and she was very aware of that fact. She was an uncontrolled smiler now.

Vanessa had done that to her in under a week. Impressive. Points to her.

"Hey," Vanessa said as she approached the counter, all big smile and rosy cheeks.

"Hi there. You look all winter cute." It was true. Vanessa wore a white puffy coat with a purple hat and no gloves, over jeans and ankle-high winter boots. "Did you walk here?"

"I did." There was a slightly breathless quality to Vanessa's voice that Grace zeroed in on, and it took her brain in other directions. Other naughty directions. Because that's what had happened over the past few days. That's what the wooing had done. All the food and the conversation and the chaste cheek kissing. It was all wonderful, but it had also turned her the hell on and left her that way. Keyed up. Wanting. Part of her wondered if that had been Vanessa's plan all along. Another part of her didn't care because she was too aroused to think logically. She blinked rapidly as she realized Vanessa was still talking. "I walked Delilah earlier, and it's so pretty out. But I don't think winter is my dog's favorite season." She laughed then, just a soft one that came through her nose like a happy version of a scoff. "So I took her home and thought I'd walk some more on my own. Get some fresh air. And somehow…" She looked around, raised her arms, and dropped them again. "I ended up here."

"Imagine that."

"Imagine that."

And they stood that way, looking at each other for a beat. And another.

Vanessa pulled off her hat, and her blond hair was staticky. She smoothed a hand over it. "Listen, it's New Year's Eve."

"You are correct. It is."

"Do you have plans?"

"Oliver is with his dad tonight." She felt the slightly depressed tone in her own voice. There were fireworks downtown, and they could be seen from Michael's office building, so he'd asked if he could have Oliver and take him there. He was kind about it, knowing that would mean he'd have Oliver for both Christmas Eve and New Year's Eve. He'd even invited Grace to come along. In the end, she'd looked into her son's pleading eyes, and there was no way she'd take fireworks away from him.

Vanessa nodded. "Okay. And you? Do you have plans?"

There was so much she could've said right then. She could've detailed the food she'd purchased, how she had vowed to eat like a pig and watch a couple scary movies, how she knew it was possible she'd be asleep by ten, but she'd try her damnedest to stay up until midnight, and if she managed to do that, she'd open the bottle of champagne currently chilling in the fridge and ring in the New Year all by herself. She could've said any or all of that to Vanessa. But those blue eyes sparkled with hope, and those gorgeous dimples were trying hard to make an appearance, and all Grace could do was slowly shake her head.

"No. It's just me and the seventeen pounds of food I bought." At Vanessa's wide eyes, she nodded. "That's right. I'm having a foodfest. You?"

"Well, I'll be at my cousin's bar for a while. I always go for holidays and big events to help support her, but I wasn't really planning to stay all night." She tipped her head and wet her lips. "Do you think it would be okay if I crashed your foodfest?"

And suddenly, that was the most perfect idea ever. Like it had been planned all along. Or better yet, like it was a reward, because if she was being honest, she had to admit that Vanessa had been working her ass off all week, making up for missteps, showing how much she meant her apology. Showing Grace how much *she* meant. It really was a no-brainer.

"I think I'd love it if you crashed my foodfest."

"Yes!" Just when she thought Vanessa's smile couldn't get any brighter, it did. By lots of watts. Superbright. Hands on the counter, Vanessa boosted herself up, so she could plant a quick kiss on Grace's lips. "See you tonight."

And just like that, like a wind that had blown in, Vanessa blew back out again. Grace watched her go, fingertips at her lips, easy smile on her face.

"She's like a hurricane, that one," Ava said, shaking her head, but a hint of a smile tugged gently at the corners of her mouth. "Always whooshing in and whooshing out." She *tsk*ed and shook her head some more, and Grace just grinned like the lovesick fool she was beginning to realize she was. "Glad to see she's coming around, knows what she's got with you."

Grace felt her eyes go wide as she turned to Ava.

"What? I'm too old? I don't see things going on around me?" Ava scoffed, but there was no anger in it, and Grace was sure she saw another hint of a smile as Ava turned away to pull some carnations from the cooler.

Grace turned her gaze back to the front of the shop. Vanessa was long gone, but her essence still hung in the air somehow.

What a weird, wonderful week...

Chapter Twenty-three

Martini's was a madhouse. The music was thumping, the mood joyous. Terry the bouncer manned the front entrance. Three bartenders—one of whom was Julia—were smoothly moving around each other as if choreographed, lifting glasses and doing turns, flipping bottles and shaking shakers. It was like watching a dance, and Vanessa was riveted.

"I haven't seen you all week." Amelia bumped up against her. "How've you been?" She'd had a few of the New Year's Eve specials—the Resolution, Julia had named it, some concoction of vodka, blue Curaçao, and some other ingredients—and her eyes were a teeny bit glassy.

"You're not driving, right?"

"Uber, baby," Amelia said and held up her drink.

"I've seen Grace almost every day this week."

"And how's that going? She forgive you for being a dumbass yet?"

A week ago, that comment would've pissed her off. But now, she just grinned. "I think she might have." God knew she'd worked her ass off all week to show Grace how sorry she was, and the truth was, she'd deserved it. She'd deserved Grace's anger, and she'd deserved to have to work to win her back. And she was okay with that. Something had eased in her. Something had shifted. She had no explanation, no clear idea of it, but she knew it was good. "I will do whatever I need to do to get back on track with her."

Amelia tipped her head to one side. "And what does that mean, back on track?"

Vanessa looked at her. Smiled. Shrugged.

"Oh," Amelia said. Then, "*Oh.* Got it." And she bumped Vanessa with a shoulder. "Well, I hope you get there. You deserve to be happy."

And Vanessa knew she meant it because there was no sarcasm, no hint of envy or jealousy. Nothing but happiness. "Thanks, Meels."

There was a lightness about her tonight. She was perfectly happy to sit at the bar on her own—or with Amelia when Amelia didn't find a friend or family member elsewhere in the bar and scoot off to chat—and just be. She drank club soda with lime because she didn't want to show up at Grace's intoxicated. Julia had given her a nice bottle of champagne from The Bar Back. Not a ten-dollar bottle. Something decent. Brut. Respectable. She watched the crowd, watched the pride on Julia's face even as she ran around behind the bar, recognized various cousins among the customers and loved how they showed up to support a family member. Around ten, she finished her drink and slid off the barstool. Julia waved away her money, so she left a twenty-dollar bill on the bar anyway and dived into the crowd like a surfer paddling herself through the ocean waves.

Amelia was talking with their cousin Marco and caught Vanessa's eye as she headed by. Grabbing her around the neck, she hugged her tight and whispered, "Good luck tonight. I'll text you tomorrow. Happy New Year." Then she kissed Vanessa's cheek and let go. Vanessa swam her way to the back of the bar and through the closed door to The Bar Back where Savannah sat on the couch studying and Delilah lay sleeping on her dog bed.

"You off?" Savannah asked, looking up from her laptop, eyes bloodshot, diamond sparkling on her finger.

"I am." Vanessa pulled her coat off a hook and looked at her newly engaged, soon-to-be cousin-in-law. "Two things. One, thank you so much for taking my girl tonight." She bent down and gave Delilah about a million kisses on her head. Asking Julia and Savannah to take the dog overnight had been presumptuous, she knew, and she really hoped she hadn't jinxed herself by doing so.

"Listen, I want a dog, and your cousin is a hardhead about it, and this is a good way to show her how awesome it could be. So thank *you*."

"And two, put the work away and go celebrate with your fiancée, okay? It's New Year's Eve. Give your big brain a break." She shifted her kissing target to Savannah's head.

Savannah slammed the laptop shut. "Yes, ma'am." Their eyes met, and Savannah's were soft, loving. "And I hope things go the way you want them to tonight." She squeezed Vanessa's hand. "Go get your girl."

❖

Had she ever been this nervous?

Grace was pacing. Honest-to-God pacing. She didn't think people really did that, but there she was, wearing a path in the carpeting in her living room, back and forth, back and forth. It was just after ten, and Vanessa had texted to ask if it was okay if she headed over.

Did the house look okay? God, she wanted her own house one day, not half of somebody else's. Mr. Garabaldi was a nice enough man, but the fact that there was somebody just on the other side of the drywall who could bang on the wall or make noise she could hear or could hear any noise *she* made…It was starting to grate on her. One day…

She gave her head a shake. The tangent had been good, had taken her out of her head for a good ten seconds. But Vanessa would be here very soon, and she looked around, grading her space. The small table between the kitchen and living room was covered with munchies. Cheese and crackers, shrimp and cocktail sauce, chips with salsa, stuffed olives, a little dish of chocolates, a bottle of champagne chilling in the silver ice bucket she'd gotten as a wedding present and had used maybe twice.

"Sweet mother of God, Grace, how many people do you think are coming?" she asked herself quietly. But it was much too late to make any changes, as headlights flashed through the front window and across the ceiling before going out altogether.

Vanessa was here.

A glance down. A smoothing of hands over her hips. She'd changed from the comfy sweats she'd slid into after work to a cute pair of dark jeans and a mint sweater that she knew accented her eyes. Her hair was down, and she gave it a quick finger-comb, grabbed a tube of gloss from her purse and quickly ran it over her lips, as she heard Vanessa's footsteps crunching through the snow out front.

God. She was here.

Her heart was going to hammer itself right out of her chest. She was sure of it. Big breath in, slow breath out, reach for the doorknob.

She pulled the door open before Vanessa could knock. Was that too much? Had she given herself away? Vanessa started, clearly surprised. But her wide eyes settled on Grace, and a slow smile formed, and those dimples showed up, and Grace felt her world steady and balance.

"Hey," Vanessa said as she stepped into the entryway. "You look amazing."

Grace felt herself blush. When had that happened? When did she become a blusher? "Thanks. So do you," she said truthfully as Vanessa unbuttoned her black wool coat. Her cheeks were rosy from the cold, her blue eyes sparkled, and her blond hair was down with a little wave to it, probably because of the snow in the air. Before she could stop herself, she reached out and fingered the ends, sifted the strands. Then, catching herself, she blinked, gave her head a small shake, and took Vanessa's coat. "Come in. Please."

Vanessa had a bottle of champagne in her hand and held it up. "Recommended by my cousin the bartender."

"You didn't have to do that. I have some chilling, but if yours comes recommended, let's switch them out."

Vanessa walked farther into the room and glanced at the television. "You're watching *Elf.*"

"Yeah. I was inspired by a certain someone recently. I can turn it off." She took a step toward the TV, but Vanessa stopped her with a warm hand on her arm.

"Why would you turn it off?" She stood and watched. "I love this movie."

"Yeah?" Grace was shocked. "Michael is the only guy I know who doesn't like Will Ferrell, so he hates this movie."

"Has he ever actually *watched* this movie?"

Grace shook her head.

"And has he not heard Zooey Deschanel sing in it?"

A laugh shot out of Grace, and she nodded. "Oh my God, right? That's my favorite part." Their gazes held, and Grace felt butterflies and flying saucers and all kinds of floating things in her tummy, kicking her apprehension—and her arousal—up several notches. "Do you want to finish watching it with me? It'll be over just before midnight, and then we can pop the champagne…" She let the sentence trail off, worried she was coming across as too commanding, but Vanessa's smile grew.

"You know, I was thinking that we'd talk, but—"

Grace held up a hand, traffic cop style. "Can I say something before you finish the *but*?" At Vanessa's nod, she reached deep, grabbed onto the honesty in her heart, and pulled it up. "We have talked all week. And it's been great, don't get me wrong. I love talking with you. But I think we've been talking so much because you're still trying to find your footing with me." She could tell by the visible swallow that she was on the right track. "I just want to say this—you're forgiven, Vanessa. I forgive you. I told you how I was feeling, why I was hurt, and you really listened. You *really* listened. I can't remember the last time I felt that way about my significant other. You listened, and you did your best to fix it." It was Grace's turn to swallow the lump of nerves sitting right in the center of her throat. "Look, this won't be easy. We've got your job. We've got my son. We've got obstacles, okay?" She laughed, needing a touch of levity. "But for tonight, do you think we could just curl up on the couch together, watch a movie, drink some champagne, and ring in the New Year?"

Vanessa's eyes had welled up, which made Grace's do the same, and she said, so quietly that Grace had to lean in to hear her, "I'm your significant other?"

Grace barked a laugh. "*That's* what you took from my whole speech?"

A snort. "Um, yeah."

They stood. Quiet. Smiling like goofs.

Graced tipped her head to the side, not wanting to admit that the phrase had slipped out without her thinking about it, but also not sorry she'd said it. "I mean—"

It was Vanessa's turn to interrupt, and she held up a hand the same way Grace had. "You know what? Let's not worry about it tonight. Let's do what you said. Let's cuddle on the couch and watch TV and pop some bubbly in a bit. Yeah?"

Grace nodded, feeling relief and joy and contentment and so many other happy things she couldn't even voice.

"First, I need to eat my weight in shrimp." Vanessa headed to the table and fixed herself a plate like she'd done it a hundred times before.

Grace had a vision then. A vision? A premonition? A prediction? She had no idea what it was, only that she could easily see this being a regular thing—down the line, when Vanessa was no longer Oliver's teacher—but with a few additions. She could see Vanessa helping herself to food, Delilah sprawled on the floor, snoring happily, Oliver near the coffee table, LEGOs spread out all over the place, and those feelings intensified. The joy. The contentment. The happy.

And when she looked at Vanessa, Vanessa was looking back at her, eyes soft and welcoming, dimples saying hello because of the warm smile on her face.

Vanessa held up a shrimp. "Want this?"

Grace smiled, then reached for the little cocktail-sauce-covered crustacean and Vanessa's hand and held on tightly. "I do. I want this very much."

Epilogue

Four months later

"What's wrong?"

Vanessa saw Grace's expression and was instantly on alert, like she'd gotten a shot of adrenaline or an electric shock. Grace sat at the little table in her duplex, phone in her hand, staring off into space. She turned her head slightly, so she gazed in Vanessa's direction, but she didn't say anything. Just blinked.

"Hello? Girlfriend freaking out over here." Vanessa pulled out a chair and sat down. In the time she'd know Grace, in the last five or six months since she'd dated-slash-slept with-slash-fallen for Grace, she'd never seen this expression on her face. It was…Vanessa tipped her head, squinted. Shock. Disbelief. Confusion. And back to shock.

A clear of her throat and Grace finally focused on her. "Sorry. I just…I'm a little bit numb."

"Is everything okay? Is Oliver okay?" Vanessa lowered her voice. "Did somebody else die?" And she winced.

Grace's chuckle sent relief through Vanessa's system, and she felt her breath return to normal. The past couple of weeks had been hard on her girlfriend. Ava Green, owner of The Petal Pusher flower shop, had had a sudden heart attack in her sleep and died right there in her bed. Between mourning a woman who gave her very mixed feelings and worrying about finding a new job, Grace had been stressed to the max.

As if reading Vanessa's mind, Grace took her hand. "I haven't exactly been a pile of puppies to be around lately, have I?"

"Sure you have. Cute. Cuddly. Slightly aggressive with a tendency to bite a little too hard…"

That got a laugh. "I'm sorry."

"Baby. This is life, right? We're gonna have stuff."

"We certainly have stuff, don't we? What's today?"

"April seventeenth," Vanessa said.

"Only two more months."

"Only two more months." And they both grinned widely at that. They'd been seeing each other, exclusively but quietly, for nearly four months. Their close friends knew. Some of their family knew. But Oliver didn't. They'd decided to wait until he was no longer Vanessa's student before they relaxed things and went public, as Grace jokingly called it. They weren't hiding so much as keeping things private. At least, that's how they looked at it.

"So, are you going to tell me what put that look on your face?" Vanessa asked.

"What look?"

"The one that makes me wonder if somebody told you there would be no more flowers in the entire world."

Grace wet her lips and seemed to gauge how she wanted to say what she was about to say. "Oh, there will most certainly be flowers. And I will be the boss of the flowers."

Vanessa frowned, gave her head a shake. "I don't know what that means."

"Ava left me the flower shop."

Blink. Stare. Blink.

"What?"

"That was her lawyer on the phone. He called to tell me that her will says The Petal Pusher is mine." The disbelief in Grace's voice was clear. Vanessa knew she'd thought Ava hadn't even liked her that much. "She said I had a passion for flowers the way her father had, and she was sure she was leaving the shop in the best hands."

"Holy shit."

"Exactly. Exactly that."

They sat staring at each other, blinking, staring, until they both burst into laughter. The pride on Grace's face, the sheer joy that was clear in her beautiful green eyes, they were everything to Vanessa. "This is amazing," she said, standing up and pulling Grace to her feet and into a hug. "I'm so proud of you, baby," she said in Grace's ear and felt Grace's arms tighten around her.

"I can't believe it," Grace said, suddenly sobering and ticking things off on her fingers. "Oh my God, there's so much to do. I have to work out the paperwork with the lawyer, get everything set up for taxes and such, hire a couple new people, and I have so many ideas to increase business. We're gonna need to update that seriously old computer system, and I think I'll paint the main shop area. One of the coolers is shot…" Her eyes went a little glassy as, Vanessa knew, she began to work things through in her head. Before she could say anything, though, Grace turned back to her and grabbed her face in both hands. "If I didn't have you, I'd be freaking out right now. But I'm not. Know why?"

"Tell me."

"Because you give me strength. You make me feel like I can do anything."

"'Cause you can."

"I love you so much. Do you know that?" She pressed her lips to Vanessa's in a sweet kiss.

"I do. And I love you back. So very much." Another kiss and then Vanessa said, "We need to celebrate. I'm gonna call the cousins." She pulled out her phone, then glanced up at Grace. "Can I call the cousins?"

Grace snorted, as if she'd ever tell her not to. "Call the cousins."

An hour later, they were in The Bar Back with Amelia and Savannah, pouring champagne into clear plastic cups. Julia had been helping bartend out front but came back to join in the celebration. Her dark hair was a mass of curls around her head and her cheeks were flushed.

"Busy out there?" Vanessa asked.

Julia nodded. "Crazed, which is great. But I wouldn't miss this for the world." She picked up a full cup and held it aloft. "To another small business owner joining the club."

"Yes!" Savannah said with a huge smile. "We're so happy for you, Gracie."

Grace felt herself blush, loving the nickname coming from this group.

They touched glasses and everybody sipped.

"You guys," Grace said, and her eyes filled with tears, and when she turned to Vanessa, hers had welled up.

"Stop that, you're gonna make me cry, too," Vanessa said and wrapped her arm around Grace's waist, pulling her close. She pressed a kiss to Grace's temple. "I'm so proud of you."

"For what?" Grace felt like the pride was misplaced somehow. "I didn't do anything. This just fell in my lap, really. I didn't even think she liked me that much."

"Clearly, she did," Amelia said.

Julia agreed. "I was telling my parents about it, and they said Ava's father was passionate about his shop, and Ava was the same way from the moment she took it over. Her personality wasn't always... welcoming." A couple chuckles went around the room. "But she loved that flower shop. She never had any kids, and my mom said that shop was her baby. She obviously trusted you with her most precious possession."

"Pretty cool," Amelia added.

"I can't wait to see what you do with the place," Savannah said.

They spent the next fifteen or twenty minutes talking about the shop and Grace's ideas for it. She told them how she had mentioned a few things to Ava during her two years working there. "They showed up in the will," she told them, still slightly in awe. "The lawyer read the passage to me, and she mentioned how much Ava admired my"— she pretended to search for the word, when in reality, she knew it well because it had burned itself into her brain—"my ingenuity."

"A good thing to have when you own a small business," Amelia said.

"Which you now do," Savannah added.

"I do."

They chatted some more. Drank a little more. Julia went out front and came back a few times. Delilah snored in her dog bed in the corner. And as Grace looked around the room, this back part of a bar where so many important conversations had happened and she had a feeling so many more would, she felt the one thing she'd been looking for, the one feeling she'd never seemed to be able to find—she felt like she *belonged*. Like these were her people. Vanessa, yes, absolutely. But also Julia. And Savannah. They were already looping her in on their wedding plans. And Amelia, who carried a sense of sadness that Grace wondered if the others saw as clearly as she did. Her heart warmed. She had no siblings. She wasn't that tight with her parents. These women, these four women, they were her family. She knew without a shadow of a doubt that when she was ready to let Oliver in on the details of their relationship, these women would take him in and love him to bits. He would instantly gain three aunts, and she knew they'd love him like he was blood. There wasn't a doubt in her mind.

Amelia was telling the story of a new client she'd picked up, a wealthy businessman who was going to be traveling overseas come summer and wanted her to stay in his McMansion, as she called it, with his two dogs while he was gone and some remodeling was done. As she talked, Grace gave Vanessa's hand a squeeze as their fingers entwined.

"I love you," she said quietly when Vanessa turned to look at her. That beautiful face softened, the dimples came out to play, and those blue eyes that Grace could lose herself in? They sparkled with a joy and happiness that made Grace's entire body feel warm.

"I love you back," Vanessa whispered and placed a sweet kiss on her lips.

This.

Grace inhaled quietly, let it out slowly, and couldn't have stopped the smile from blooming across her face if she'd wanted to.

This. This was it. She was home.

About the Author

Georgia Beers lives in Upstate New York and has written more than thirty novels of women-loving-women romance. In her off-hours, she can usually be found searching for a scary movie, lifting all the weights, sipping a good Pinot, or trying to keep up with little big man Archie, her mix of many tiny dogs. Find out more at georgiabeers.com.

Books Available From Bold Strokes Books

A Fairer Tomorrow by Kathleen Knowles. For Maddie Weeks and Gerry Stern, the Second World War brought them together, but the end of the war might rip them apart. (978-1-63555-874-6)

Changing Majors by Ana Hartnett Reichardt. Beyond a love, beyond a coming-out, Bailey Sullivan discovers what lies beyond the shame and self-doubt imposed on her by traditional Southern ideals. (978-1-63679-081-7)

Wisdom by Jesse J. Thoma. When Sophia and Reggie are chosen for the governor's new community design team and tasked with tackling substance abuse and mental health issues, battle lines are drawn even as sparks fly. (978-1-63555-886-9)

Highland Whirl by Anna Larner. Opposites attract in the Scottish Highlands, when feisty Alice Campbell falls for city girl about town Roxanne Barns. (978-1-63555-892-0)

Holiday Hearts by Diana Day-Admire and Lyn Cole. Opposites attract during Christmastime chaos in Kansas City. (978-1-63679-128-9)

Humbug by Amanda Radley. With the corporate Christmas party in jeopardy, CEO Rosalind Caldwell hires Christmas Girl Ellie Pearce as her personal assistant. The only problem is, Ellie isn't a PA, has never planned a party, and develops a ridiculous crush on her totally intimidating new boss. (978-1-63555-965-1)

On the Rocks by Georgia Beers. Schoolteacher Vanessa Martini makes no apologies for her dating checklist, and newly single mom Grace Chapman ticks all Vanessa's Do Not Date boxes. Of course, they're never going to fall in love. (978-1-63555-989-7)

Song of Serenity by Brey Willows. Arguing with the Muse of music and justice is complicated, falling in love with her even more so. (978-1-63679-015-2)

The Christmas Proposal by Lisa Moreau. Stranded together in a Christmas village on a snowy mountain, Grace and Bridget face their past and question their dreams for the future. (978-1-63555-648-3)

The Infinite Summer by Morgan Lee Miller. While spending the summer with her dad in a small beach town, Remi Brenner falls for Harper Hebert and accidentally finds herself tangled up in an intense restaurant rivalry between her famous stepmom and her first love. (978-1-63555-969-9)

A Convenient Arrangement by Aurora Rey and Jaime Clevenger. Cuffing season has come for lesbians, and for Jess Archer and Cody Dawson, their convenient arrangement becomes anything but. (978-1-63555-818-0)

An Alaskan Wedding by Nance Sparks. The last thing either Andrea or Riley expects is to bump into the one who broke her heart fifteen years ago, but when they meet at the welcome party, their feelings come rushing back. (978-1-63679-053-4)

Beulah Lodge by Cathy Dunnell. It's 1874, and newly betrothed Ruth Mallowes is set on marriage and life as a missionary...until she falls in love with the housemaid at Beulah Lodge. (978-1-63679-007-7)

Gia's Gems by Toni Logan. When Lindsey Speyer discovers that popular travel columnist Gia Williams is a complete fake and threatens to expose her, blackmail has never been so sexy. (978-1-63555-917-0)

Holiday Wishes & Mistletoe Kisses by M. Ullrich. Four holidays, four couples, four chances to make their wishes come true. (978-1-63555-760-2)

Love By Proxy by Dena Blake. Tess has a secret crush on her best friend, Sophie, so the last thing she wants is to help Sophie fall in love with someone else, but how can she stand in the way of her happiness? (978-1-63555-973-6)

Marry Me by Melissa Brayden. Allison Hale attempts to plan the wedding of the century to a man who could save her family's business, if only she wasn't falling for her wedding planner, Megan Kinkaid. (978-1-63555-932-3)

Pathway to Love by Radclyffe. Courtney Valentine is looking for a woman exactly like Ben—smart, sexy, and not in the market for anything serious. All she has to do is convince Ben that sex-without-strings is the perfect pathway to pleasure. (978-1-63679-110-4)

Sweet Surprise by Jenny Frame. Flora and Mac never thought they'd ever see each other again, but when Mac opens up her barber shop right next to Flora's sweet shop, their connection comes roaring back. (978-1-63679-001-5)

The Edge of Yesterday by CJ Birch. Easton Gray is sent from the future to save humanity from technological disaster. When she's forced to target the woman she's falling in love with, can Easton do what's needed to save humanity? (978-1-63679-025-1)

The Scout and the Scoundrel by Barbara Ann Wright. With unexpected danger surrounding them, Zara and Roni are stuck between duty and survival, with little room for exploring their feelings, especially love. (978-1-63555-978-1)

Can't Leave Love by Kimberly Cooper Griffin. Sophia and Pru have no intention of falling in love, but sometimes love happens when and where you least expect it. (978-1-636790041-1)

Free Fall at Angel Creek by Julie Tizard. Detective Dee Rawlings and aircraft accident investigator Dr. River Dawson use conflicting methods to find answers when a plane goes missing, while overcoming surprising threats and discovering an unlikely chance at love. (978-1-63555-884-5)

Love's Compromise by Cass Sellars. For Piper Holthaus and Brook Myers, will professional dreams and past baggage stop two hearts from realizing they are meant for each other? (978-1-63555-942-2)

Not All a Dream by Sophia Kell Hagin. Hester has lost the woman she loved, and the world has descended into relentless dark and cold. But giving up will have to wait when she stumbles upon people who help her survive. (978-1-63679-067-1)

The Secrets of Willowra by Kadyan. A family saga of three women, their homestead called Willowra in the Australian outback, and the secrets that link them all. (978-1-63679-064-0)

Turbulent Waves by Ali Vali. Kai Merlin and Vivien Palmer plan their future together as hostile forces make their own plans to destroy what they have, as well as all those they love. (978-1-63679-011-4)

Protecting the Lady by Amanda Radley. If Eve Webb had known she'd be protecting royalty, she'd never have taken the job as bodyguard, but as the threat to Lady Katherine's life draws closer, she'll do whatever it takes to save her, and may just lose her heart in the process. (978-1-63679-003-9)

Trial by Fire by Carsen Taite. When prosecutor Lennox Roy and public defender Wren Bishop become fierce adversaries in a headline-grabbing arson case, their attraction ignites a passion that leads them both to question their assumptions about the law, the truth, and each other. (978-1-63555-860-9)

Unbreakable by Cari Hunter. When Dr. Grace Kendal is forced at gunpoint to help an injured woman, she is dragged into a nightmare where nothing is quite as it seems, and their lives aren't the only ones on the line. (978-1-63555-961-3)

Veterinary Surgeon by Nancy Wheelton. When dangerous drugs are stolen from the veterinary clinic, Mitch investigates and Kay becomes a suspect. As pride and professions clash, love seems impossible. (978-1-63679-043-5)(978-1-63679-051-0)

All That Remains by Sheri Lewis Wohl. Johnnie and Shantel might have to risk their lives—and their love—to stop a werewolf intent on killing. (978-1-63555-949-1)

Beginner's Bet by Fiona Riley. Phenom luxury Realtor Ellison Gamble has everything, except a family to share it with, so when a mix-up brings youthful Katie Crawford into her life, she bets the house on love. (978-1-63555-733-6)

Dangerous Without You by Lexus Grey. Throughout their senior year in high school, Aspen, Remington, Denna, and Raleigh face challenges in life and romance that they never expect. (978-1-63555-947-7)

Desiring More by Raven Sky. In this collection of steamy stories, a rich variety of lovers find themselves desiring more: more from a lover, more from themselves, and more from life. (978-1-63679-037-4)

BOLDSTROKESBOOKS.COM

Looking for your next great read?

Visit BOLDSTROKESBOOKS.COM
to browse our entire catalog of paperbacks, ebooks,
and audiobooks.

Want the first word on what's new?
Visit our website for event info,
author interviews, and blogs.

Subscribe to our free newsletter for sneak peeks,
new releases, plus first notice of promos
and daily bargains.

SIGN UP AT
BOLDSTROKESBOOKS.COM/signup

*Bold Strokes Books is an award-winning publisher
committed to quality and diversity in LGBTQ fiction.*